Mean Spirit
A Tipsy Fairy Tale

E. Chris Garrison

Cover art: Anne Rosario

Cover art in this book copyright © 2020 Anne Rosario & Silly Hat Books

Editor: Linda Sullivan

Copy Editor: Amy E. Garrison

Published by Silly Hat Books

ISBN: 978-1-953763-22-8

www.sillyhatbooks.com

Publisher's Note:

Mean Spirit is a work of fiction. All names, characters, and places are the product of the author's imagination, used in fictitious manner. Any resemblances to actual persons, places, locales, events, etc. are purely coincidental.

First Edition

Other books by E. Chris Garrison

Reality Check: A Tale of Quantum Entanglements
Alien Beer and Other Stories

Trans-Continental: Girl in the Gears
Trans-Continental: Mississippi Queen

Blue Spirit: A Tipsy Fairy Tale
Restless Spirit: A Tipsy Fairy Tale
Mean Spirit: A Tipsy Fairy Tale

The Road Ghosts Omnibus

Contains:
Book One: Four 'til Late
Book Two: Sinking Down
Book Three: Me and the Devil
Short Story: Spectral Delivery

Dedication and Acknowledgements

Mean Spirit is dedicated to Sara Larson, who gave me the idea to include pukwudgies as a part of Skye's adventures.
I'm just sorry you never got to see it.

Chapter One

Every time I feel myself start to backslide, I visit Raven's grave. Except her name wasn't Raven, that's just what the vampires called her. Outside of the game, her family knew her as Jessica Fowler. Annabelle, the L.T., Frannie and I went to her funeral. A lot of the gamers did, after what happened at Big Con. I hardly recognized some of them out of costume. Everyone seemed so much smaller and more awkward in our funeral clothes. Frannie called them "muggle clothes".

I'd been playing as a pretend vampire with these people for years, ever since Stuart brought me to Indianapolis from Chicago. The game had always been my life, a saving grace to a more miserable mundane existence. You'd think having a connection to another, real paranormal world would have dulled the thrill of that. But instead, it made me feel just a little less crazy. The made-up fantasy world I shared with the gamers in Indy put me among people who at least *wanted* to believe in other worlds, magical creatures, and adventure. Most of us knew why we did this:

Reality sucks.

I can't hold a job, and the ones I do get are mind-blowingly boring. I blew the one great job I did get as a promo girl for Fantasy Free Form, an online sword-and-sorcery game. I did a good job at it, but the *other* best job I ever lost—as a paranormal investigator—got in the way. Both happened at Big Con, which is where Raven, aka Jessica, had died.

And that was my fault.

Oh, sure, everyone says it wasn't. They tell me, "Skye, you didn't *make* Raven nail the trolls, she did it herself. The big troll killed her, not you."

But people follow me. My friend Bask, the Transit King, says it's in my blood, from the long line of MacLeods before me. Bask is always true to his word, but he's also a notorious teller of tall tales. He might be fluffing me up, or he might mean it. I've led friends into battle a few times now, people who mostly haven't fought before. I lost Stuart in one fight, and now some girl we called Raven that I didn't really even know.

But still, I visit her grave, maybe every week or two. Annabelle takes me sometimes, when she's off work, or sometimes Leslie does. The bus schedule is complicated getting to the cemetery from Broad Ripple where Annabelle and I live, but I make the trip anyway.

I kind of have to. I told Annabelle—no, I'd *promised* her—that I'd straighten up. Sure, my drinking lets me see into the other world of trolls and goblins and fairies (but don't call them that), but it's lost me too many jobs, and I've made some terrible decisions while in that state.

Like the ones that got Stuart and Raven killed.

Bask didn't go to Raven's funeral. He doesn't mix with humans much outside of the bus. He's kind of a fairy Godfather, riding the bus lines, giving out magical favors, in return for the promise of another favor--anything he asks--somewhere down the line.

He's a sweetheart so long as you keep that promise. I always thought of him as a funny little gnome, a kind of creepy uncle at worst, and a mentor at best. He called me his knight, and I've done things for him, since he'd always been kind to me.

I'd hoped he'd make the funeral, and I'd asked him to get off at the Crown Hill Cemetery bus stop to go with me to visit her, but he's always said no, and won't say why.

Maybe his folk don't treat death the way we do. I mean, he'd led me to fight Queen Howl, who he revealed as his wife, after I'd separated her head from her shoulders with a magic sword he'd helped me claim. He never seemed to miss her. I wonder sometimes if he'd miss me if I'd died in Raven's place.

This time, I'd brought a twenty-sided die to place on Raven's grave. The chill November wind cut through my denim jacket and reminded me that leggings might not be warm enough for these trips as the month went on. I rolled the die on her flat stone, across her name, and it came to rest with 1 facing me.

"Hope you got a good roll," said an unfamiliar voice. I turned to see a woman approaching me, her boots crunching on the crispy leaves. She had curly brown hair, little oval glasses, and freckles across the bridge of her nose. The warmth of her smile pushed back the chill air just a bit.

I picked up the twenty-sider and pocketed it. "Natural one. Bad luck. She was a gamer, I thought she'd appreciate a die roll in her honor."

The woman nodded and held out a hand to me. "Cassie Fowler. I'm Jessica's big sister. I've seen you out here before."

I nodded, and tears threatened at the corners of my eyes. I stared at her outstretched hand and realized she wanted to shake. I took her hand and just held it a long moment. Her fingers were warm and soft. "I'm so sorry," I stammered. "I can't tell you how sorry I am."

Her smile faded and her eyes slid back to her sister's grave, and she let go of my hand. "Oh, now I know you. You're Skye, the vampire girl who talked at Jessica's funeral. Kept calling her the wrong name."

I wanted to run, maybe find an open grave to throw myself into. "Uh huh. Raven. That's what she called herself."

Cassie stuck her hands in the pockets of her green hoodie and looked at me. "Skye, at her funeral, you made my sister out to be a hero. Jessica always did get carried away. But on that day of the riots, it was more than just a game, wasn't it? More than just what Homeland Security told everyone. A big fight between gamers, football players, and motorheads? I mean, everyone saw that thing on TV. I saw Monument Circle before they cleaned it up and started renovations. I know there's more. Won't you tell me about it? If my sister was a hero, I need you to tell me what really happened, Skye."

My phone chimed. I pulled it out and peeked, not sure how to tell Cassie how her sister had killed a troll and then had been killed by the very *thing* she'd seen on TV. An ancient stone troll as big as an elephant had tossed Raven/Jessica aside like a doll.

So which is better? The comfortable lie she'd been told, or the impossible, unbelievable truth I'd witnessed?

"Cassie, uh, I don't know how to say this, but here goes. Would you believe me if I told you that monsters are real?"

Her eyes widened. "Monsters? Like the bogeyman?"

I shook my head. "Well, not like that, but yeah. Animal people. Trolls. Fairies."

She laughed. "Fairies. Really? Come on, Skye."

"Only don't call them that," I said. "It's sort of a slur. They don't like fairy tales; the 'lords and ladies' say we put them in a bad light. If you ask me, some of them deserve everything the Brothers Grimm had to say about them."

Cassie met my eyes for the first time, and I had to stop from taking a step back. Her eyes contained storms and depth; being the focus of her attention was almost too intense. Then, she smiled with those eyes and looked away. "I don't know if you're teasing me, but I believe in a lot of things. Fairies, ghosts, gods and goddesses, and magick."

"Sometimes I wish it was just pretend, like in the vampire game. But magic and monsters are all around us. You just have to have the knack for *seeing* them is all."

Her eyes laughed, and she pursed her lips. She studied me again, and then said, "I know."

"You do?"

She nodded, and then pushed her glasses up her nose.

"Can you see things right now?"

She shook her head. "I only get glimpses. More like impressions. One person might have an aura around them that warns me they're bad news. Another might feel so much larger than what my eyes see. You, you've got this lovely purple aura around you, Skye, like the deepest part of the sunset."

Warmth came to my cheeks despite the chilly air around us. "I see those things, too. Out of the corners of my eyes, when I'm not really paying attention. So hard to see things directly. I used to see a *lot* more."

She stuck her hands in her hoodie pockets and shivered. "Oh? What happened? Why don't you anymore?"

It was my turn to break eye contact. "I quit drinking."

Cassie sighed. "Oh. I thought you were being real. I meant what I said. I believe."

I looked up and met her eyes for just a second before she looked away. "No, Cassie, that's not what I meant. I have this power. I got it when I was drunk, years ago. Something attacked me, took over my body, forced me back into my head somewhere dark. Friends saved me, and a Wiccan girl I know patched up the damage it left behind. Sorry, this must sound crazy."

She nodded. "Yeah, kinda."

I pushed on. "This is why I don't talk about it much. On that day, a bit of me broke off, a little piece of my soul became something new. It was like I became twins, only the other part is little and lives in the other world as a spirit. She appeared to me the next time I drank. I call her Minnie. I miss her so much. I only see her in dreams anymore."

Cassie held out a hand again. I looked at her and she reached to take my hand in hers. "Come on, let's walk together."

I said a silent goodbye to Raven and let Cassie lead me along the roadway in the cemetery. We passed standing stones, tall obelisks, and low stone coffin-like monuments. We stopped at one marked HARPER, and she let go of my hand.

"This is my great-grandparents' plot. My mother's mother's mother; Mamaw Isobel died when I was three years old, but I remember her."

I watched her gaze at the weathered old stone. "I don't remember that far back."

Cassie shrugged. "Mamaw told me I was special, and that I shouldn't ever stop looking at the world differently than everyone else. When I moved out of my parents' house to live with my first husband, mom's mom gave me a box addressed to me from Mamaw. Grandma told me it was trouble, and if I was smart, I wouldn't open it, or better yet, give it to Goodwill."

"What was inside?"

She glanced up at me. "What makes you think I opened it anyway?"

"I don't really know you, but you seem like you'd be too curious to resist. I know I couldn't."

She stuck her tongue out at me. "Well, I kept it under my bed for a week before taking it out one day when my husband was at work. Inside was a handwritten book, a little dull knife, a ceramic bowl, and a mirror."

I smiled. "She was a witch?"

She nodded. "Yes. Not exactly Wiccan, but close enough. Something outside the usual traditions, very personal and old. I never let my first husband see it. I learned all kinds of herb lore and how to look for signs in nature. Like look over there. See those two crows over there? The number means things. 'One for sorrow, two for mirth, three for a wedding, four a birth--"

I interrupted her by pointing behind her. "What does a bazillion crows mean?"

The sky darkened as a great cloud of black birds formed a swarm that undulated as it grew in size. The two crows nearby squawked and flew at us and we both screamed and fended them off.

"It means run like hell!"

We took off running. I threw a glance behind us, and it was as if night had fallen, and the air filled with the cacophony of more crows than I'd ever seen in my life.

Chapter Two

The birds outpaced us, and the world became wings and crow calls. Cassie grabbed me and we stopped. She planted her feet far apart and raised her arms in a "Y" and shouted a string of words I didn't catch, but which sounded like a command.

The crows stayed maybe six feet away from us in all directions. We were inside a giant snow globe, with frantic black flakes shaken and swirling and swooping outside the glass.

Then, an archway of daylight and grass appeared before us. A lumpy figure, like a small troll, strode into our bubble, eclipsing much of the light.

A woman's laughter burst from the silhouetted figure, and she threw back a hood and spread her arms, showing her to be just pudgy, not trollish. Her hair flew wild in the wind of the crows, and she held up a cane by its middle and shook it at us.

Her raspy voice carried over the din. "Well, I have found myself a knight and a bishop here on the playing board, what moves are they making for the White King? They're in check by the Black Rook, hmmm?"

I couldn't make out Cassie's face, she spat her words at the woman. "This isn't a game board, and we're not pieces. This is a cemetery! Even the dead find rest here, how *dare* you attack us here!"

For once, I wasn't the weirdest person in sight anymore. "What the crap, lady? Call off your birds, okay? We're here to mourn, that's all."

A light sprang from the end of the cane and now all our faces lit with its yellow glow. The woman seemed far younger than her voice, her short black hair a floating mess in the wind.

"Who might they be visiting, and who are they?"

"My name is Skye MacLeod, and I came to pay my respects to my friend Raven."

The woman closed the distance in a blink, her nose to my nose, her breath smelling of roses and sickly-sweet rot. "Skye? Raven? Ha! Good, good! The Toppled Knight mourns her pawn."

Fury rose in me, bird swarm or no.

But before I could say anything, Cassie shouted, "She was *not* a pawn! Her name was Jessica, and I'm her sister Cassie! Now call off your flock!"

The bird lady moved from my face to Cassie's in the blink of an eye. "Cassie, daughter-daughter-daughter to the Eastern Harper. We smelled the craft, didn't we? Oh yes, we did. The Timid Bishop it is, not sure of her direction, hmm?"

Then, as quick as she'd come close, she blinked to the archway. With a clap of her hands the bird woman cried, "Come to Mother Wren, darlings!"

The bubble around us popped, and birds fell in like flapping, cawing hailstones. Cassie and I crouched and covered our heads with our arms while the crows flailed us with their wings and screeched in our ears.

And then, silence.

I opened my eyes and all that was left of the swarm of crows was an expanding avian cloud that thinned and dispersed like smoke as I watched.

Of Mother Wren, there was no trace.

Cassie fell back on the ground and leaned on her family's stone and laughed.

I stared at her. "What's funny about that? Do you know that crazy lady?"

She nodded and held up a finger as she struggled to get her giggling under control.

I stood up and brushed off feathers and dirt that had blown onto my clothes in the maelstrom of blackbirds.

"I don't know her personally, but Mother Wren's a legend. She's supposed to be seen around the city parks, or on the Circle or most anywhere, really, feeding pigeons and crows. I knew there had to be some truth to it, but I had no *idea* she was like that! Wow!"

"What's her problem anyway?"

Cassie shrugged and pulled herself to her feet with a grunt. "Don't know. Maybe she was expecting someone else. Are you a knight, like she said?"

Mother Wren's words came to me: *Toppled Knight.* I sighed. "That's a long story, Cassie. I did work for a King for a couple of years, and he called me that, until Big Con. I won that battle but lost the war, you might say. We parted on good terms, but I was fired by two bosses and a King that day, for doing what I had to do to fix my own blunders. He calls me Oathbreaker now."

Cassie's mouth formed a little "O" and she nodded. "Guess that's a bad thing among the fairyfolk, huh?"

"Yeah. 'Specially if you're one of them."

Cassie laughed. "Oh Skye. You're asking too much. *You're* a fairy? Sorry, but I think I'd notice that. Where are your wings?"

My turn to laugh. "Just a touch of fairy blood, from a dozen generations or more back. In Scotland. Minnie might have gotten the lion's share of that part of me, too."

"Skye. Like the Isle of Skye? Of course, your last name!"

I nodded. "When I was little, I thought my name was a cruel joke by my parents. Skye, head in the clouds, the kids would say. I always was taller than everyone else back then."

Her eyes twinkled as she looked up at me. "Still are, looks like."

"Well... Not taller than *everyone*, but yeah. Cassie, I think I've missed my bus, and I don't want to be here anymore. I don't suppose I could beg a ride to Broad Ripple, could I?"

She beamed at me. "Sure! But hey. I mean, maybe it's a bad time to ask... I don't know..."

Her eyes roamed all around as we walked, shy all of a sudden.

"What, what is it?"

"Well, I was thinking, my next stop was Eagle Creek Park."

"Oh. I guess Broad Ripple is a little out of the way."

She peered over the top of her glasses at me in an owlish sort of way. "Do you believe in ghosts, Skye?"

I had to laugh. "You have to ask what I'll believe after our visit with crazy crow lady and her flying circus?"

Cassie stuck her tongue out at me. "There're things and then there're other things. Do you know about the *GhostBus*?"

I shook my head.

"Well, there's this paranormal investigator who travels the country in his RV with his dog, checking out reports of hauntings. He's got a YouTube show. You know, he's the rival of that one couple. They're all out of Memphis."

I stopped walking and folded my arms. "Larry Fisher."

She stopped and peered at me with concern. "Yes, that's him. What's wrong?"

Images sprang to mind of Larry holding my friends at gunpoint while the demon kept me pushed back, a prisoner in my own head. Then the stories they told later of him sabotaging their web show. "We've met. We're not exactly friends."

Cassie pouted. "Oh. Well, I would have liked to have taken you with me, since we only just met, but I can see there's bad blood there."

Her pout tugged at my heartstrings the way only my Annabelle could do. Cassie was too cute to refuse. "Well, it's been years. What's he up to?"

Her smile was like the sun coming out from behind a cloud. "Well, he's being very secretive, but I got a Facebook invite for a live event in about a half hour at Eagle Creek. We could be on his show! Besides, you have to meet his puppy, he looks like such a sweetheart!"

I kept further concerns about Larry to myself and let her lead me on the path toward the exit. Crown Hill is one of the largest cemeteries in the world; you could spend all day wandering its acres of grassy hills and monuments.

Something moved in the corner of my eye.

I stopped and turned to look. Nothing seemed out of place, just more stones and statues and mausoleums stretching off into the distance.

Cassie stopped too. "What is it, Skye?"

I shrugged. "Not sure. Maybe it was just leaves in the wind."

"I don't know. It seems pretty still now."

We walked further along, and then I saw the movement again. I whirled and still caught nothing.

Cassie shivered. "Skye, have you ever watched Doctor Who?"

"Hmm? Yes, why?"

"I'm pretty sure that angel statue in front of us was right back where we stopped last time."

"Holy crap. When I said monsters are real, I didn't mean television monsters, too. Just in case, do you have anything iron on you? It's made me itchy since Big Con."

I kept an eye on the angel statue in case it moved while Cassie rummaged through her purse.

"Uh... so steel doesn't count? It's mostly iron, right? But not for this purpose?"

"Right. Steel is irritating, iron is deadly."

She came up with a heavy-looking metal pendant. It bore a five-pointed star made in an overlapping Celtic style. The recessed crevices of the design were black, while the relief shone like silver. "This is just chromed over iron. I know because it rusted and I had to have it re-plated. Will this do?"

She swung the pendant back and forth on a loop of leather cord. She took a step ahead of me, toward the statue.

"Careful!" I said. "If you burn it, it's going to fight back."

"But it'll hurt, right? I think I want to test whether it's some gargoyle that's following us without invitation. Maybe teach it a lesson."

Cassie took a step within arm's reach of the angel and let the pendulum swing back and forth toward it.

That's when the statue moved. Just a twitch, but I caught it, and judging from Cassie's shriek, she had seen it too.

"Ah ha!" I cried. "We caught you! You can stop pretending now. Who sent you? King Bask?"

It played possum, silent and still as though we'd never seen it move.

Cassie caught her breath and took a step even closer. Now I worried what the angel might do to her if it decided to grab her. I'd seen wicked granite claws on some of the downtown gargoyles. And they had no love for me, since gargoyles are a type of troll, and I'd had to go to war with the trolls. And killed their godlike Chained Lord. With a little help from Bask. And my army of bikers and nerds. *And Raven.*

Cassie spoke in the same deep voice she'd used earlier when she set up that magical snowglobe around us. "Begone! Bother us no more! Or face the bite of cold iron!"

The angel-gargoyle turned and ran as best it could, grinding and thumping at a slow trot.

Cassie appeared to be shaking, maybe sobbing, and she bent over at the waist, hands over her face, which reddened with emotion.

I touched her shoulder. "Cassie, it's okay, it's going away! You saved us! What's wrong?"

Giggles burst forth from my new friend, and she came up with tears streaming down her face, eyes squinting in laughter. "Oh Skye, I can't believe that worked."

"What? Trolls can't stand iron. None of the otherworldly folk from that realm can."

She pulled her hands down, revealing fogged glasses. She dangled the pendant in front of me. "This is just painted pewter. I got it on eBay a couple years ago."

I tried to hold it back, but I couldn't. We both burst out laughing together.

"That was kinda crazy," I said, gasping for breath. "I mean, what if he didn't fall for your bluff?"

She shrugged. "Then we'd be where we were to start with. Now he's gone. And look!"

She put a hand out to me, balled in a fist, and then opened her fingers to reveal something glittering in the sunlight.

In her hand rested a key, made of some translucent material, like frosted glass, or quartz. The key was like an old cartoonish skeleton key, and it reflected light in such a way that it was difficult to look at for long.

Chapter Three

Cassie peered at me over the rims of her glasses, though they'd cleared of fog. "You should take it. I don't know what to do with it."

I shook my head and put my hands behind my back. "No way. I can't afford to get wrapped up in magical business right now. I've promised myself, and Annabelle, that I'll stay off the booze. And that means no paranormal second sight for me."

She tilted her head and smiled. "Says the girl who just met a witch, a crazy magic bird lady, and a gargoyle in about fifteen minutes' time."

I ruffled my hair as though washing all the crazy out of it. "I know! I can't get away from it! And it's worse, 'cause I can't *see* anything until it's up in my face! I feel like I'm walking around in the dark being poked by things I can't see. I'd kill for a drink right now. Just in case there are more *things* we can't see."

"Seems like you saw that statue move, at least. Maybe I can help you work on owning your powers without drinking."

I took in a deep breath and blew it out. I squinted down at the cute little witch. "Yeah? How?"

She smirked. "I have no clue. Let me think about it. Meanwhile..." Cassie held out the key again. "I'm not keeping this. Seems like the angel came to see you, Skye."

I held out my hand. She dropped the key in my palm, and it sat much heavier than I'd expected. My breath misted on its surface as I held it closer to look. Even though it glowed, it could have just come out of a freezer.

Cassie took my other hand. "We should go before anything else happens. And I don't want to miss Larry and the *GhostBus*."

I shoved the key in my purse and let her pull me along. She made a fast pace for someone head and shoulders shorter than me. We passed under the bridge separating the old south side of the cemetery from the newer part on the other side of 38th street.

She took me past the Eternal Flame and the main building of the cemetery to the parking lot.

Somehow, I knew which car had to be Cassie's. Sitting by itself on the far end of the lot was a Volkswagen Beetle. Not one of the new space age ones, but the kind that hadn't been made for decades. It wasn't the kind of car that made me so sure it belonged to her. No, it was the mass of bumper stickers on the back that made the blue paint underneath difficult to make out. I only got a glimpse, but there was a "My other ride is a broom" sticker alongside one that urged me to "Hang up and drive!" I smiled when I noticed a "University of Catan" sticker.

She noticed me reading. "What? I like stickers!"

"I can tell! I like the rainbow stripe, personally."

"Oh! So, the Annabelle you mentioned...?" She made a silly, outrageous wink at me.

A grin split my face and I hugged myself. "Yes. She's my girlfriend. She's a *firefighter*!"

She unlocked the passenger side door and opened it for me. "Oooooh! That's hot! You'll have to introduce me." She waggled her eyebrows.

"Sure. I think she'll like you. She usually likes my friends."

As we sat in her car together, Cassie blushed. "You're so sweet. I'm glad I met you, even if it was at my sister's grave."

The warm glow fled me as cold guilt washed through me. I looked away, out the window, as she started the car. It took her a couple of tries, during which the elderly Beetle coughed and backfired. After she loudly questioned its parentage, it burst to life, and we zipped out of the parking lot and onto the city streets.

I have to admit, I'm a lifelong pedestrian. I grew up in Chicago, taking the Ell and buses everywhere. Since moving to Indy, I've adopted the bus system here, though it's not nearly as frequent or convenient. I'm lucky to have friends who don't seem to mind giving me rides, though I try not to wear out my welcome.

Sudden muffled music from my lap brought my grin back. The theme to "Chariots of Fire" played, and I dug my phone out of my purse. My fingers brushed something icy inside, and the image of the key sprang to mind.

"Hey there hot stuff!" I said, answering Annabelle's call.

Her voice came as a relief. Annabelle's been so good to me since Big Con. "Hey baby! What's shakin'?"

"Oh, let me tell you. Crown Hill is the paranormal place to be today."

She groaned. After all the crap we've been through with fairy creatures and strange magic, it gets to be a conditioned response.

I laughed. "I know, I know. But don't worry, I haven't had a drop to drink. It must be my magical personality drawing them."

Cassie raised her voice so she could be heard over the phone. "I'll say! Wooohoo!"

On the other end of the line, Annabelle coughed. "Who's that?"

I rolled my eyes at Cassie, but I put a little tease in my voice. "Oh, that's just this witch who picked me up. She's taking me away with her to look for boogeymen in Eagle Creek Park."

I could almost hear Annabelle's face cloud up. "A witch? What's going on, Skye?"

Cassie called out, "I might just keep her for myself! Eee hee hee!"

"Skye..."

I laughed. "She's Raven's sister, Cassie. We've hit it off. She's a terrible flirt. You'll adore her."

Cassie stuck her tongue out at me and then looked forward as her light changed. The Beetle complained, and then lurched forward.

Annabelle sighed. "Uh huh. Well, don't you let her cast any charms on you. You're mine, remember?"

"I remember, babe. I'll let you know when I'll be home, shouldn't be too much later. Love you!"

"Love you, too. Be careful."

"I will."

I hung up as Cassie made loud kissy noises.

I clicked my phone off and glared at Cassie. "Are you *always* this obnoxious?"

Cassie giggled and gave me a raspberry. "Sure, why not?"

In a little while, we pulled up to the turnstile for Eagle Creek Park. Cassie flashed a member card and they waved us on past.

"Come here often?" I peered around as she drove deeper into the park, past a parking area and onto a side road.

She nodded. "City witch's gotta keep in touch with nature somehow, right?"

"Ever been to Holliday Park?" I thought of Queenie's hidden castle and her frogman minions. Then I remembered its current proprietor: my former boss and mentor Bask, the Transit King.

"Uh huh. Love that place, but parts give me the creeps. Always feel like I'm being watched."

"That's 'cause you are. So much goes on there that mortals can't see."

"Oh, so now you're not a mortal?"

I laughed. "Pretty sure I'm mortal. I just have one foot in the other world and a wee bit of fairy blood."

"Yeah that's what you said. Must be super cool!"

"You'd be surprised how unfun it can be sometimes."

"Oh, I don't know!"

She pulled the little Beetle into a picnic area with a large field, a parking lot, and a shelter house. Parked across maybe a dozen spots was an enormous vehicle with GHOSTBUS painted in drippy green letters across the side.

I squinted at the *GhostBus*, which was clearly a converted schoolbus from before my childhood. Black paint covered the lower half of most of the side windows. Red Christmas lights along the tops made the interior glow with a dim, warm light.

A few other cars had parked nearby, and people in black hoodies milled around. The hoodies had cartoon ghosts or bore cute slogans about the paranormal. Some of them waved around electronic boxes with flashing lights. Others held pendulums or walked around, led this way and that by the pointing of metal rods held out before them.

Ghost hunters.

I scanned the people, looking for familiar faces and didn't see anyone. It made sense. All the ghost hunters I know would drive a hundred miles out of their way to avoid Larry. Seeing as he'd kidnapped a few and let others—like me—get possessed by a demon as a part of a moneymaking scheme years ago.

"Guess I'm the only one stupid enough to go see Larry on purpose."

Cassie, who'd been halfway out her door, paused and studied me. "Why? How bad are things between you and Larry?"

I shook my head. "He's bad news is all. He's hurt a few of my friends. Guess I owe a lot of who I am to him, in a backwards sort of way. Let's go."

I hopped out of the car and followed her toward the ghost hunters.

As if the show had been waiting on us, the door of the *GhostBus* swung open. A creature burst out and dashed past the first few ranks of ghost hunters and made an arrow right for Cassie.

I yelled and grabbed Cassie to pull her out of the way, but she was making kissy noises and holding out her hands. "Who's a good puppy? Yes you are! So good to meet you, Jimmy puppy!"

The creature turned out to be a beautiful golden retriever who slobbered all over Cassie's hands in greeting. He barked once at me but seemed unconcerned overall.

"Well what have we here? Haw. Never thought I'd see you again, girlie." I'd know Larry's drawl anywhere. I shivered as forbidden nightmares welled up from their prison deep inside my guts.

I looked up into the weathered grinning face of Larry Fisher. His brown eyes glinted in the shadow under his black leather cowboy hat. His too-white teeth gleamed as only a predator's can.

I wanted to punch that smug expression right off his face. "Hey Larry. Got anyone I know chained up in that bus, or are you still looking for someone's life to ruin?"

He affected a wounded posture, hands crossed over his chest. "Skye, you're lookin' at a reformed man here. What I done,

I did out of desperation. Out of blackmail, even. Don't you b'lieve in second chances?"

I folded my arms. "Sometimes. From all I hear, you've run out of second, maybe third chances with a few people I know. You better be glad Frannie didn't join these folks. She'd haunt you good, make you pee your pants on camera. I'd pay your subscription fee to watch that."

Larry's grin disappeared and he whistled to his dog.

Larry scratched Jimmy's head with genuine affection. To Cassie, he said, "Ma'am. I see you met Jimmy. He's got good taste; with his endorsement, I figure I won't judge you by the company you keep just yet."

Cassie bit her lip and looked from Larry to me and for once, had nothing to say.

Jimmy barked once and eyed me. I expected a growl, but he just watched.

"Larry Fisher, meet Cassie Fowler. She's a fan. I'm just along for the ride."

Larry held a hand out, and Cassie accepted it. They gazed at each other a long moment, then parted.

"Nice to meet you," said Cassie, in a softer voice than I'd heard her use so far.

Larry flashed her a grin and let his eyes slide right past me as if I wasn't there. That was fine by me.

He turned to the crowd and greeted them with a whoop. "*GhostBus* fans! Welcome!"

The couple dozen people around us cheered and waved their arms.

He waded through them with Jimmy in his wake. "Y'all are too kind, comin' out to see me. Tell me, who all here knows somethin' about ghosts?"

Everyone cheered louder. Everyone but me.

"Now, I knew that. But who here knows somethin' about the little people?"

The ghost hunters paused and looked around at each other.

I raised my hand.

Larry narrowed his eyes and laughed. "Haw. Skye, right? What d'you know about little people?"

"Well, there's all kinds, aren't there? Goblins, for example. Redcaps." I thought of my Minnie with a pang of loss, not having seen her in weeks. "Unique fae folk too, who just happen to be small."

"Hah. Yeah, sounds like you know your fairy tales."

"Some of them aren't complete bullcrap, Larry."

He touched the rim of his hat and coughed. "Well now, that's just why I'm here today. The Delaware Indians used to have a name for a nasty type of little people. Mean spirits that haunt the woods, spoil your milk, burn your crops. The stories say the little bastards'd push you off a cliff just for a laugh."

Someone called out, "Gremlins!"

"Yah, that's pretty close! But the Delaware, they called these little monsters 'pukwudgies'."

Laughter filled the air.

Chapter Four

"You're the expert, Skye, what d'you know about pukwudgies?"

I drew breath and said, "I *think* they're like pookas. But they're supposed to be way up in New England, aren't they?"

Another girl piped up. "You mean like the Hobbits up in Mounds State Park?"

Larry touched his nose and pointed at the girl. "Yep, that's what I'm talkin' about. There's a history of pukwudgie sightings up in Mounds, near Anderson. Only place outside of New England. Figure it's linked to the Mound Builders. I spent a few days up there, scouting around, listening to stories. Jimmy and me looked around for tracks, but we came up empty. Well, other than spottin' some jumbo-sized raccoons walkin' on two feet. That, and a slashed tire on the ol' *GhostBus* while we were sleeping."

He paused for dramatic effect while everyone peered at the *GhostBus*.

"But that's hearsay. A personal experience. Not evidence. Got nothin' on camera, and without that, it's just stories, people."

Jimmy woofed and wagged his tail. Larry patted his head.

Cassie raised a hand and said, "So if they're supposed to be in Mounds, why are you here? Just visiting fans?"

Larry grinned and touched his hat. "Well now, thanks for askin', darlin'. Sure, I love to meet y'all, but I'm still on the hunt. Word up at Mounds was that the puks have gone missin', those who see 'em regular haven't seen 'em in a month. I just about gave up and drove on back to Memphis, but what did I see on the Kindred Spirits messageboard but a 'pooka' sighting right here in Eagle Creek Park. Not just a sighting, neither. Naw, it was a full-on mugging!"

I rolled my eyes. To Cassie, I murmured, "Pretty sure if there'd been a monster attack in Indy, I'd have heard about it."

Cassie shushed me, eyes only for Larry.

Larry went on, "Lady says she came out here for Halloween to find some nature spirits, out in the wild. While the veil's thin, y'know. As she sat in the woods with her incense, she says some big raccoons surrounded her and changed before her eyes; them critters chased her away from her ritual stuff and her purse. Says they looked like mean little men, 'cept they had spikey quills, claws, and squinty eyes. She got all scratched up, and she busted her ankle runnin' away. She was lucky, since it was pukwudgies."

No one laughed at the name now.

Against my better judgment, I spoke up. "Sounds like something best left alone."

Larry stared at me a long moment and nodded. "You're right. But that's not what me an' Jimmy are about. We look in places no one else would for things no one else knows about. Now. I've heard things about you, Skye. Rumors. Hear you'd be pretty useful, lookin' for paranormal critters like these. Don't s'pose I could buy you a drink and talk business?"

Buy me a drink? Is that just an expression, or does he know what he's saying? "Don't know what you've heard, Larry, but I'm on hiatus as far as the paranormal's concerned."

"Haw. Fair enough. But it's a payin' gig. I'll foot a consulting fee. I'll be here a few days, campin' out. Come see me if you change your mind, 'kay?"

I shrugged. Money was tight at home, but working for Larry? I don't know how I'd look myself in the mirror again.

He raised his voice and swept an arm to take in the rest of the crowd. "Any of you who want to camp out here by the *GhostBus*, I know nights are gettin' cold, and Thanksgiving's comin' up fast, but we'll have fun, I promise. Now, I'm gonna sit in the shelter for a bit, and we'll do some interviews for the show, so come on if you've got stories to tell!"

Larry led them like the pied piper of ghost hunters. I had to catch Cassie's arm to stop her. "Cass, I'm going to sit this one out, okay?"

She bit her lip and looked from me to the receding Larry and back.

I smiled at her. "It's okay. I'll go for a walk, meet you back here in a half hour?"

She nodded and waved and dashed off after the others.

I found a path into the woods, despite Larry's story of the pukwudgie mugging on my mind. As much as I liked Cassie, right now I'd like to be elsewhere. Home, maybe, so I could wait for Annabelle and surprise her when she got home. Or on the strip in Broad Ripple, maybe run into Leslie. Leslie'd know how to put things into perspective, he always does.

Of course, where I'd prefer to be is downtown at Heath's brewpub, sampling one of his seasonal brews. I missed him and I missed the sweet buzz his beers gave me.

I missed my Minniekins. I had the sense, here and there, that she might be on my shoulder, in my purse, or just sitting quietly nearby. Having gone dry, my shadow was mostly just the absence of illumination caused by my body blocking a light source. What frustrated me was that I *knew* she could animate my shadow to get my attention, but I hadn't seen so much as a wave from her.

I found a fallen log to serve as a seat. I drew in cool air and let out tension and stress. I listened to the wind in the trees, the last leaves on the branches rustling as they clung for dear life. I closed my eyes and thought about Minnie. I murmured her name over and over. I pictured her dancing on my knee, I remembered her hefting a shot glass like a stein in a toast. I filled my mind with the sound of her laughter, like the twittering of little birds.

The twittering became more and more tangible, so much so that I opened my eyes and found Minnie dancing on the log next to me.

I almost grabbed her up to hug her to me like a little teddy bear, but I know she hates that. "Minnie!"

She waved a hand and watched me close. "You can see me? Nice trick, Skye!"

I looked around. The path was lit by the moon, the trees outlined by stars. "But why's it night? That's hours away."

She put hands on her hips. "A couple months off, and she's a noob all over again. Hello, Skye, you're dozing in your world. Welcome to my side. Now don't get too excited, you might wake up, okay?"

I nodded. "Gotcha. So, what's going on? Today alone, I've--"

She waved a hand. "I saw, I saw. Good thing you met the witch. Very handy, that one."

"But why, Minniekins? I've been out of the game. What's going on?"

Minnie began ticking off points on her pudgy little fingers. "Okay first, no one ever knows what Wren's up to. She's weird. If I had to guess, she's hoping to use you against Bask."

"But Bask's been avoiding me."

"You and me both, babe. I've taken a few solo bus rides and even wandered Holliday Park, but he's not shown his face. Personally, I think he's up to something."

I sighed. "I miss him too. Before I screwed everything up, we'd gotten so close."

She shrugged. "Maybe. Close can be too close with that guy. Just ask his wife. Oh wait, you can't, she's dead."

"In my defense, she wasn't a very nice person."

"Yeah, yeah, I hear you, sister, I was there. It was her or you and a bunch of civilians. Can't say I miss her either. But it was the Transit King who set all that up."

"So, what about the gargoyle? And the key he dropped?"

Minnie shook her head. "Trolls are in chaos since the big guy bit it after T.K.'s big bus flattened him. They're without a king and from what I hear, in all out subterranean war against the goblins."

I winced. "You think they'll stand a chance?"

Minnie waved a hand. "Eh, never heard of the goblins being genocidal, they'll survive once they take their beating."

"No, I meant--"

She laughed. "Without their brains, those big oafs keep wiping holes in the ground, mistaking them for their asses."

We laughed together for a long minute. The darkness flickered light and back again.

"Whoops, almost lost you there, Biggun. You gotta find a more reliable way to do this, you can't go through life half asleep."

"You're right. Cassie thinks she can help me."

"What, with a spell?"

I shrugged. "Didn't say. We'll see, I guess. What about these pukwudgies. Are they real?"

Minnie's smile disappeared. "As a heart attack, babe. You've been tailed by one."

"What! And I'm sitting here daydreaming in the middle of their woods?"

"I've got your back, Skye. It's just watching, looking like an overgrown raccoon right now."

"Right now? They can change appearance?"

"Believe it. And not just some lame glamour to fool mortal eyes, but genuine shapeshifting. They're all over the woods, and they're pissed about something."

A pair of lights shone in the dark in the underbrush behind Minnie.

"Oh, you ought to know about the Kelpie, too--"

"Eyes, Minnie, behind you!"

The lights flickered once and went out.

Minnie turned around to look, then back at me. "I don't see--"

A scream, like a small child in pain, preceded a spiny animal the size of Jimmy the dog bursting from the bushes, mouth full of sharp teeth bared.

Minnie vanished, and daylight slammed in place of the dark. The creature remained, charging me.

Even as I bolted down the path with the thing nipping at my heels, I wished for the Fairy Hilt so I could defend myself. Or my trusty iron poker. Anything.

It had wild, preternatural speed driving its clawed feet, but I had my giraffe legs taking me in long strides ahead.

I pounded down the path, cold air tearing at my lungs. I didn't dare to look back. I just ran and hoped it gave up before my breath gave out.

I burst from the woods and into the picnic area. Larry darted from the shelter house, toward me. I angled to avoid him.

Jimmy bounded out of the shelter after his master and bayed like a hound on the hunt.

Crack!

A shot rang out, and I whirled around to see Larry firing a second shot from a pistol at the spiny beast. The creature stopped in its tracks, and I glimpsed red in its pelt before it turned and ran back the way we'd come, into the woods.

Larry fired after it twice more and swore.

Dizzy and out of breath, I lost my footing and fell to the grass.

Cassie appeared at my side, her eyes owlish and her mouth open in shock. "Skye! Are you okay?"

I nodded and held up my hand while I caught my breath. She took my hand and pulled me to my feet.

"Was that?"

I nodded. "Think. So. Mean. Little. Bastard."

Larry ran up to us. "Damn, Skye, I knew you'd be handy! Sure about that job?"

I shook my head. "Not sure. I'll think. About it."

Out of the corner of my eye, I'd swear I saw my shadow wave and thrash around. When I looked, it was just me, hair blowing in the wind.

"Tell you what, girl. Come on back tonight, after these folks have gone home. Maybe just sit around the campfire with me and ol' Jimmy and talk. I'll give you a hundred just for an hour's consult about what you saw, okay?"

"Larry, if you were anyone else--"

He held up his hands, glanced at the curious people in the shelter, then said in a low voice. "Look, I can't apologize for that no more. I did you wrong. I did a lot of people wrong. You can ask Frannie. Or ask your buddies Lizzie and Brett. None of them's got no love for ol' Larry, but they can vouch that I'm tryin' to do better."

"Last I heard, Larry, you'd upgraded from kidnapping and consorting with demons to working for an unethical, sociopathic bastard who had you breaking all sorts of laws."

Larry flashed me the briefest of grins. "All true. But I saved their bacon, even after that Brett went psycho on me. See the angle my nose points? I've got him to thank for that. But I still helped 'em get away. And I've gone straight since then."

"I'll think about it. Now go away. I'll be back later if I'm stupider than usual."

He touched his hat and left without another word.

Cassie stared at me, eyes still owlish.

"What?"

"Is all that true?"

I nodded. "That and more. At least I hope the part about Brett breaking Larry's nose is true."

"Who's Brett?"

"A ghost hunter I know. If I've got one foot in the fairy world, he's got one foot in the grave. Him and Frannie both."

She whistled. "Do you have any *normal* friends, Skye?"

I smiled at her. "Not so far."

"Hey!"

"Oh excuse me, Glinda the Nerdy Witch of Naptown, you're my only *normal* friend."

"What? Take that back!"

We laughed and hugged.

She glanced at the woods, and then at her car and then at the dimming November sky. "So, we probably better get you home, huh?"

"Maybe. But Cassie, I think I'll take you up on that offer to help teach me to work my mojo without booze."

She wet her lips and studied me. "Sure. But not today. It's getting too late."

"It's a daytime kind of thing?"

"Well, yes. That, and it gives me a reason to see you tomorrow."

I smiled, and we got in the car. I gave her directions the whole way back to the apartment Annabelle shared with me, just south of Broad Ripple.

As I hopped out, Cassie said, "It was nice meeting you, Skye. Can I ask you to do something for tomorrow?"

"Sure, whatever you like."

"I want you wear something loose and freeing, something that makes you feel like a goddess."

I giggled. "I can do that."

"Also, I need your number, so I can call you when I get off work in the afternoon. I'm on an early shift."

I held fingers to my lips. "Oh, this is all so sudden."

She gave me a raspberry. We laughed, and then exchanged digits.

"Oh, and Skye? Watch that aura. It's been tingeing a little dark since the woods. Watch your back, okay?"

Chapter Five

After Cassie dropped me off, I fidgeted around the apartment. I texted Annabelle, who told me she'd be off at 7. Since that was still an hour and a half away, I went for a walk.

Sure, maybe I was crazy to go off on my own after the events of the day, but I couldn't just sit still, either. I wandered up the street to the Monon Rail Trail and let it take me toward the strip.

Each step took me deeper into gloom, both from the setting sun and the trees looming up around me, nearly meeting above. The glimpses of sky revealed incandescent wisps of cloud, fading from pink to red to deep purple. I caught a fleeting glimpse of birds or bats flitting high above the trees, black against the sky. Something small scurried and rustled in the leaves in the brush alongside the trail, away from the pavement.

I'd have found comfort in the sounds of nature, but at the moment, I craved the company of other people, the solidity of cars and buildings, the predictability of traffic patterns. Nature hadn't been on my side today.

The sudden nearby flapping of wings sent me into a panic. Thinking of Wren's minions, I threw myself off the path, catching my leggings on some thorny vines as I did.

Instead of a thousand crows, my eyes made out one great bird; maybe it was a hawk or a buzzard, its wingspan as wide as I am tall. Then my vision blurred and a man in a cloak stood before me.

He let out a gasp like a gust of wind. "Hah. Didn't mean to scare you that way. Come on out, child."

Thunder rumbled in his voice, and yet noises around us calmed to a hush usually reserved for the first big snowfall of the year. The invitation contained no questions, just the patient expectation of obedience.

Me being me, I said, "That's okay, I like it here among the brambles. I've had enough of fairies for one day."

The big man harumphed, and wind stirred the leaves around me. "I would take it as a courtesy, *fairykin*." He spat the last word like an accusation.

The thing about fairy folk is that they trade favors and courtesy like money. If this guy said it was a courtesy, I could count it as a little favor. So, if I did as he asked, I was safe enough for the moment.

I stepped out onto the path, untangling thorny vines from my legs, cursing under my breath.

He raised a hand and placed a ball of dim light in the air above his head. It hung there like a tiny moon, pulsing with a soft cold light.

It was Santa Claus in a black trenchcoat and a broad-brimmed hat. A younger or drunker Skye might have laughed or made a wisecrack about it not being Christmas until after Thanksgiving. Then again, he gave off a sense of quiet power like storm clouds blotting out the sun, so I might even have thought twice.

I couldn't resist a little snark, just the same. "It's been a long day. I'd ask you to get a drink with me if I wasn't off the sauce for a while."

His eyes were not merry, his belly did not jiggle like a bowl full of jelly. He did smile, but not with his eyes. "Another time, then, I would enjoy the experience. I came to warn you, Knight MacLeod. Forces are in motion, and you might be tempted to meddle, as you have before. Do not."

"Everyone seems to know my name, but I don't remember being introduced."

He blinked, and it seemed to me this might be the first time since he arrived. "You may call me Earl."

"Pleased to meet you, Earl. I've been doing my damnedest not to interfere, or even *talk* to fairy folk for months now. But if I keep getting told what to do, I might just be getting curious."

His massive eyebrows knit together as his face clouded. "That would be inadvisable. Your Transit King would tell you the same."

I let out a frustrated noise. "Transit King! Is that what this is about? Tell that little bus tyrant I'm sick of his games. If he sends another fairy after me, so help me--"

"You should not use that word so freely. There are many who would take offense."

I snorted. "Fairies is as fairies does, bub. Approach me like a person sometime, with a little respect, instead of throwing magic around to impress or intimidate me, okay? It's bad enough I'm on the wagon, but to be reminded constantly that I'm nothing special without regular doses of ethanol, that's just a slap in the face."

"I am warning you--"

"No! I'm warning you, get out of my face. Leave me alone or you'll find I'm full of ways to make your life miserable, whoever you are."

He pulled himself up to an impossible height, eclipsing his tiny glow-moon, and seemed to expand to fill the path. His eyes flashed like lightning, and his low voice rumbled like a freight train. "I am the Wings of Winter, the holder of the Ice Chalice, the Lord of the Sky in this city and beyond. Mind your manners, mortal, or you may find it difficult to face the open sky ever again."

Have you ever been there when lightning struck? The pure primal terror of the sound can make your muscles move on their own and send you fleeing and screaming without you being involved in the decision.

This was like that, only I'd faced down the Chained Lord and Queen Howl, and I'd even defied Bask, the Transit King. I held strong, like my family motto. I drew breath. "And I am Skye MacLeod of the MacLeod Clan, former Knight of Bask, and protector of mortals from the likes of you. Begone or I will take up the Fairy Hilt and so help me, I'll do to you what I did to the big supernatural bullies before you. Goodbye, Earl."

Pushing it a wee bit far, I snapped my fingers in his face.

Upon reflection, that might have been a poor choice. It's sort of comforting to know it wasn't caused by alcohol this time.

His cloak became feathered and wide, touching trees on either side of the path. He raised his head and let out a cry that would have made the King of Eagles jealous.

And with one flap of those great wings, he vanished into the sky.

I made it to Broad Ripple proper without any further encounters. The pub on the corner exerted a gravitational pull on me. Just one drink, and I could have a nice chat with Minnie. Just one, and maybe I could hold onto the buzz long enough to see those pukwudgies coming. Just one drink and I wouldn't be worried about invisible gargoyles, trolls, or fairy royalty taking me by surprise.

But no, I was a good girl and passed it by, along with some of the more obnoxious bars along the road. I snubbed the Starbucks, like I had every day since I'd been fired from there.

No, my feet took me to the Cafe' Expresso. The name of the place made me wince every time, but the menu made it clear to grammar nazis that the misspelling of the word "espresso" was a deliberate play on words.

A favorite haunt since my self-imposed dry spell, I'll admit the place helped fill the gaps with another bad habit. At least my soy chai lattes aren't going to get anyone killed. I bellied up to the bar since there wasn't time to settle into a booth and get cozy. The hunky barista behind the counter took my order and set about concocting it.

"Hey, Skye."

The woman to my left brushed blue bangs out of her eyes and gave me an impish smile.

"Blue! I didn't know you were in town!"

She shrugged. "Thanksgiving. You know how it is."

Blue and I have a bond; we've both lost parents. She still had her dad, but he lived out in New York or something. Thanksgiving was never an easy time for either of us, and last year, we'd both gotten tangled up in some nasty supernatural business.

I raised an eyebrow. "Hope Rebecca doesn't have you working this year."

Blue studied me. "You still on the outs with her?"

"She's kept away since Big Con. I figure if she wants to talk, I'm a lot easier to find than she is. For a while, I thought she kept me on because I stood up to her, but that's really why she fired me."

Blue sipped at a soup bowl sized mug of foamy cappuccino and sighed. "I haven't forgotten how you stood up to her for me that one time, Skye."

I smiled. "Yeah you could be on the same list I'm on now. Whatever. It's cool. I mean, I've got some information for her if she's interested, but I'm not crawling to her to beg for work, either."

Blue pursed her lips, then said, "What kind of information?"

I waved a hand. "Pukwudgies, for instance."

"You mean in Eagle Creek?"

"What? Yeah. Larry Fisher's out there with his *GhostBus* talking about them. One nearly bit a chunk out of me earlier today."

Blue leaned in closer. "So they're real? I thought Rebecca was pulling my leg, sending me on a wild goose chase."

"So, she did send you on a job, just a couple days before Thanksgiving? Typical."

Blue swept her fingers to one side, dismissing my words. "Nah. I was here anyway. We're having a Very Perionne Thanksgiving. Chip's driving up and bringing his dad, and my dad's flying in. You and Annabelle could join us, if you're not doing anything?"

Oh, how sweet! "Tempting, and thanks for inviting us, but Annabelle has to work that night, so we're just having turkey pot pies or something at a casual Friendsgiving party around noon before she takes off."

"Gotcha. I gotta be honest with you, Skye, I asked Rebecca about taking you along on this job, and she said not to bother you. What's up with that?"

"You mean other than the disaster at Big Con? Well, I'm sure she knows I'm not drinking, and therefore I'm powerless."

Blue snorted. "Didn't see you use powers last Thanksgiving. Or drink."

"Yeah. Maybe Rebecca had me in reserve, in case there was a spirit world connection?"

"Tell me, what powers do I have, Skye?"

"Well, there's... I mean, you can..."

She sipped and wiped foam from her lip, revealing a grin. "I'm just a tough girl who's seen a few things that go bump in the night. Same as you without your powers."

"I'm not so tough. I'm kind of a nerd, Blue."

Blue rolled her eyes. "You've met my boyfriend. But do you get *all* your courage from alcohol? No, you were cold sober when the shit hit the fan, and we wouldn't have made it out of that mess without you."

"You make a good argument, kiddo. So why do *you* think Rebecca left me on the bench for this and called you in?"

"Beats me. If I had to guess, I'd say pride got in the way."

"See? You get it. Rebecca's so full of pride, it gets in her way."

Blue drained her mug and stood up. "Did I say Rebecca's pride? I think you two bonk heads because you're so much alike. See you around, Skye."

"Wait, what about the job?"

She smiled. "The job's mine. You'd have to talk to Rebecca if you want in on it. Later!"

Blue bounced out of the Cafe Expresso and into the night.

Chapter Six

"You want to do *what*? No way, Skye. That's crazy." Annabelle threw herself in the orange plush chair in the living room and gnawed on a slice of formerly frozen pizza. She looked everywhere other than at me.

"Larry's not to be trusted, I know. But he'll pay me to, I don't know, be a paranormal lookout."

"Without drinking, Skye?"

"Without drinking, scout's honor!"

"You were a girl scout?"

"See? I'm full of surprises, baby. And yes, without drinking. You know I can see stuff out of the corners of my eyes. I've got that spidey sense sort of thing, too. And like Blue said—"

"Blue is one of the only people I know that's more reckless than you, Skye. I blame Burton. She's too easy and free about putting other people in danger. Maybe she's the worst out of all of you."

"But Belle, this isn't with Rebecca."

"Because working for a sociopathic kidnapper is a step up?"

I set my slice of pizza down on the table on a paper plate and crouched next to her. "I might be without powers, but so's Larry. He's not hanging out with demons or under anyone's thumb. He feels lighter, calmer. And he's got a dog!"

"So? Lots of people have dogs."

"But the dog loves him. If you can't trust people, look to their animals. How they treat pets says everything about them. Maybe Jimmy's been a good influence?"

She tore another bite off and chewed for a while. Then, she said, "I just can't believe you're defending Larry of all people. Even reformed, he's the worst, babe."

I shrugged. "I don't have to like him or trust him. It's just a job."

"What about the little monsters with the spines and claws? This is the kind of thing you stopped drinking to avoid."

"No, I stopped drinking because it made me stupid, and I screwed a lot of things up. It wasn't the drinking that made me special. It just brought that specialness out. I want that back, Belle. I miss my Minnie, I miss being a part of that world."

She stared out the window. "What about this world? What about us, Skye?"

I groaned. "Why does it have to be one or the other. What if I asked you to choose between me and firefighting?"

"That's not the same--"

"Yes it is! It's your calling, it's what you love to do. It's part of who you are. Just like the fairy world's in my blood. Literally!"

"If Bask didn't lie to you about that, too."

I walked across the living room between her and the window to face her. "Bask makes up stories, but you know better. You've seen what I can do."

Annabelle scrunched up her face. "Yes, and it's dangerous. I don't want to wake up some day and hear you got eaten by a Grue on some whack-a-doodle mission from Carmen Sandiego."

I almost laughed at that. Rebecca was known for her red hair and fedora. But I knew it was bait, and I refused to be lured off topic. "You think I'm not worried when you go out on runs? What if a burning house collapses on you?"

"Babe, we're trained for that."

"And both T.K. and Rebecca took me under their wings and trained me! I'm not just some paranormal padawan anymore."

One corner of her mouth quirked. "But you are not a Jedi yet."

I sighed and stomped back to the dining area and nibbled on my rapidly cooling food. "If you tell me not to go, I won't. But Belle, even if I don't get my special sight back, this is my calling. I'm like Iron Man without the suit, but Tony Stark is still pretty bad ass."

"What are you going to do, sass the pukas to death?"

I crossed back to the living room and picked up the iron fireplace poker. "It might not be my ancestral blade, but it'll do against fairy folk."

"I thought that burned you now?"

My fingers did tingle, even holding the iron through a wooden handle. "It's fine. Look."

I held the length of the poker against my forearm. The sensation of electricity crawled all along where the metal touched me, but not the searing burn I got when under the influence of the Transit King's powerful "wonderbooze". After a few seconds, I pulled the poker away and showed her.

"Looks like a sunburn to me."

"So? I'll just keep the metal off my skin. Or maybe put on some SPF 30."

"I still think this is a stupid idea."

"I don't have any other jobs lined up."

"Heath's offer stands. He needs an assistant brewer."

I rolled my eyes. "Because working at a brewpub helping make delicious beer would help matters so much."

"Fine. You win, Lady MacLeod. Go off on your damn fool crusade with Indiana Bonehead and the Hedgehogs of Doom. Just wear a sweater. It's getting down below freezing overnight."

I laughed.

She scowled.

I took her pizza plate from her and set it aside, then curled up in the elderly orange chair with her. The chair groaned and something popped in its internal woodwork.

She pulled my face to hers. "You damn well better be careful out there. Hear me Skye?"

"Shut up," I said, covering her mouth with mine. She responded, and I lost myself in a kiss even more delicious than the visions of Heath's beer dancing in my head.

After some fun kissy time together, I packed up some necessities in a backpack, then threw it in the back of Annabelle's pickup truck with my bicycle and a sleeping bag.

Annabelle didn't say much as she drove me to the park. "Isn't Eagle Creek closed at night?"

"Yeah I think it is. Guess Larry's got special permission?"

We pulled up at the gate and a park ranger came out of the gatehouse and pointed at a "Closed" sign.

I hopped out and told him about Larry and the *GhostBus*. The ranger told me to hold on a moment, and I watched through the window as he got on the phone and argued with someone. After a bit, he came back and said, "Huh. Guess he's got a permit from the city. You can go in, but not the car."

Annabelle grumped some more, but she kissed me goodbye and helped me put on the backpack and bungeed the sleeping bag and fireplace poker into the milk crate attached behind my seat.

I pedaled away into the park, glad for the little LED headlight as the gloom closed in around me. The paved road flew by under my tires, and despite the icy sting of the wind on my face, I felt exhilarated and free.

"I should totally bicycle everywhere," I told myself. I flexed my fingers to keep them from going numb.

In a few minutes, I came upon the picnic area and shelter. The *GhostBus*'s red Christmas lights promised warmth, which made me pedal faster.

As I closed the distance, I noticed a flickering light under the bus, and for a moment, I worried it might be on fire. Once I stopped near it, I realized it must be a campfire on the other side, so I parked my bike, picked up the poker, and walked around the back of the bus. I remembered Larry's gun, so I called out a greeting before rounding the end of the bus.

Larry and Jimmy sat near the fire. Larry tipped back a beer bottle and raised it in my general direction.

Maybe this wasn't such a great idea after all.

"Hey Skye, pull up a log and sit awhile."

"Hey Larry. This is still a paying gig, right?"

He nodded and grinned. "Need me a consultant. My specialty is ghosts and demon-kind. We both know these pukas are a different kind of thing. Something up your alley."

I nodded. "Seems that way. How'd you get permission to camp out here?"

Larry tipped the bottle up and tossed it in the fire. "I got a guy. He fixed me up. Ranger give you any trouble?"

"Not really. Didn't seem to like it much."

"Doesn't have to. Want a beer?" He popped open a cooler behind him and fished out a couple of longnecks.

"No, but thanks."

"Aw come on. I heard about you, Skye. I hear it'll help loosen up that sight of yours."

I stared into the fire. "Someone's been running their mouth too much, I think. Does the job require it? 'Cause I'm not drinking."

Larry put one of the bottles on the ground next to him and twisted off the cap of the other. "Naw. Just hoped for a little extra insight, if you know what I'm sayin'. These vicious little bastards can hide in plain sight, so havin' some second sight might be best."

"Maybe. But I've promised myself to lay off for now. I still get glimpses here and there. Should give us some warning."

Larry nodded and took a swig of beer. "Haven't seen anything tonight, but I keep hearin' things. Jimmy's chased after shadows a couple times, too."

I dug in the dirt with the end of my fireplace poker. "So what's the plan? Sing 'Kumbaya' around the campfire until one of them charges us?"

Larry snorted and showed me his pistol. "That'd make life easy. Pow. Right through the head. Naw, these guys are the very definition of tricky. It's not gonna be anything so straightforward."

"Got anything iron, Larry? That's what's best against spirit world creatures."

"Well, yeah. Got me some horseshoes for pitchin'."

"Those might work. Most iron things will, in a pinch."

Larry popped up from his seat and disappeared into the *GhostBus* for a minute.

Jimmy and I regarded each other over the dwindling campfire. As I made eye contact, he sat up.

I smiled at the dog. "How's it going, boy?"

Jimmy opened his jaws wide in a yawn. His tongue lolled out to one side, and I got the impression he smiled back at me.

"You're a good buddy, aren't you? Is Larry good to you?"

Jimmy barked twice and wagged his tail.

I tossed a few sticks into the fire. "I guess no one can be all bad if they've earned the love of a dog."

The doors to the bus banged open and shut, and Larry walked up, carrying a rusty shovel. "Think this'll do?"

I stood and touched the metal blade; my fingers found it tingly and hot to the touch.

"Yeah, it should. Been robbing graves, Larry?"

He scowled. "Why you gotta be that way, Skye?"

I sat back down on the log. "You know why."

Larry hefted a chunk of wood onto the fire, then sat down with me on my log. Jimmy followed, but sat on his master's other side, away from me. "I'm not sayin' what I've done is right, sister. But I had my reasons. In hindsight, I'd do a lot different. Who wouldn't? How about you? Haven't you got regrets?"

I sighed and watched the flames climb higher. My eyes unfocused, and the figures of trolls seemed to dance in the flickering tongues of fire. "Of course. Sounds like you know more about me than I'd have guessed."

Larry sipped at his beer. "Might say I'm a fan of your work. It's not everyone who could unleash hell on earth and tear it a new one in the same day."

"It was a terrible day."

"But you won."

"I got someone killed. Maybe more than one. Annabelle made me promise not to read the news."

"But you won. Results matter, girl."

I turned to glare at him. "Maybe, but if that's all I cared about, I'd be as bad as the 'lords and ladies'. They don't care who gets hurt while they play king of the hill."

Larry's eyes glinted with yellow firelight. "Like the Transit King?"

I shrugged. "I thought maybe he was one of the good guys. Maybe there's no such thing in the fairy realm. He's always done good by me, but then I've made him more powerful than ever by taking out his main competitors."

Larry coughed. "What's his game, then?"

"I wish I knew. But whatever it is, some new players have come at me with attitude, and I'm not even in the game."

Larry laughed and slapped me on the shoulder. "Oh sure you're not. Out here with ol' Larry, watching for spiny bogeymen in the woods in November. Just a fine night for camping, yup."

"Maybe I'm here to figure out what game we're playing, and what the stakes are, before sliding up to the table."

The cry of some night bird, or maybe the death squeal of some small animal, cut through the chill quiet of the woods. As one, Larry and I jerked our heads to look.

"Hear that? I don't see nothin'. You?"

I shook my head and held up a finger. I fixed my eyes on Larry while I forced my attention to my peripheral vision.

Something Jimmy-sized crept toward us. Several somethings, maybe.

I lowered my voice to a whisper. "Yeah. Don't look. Keep your shovel handy."

Larry grasped the shovel with both hands and raised it at an angle, like a baseball bat.

Jimmy flattened to the ground, pointing at the creatures; he let out a growl that set all the hair on my body standing. I would not want to be on that dog's bad side.

Movement. The things dug in and bounded toward us. I stood, the campfire at my back. My shadow stretched out halfway to the tree line, and its hands waved in a Y, unlike my own. *Minnie's trying to warn me.*

Larry stood next to me. He murmured, "Might be a good time for you to get the hell back to the *GhostBus*."

I shook my head no. My shadow nodded with gusto. "Only if you're going."

Larry coughed out a short laugh. "What's the sudden concern for my welfare, MacLeod?"

"If you die, I don't get paid. Also, I've already watched an associate get bitten in half by a monster. I don't want to repeat that. Also, incoming!"

Pairs of lights grew as they bobbed toward us. I held out my poker in an *engarde* position. Larry swept his rusty shovel back and forth, fighting blind.

The several somethings became *many* somethings, and they formed a ring just a little out of our weapons' reach. The fire glinted off their eyes; where their bodies should be, inky shadows moved instead.

"I hear you breathing!" cried Larry. "Come at me!"

Something heavy landed inside the half circle of creatures, in the firelight where we could see.

A smallish body, like a hunched preteen human, lay on the grass, body covered in wicked long spines. Its eyes glazed and white, I knew it was dead. A messy splotch of brick red surrounded a puckered black hole in its belly. On its head sat a hat, constructed of leaves and woven sticks, in the shape of a crude ten-gallon hat.

"Larry, I think that's for you."

"Shit. And I didn't get them nothin'. Saves me the trouble of bagging another one, I reckon. This'll do fine."

I hissed, "Larry, you idiot. This is an effigy, using the creature you shot. Looks like it crawled off and died."

A low moaning rose among the pukwudgies.

Larry spat. "Teach 'em to mess with me."

The puks' moaning became chanting, one phrase repeated: "*Na sah fah bol dah! Na sah fah bol dah!*"

My shadow made a gesture. It drew its finger across its throat.

"Larry, I think they want you dead."

"Who doesn't?"

Jimmy's growl reached a higher register, like a teakettle about to boil. He barked and lunged toward the shadows. He disappeared in darkness, and his barking stopped with an abrupt yelp.

"Bastards!" shouted Larry, and he ran after his dog, shovel held like a bayonet ahead of him.

The circle rushed in, and I jumped back, just missing the fire. I swept at the shadows, and my poker connected with something solid; a feral scream, accompanied by the stench of burning hair and flesh stung my nostrils.

With the fire in front of me, I couldn't make out Larry or Jimmy. My blood surged hot in my veins with fear and anger. A wild, wordless cry filled the air, and it was a few pounding heartbeats later before I realized I'd made the sound.

Larry hollered back, and the night lit in his vicinity by crack of his pistol. I glimpsed the shiny gold coat of Jimmy nearby, half covered by a spiky shadowy blob.

I grabbed up a branch I'd thrown on the fire earlier and held it in my other hand, yellow flames licking as I menaced the beady-eyed shadows. A pair of eyes appeared at my side and I jabbed between them with my poker. With a sizzle and flash of bluish light, they fell out and away, a scream trailing behind.

"I didn't start this fight," I said to the eyes weaving and bobbing before me. "But the MacLeods hold fast."

I took a step and swiped a quick arc ahead of me with my iron poker. Some of the eyes winked out. I repeated the process. A pukwudgie stood too close and screeched as the tip of my weapon grazed its belly; a bright blue comet's tail followed its path.

Another shot rang out so close I stopped and called out to Larry; I jabbed in his direction and a shadow lashed out at me, claws tearing the sleeve of my denim jacket. In my surprise, I dropped the branch, and its fire went out as it hit the ground. I swatted the creature with the length of the poker. It sizzled and ran.

With the shadow gone, I could see Larry. At his feet lay Jimmy, his golden coat darkened with blood in parallel stripes along his ribs. Larry's eyes met mine.

I menaced the milling, chanting shadows to clear an area around us. "Grab Jimmy and haul him to the bus. I'll cover you."

Larry nodded and bent to scoop up his dog in both arms. He braced the shovel under his arm and pointed it forward. I told him to leave the shovel, but he took off running toward the fire and the bus.

As we beat a hasty retreat, the pukwudgies chanted louder. "Na sah fah bol dah!"

Chapter Seven

I had to poke and smack several pukwudgies with the iron fireplace tool as I made a fighting retreat. As we approached the *GhostBus*, I closed the distance with Larry, and as I feared, still more of the little monsters waited for us on the other side, between us and the door. These didn't bother with the shadow glamour; they stood like miniature spiny cavemen with manicures like Freddy Krueger.

Larry's face seemed pale even lit by the red lights from inside the bus. "Skye, grab the horseshoes from my coat pocket."

I swept my weapon in a wide arc before doing as he asked. The pukwudgies came no further, but they held their ground, still chanting, "*Na sah fah bol dah*!"

I planted the poker in the ground to ready the three horseshoes. The metal tingled in my hand like a handful of angry red-hot bees. As I flung the first at the monster closest to the bus door, I yelled, "'*Na sah fah bol dah*' yourself!"

My aim couldn't have been better if my warrior ancestors guided it for me themselves. The horseshoe clocked the pukwudgie right between the eyes and it dropped to the ground like a spiny sack of sand.

Larry edged toward the door of the bus.

The puka next in line howled its rage and led two others to rush me. I hurled a second horseshoe at the leader. It flipped through the air and landed flat on the creature's spiny chest. A blue upside-down U flashed and my assailant howled in agony and clawed at its own flesh and ran in circles, trailing the noxious scent of seared fairy meat.

The others hesitated and I menaced them with the last horseshoe, my fingertips threatening to blister with the intensity of holding the iron.

The pukwudgies fell to all fours and arched their backs, puffing out their spikes like angry cats. They seemed to grow to double their size.

I didn't wait around to see their final form; I dashed for the now open door of the *GhostBus*. Larry blocked the way, struggling up the stair with Jimmy hanging limp in his arms.

I turned my back and faced the pukwudgies, who'd each grown to double size. Black gunk dribbled from their teeth and sizzled on the ground below. Their spines shone like razor wire in the moonlight, their claws became talons that tore up the ground as they menaced me. Those eyes though, will haunt my nightmares, they shone with an inner yellow light of pure hatred.

Too late, I realized I'd left the fireplace poker behind.

"Hurry up Larry, or I'm dead!"

"Hang on!"

I flipped my wrist as though flinging the final horseshoe at them but didn't let go. They howled and jumped back. Their rage burned to new heights at this trick, and they screamed the words of their chant and leaped.

Hands grabbed me under my armpits and hauled me up and into the bus, and the metal door slammed shut; The pukas flattened on the glass and yowled as they contacted the steel of the doors; not as deadly as iron, steel still hurts fairy folk. Trust me, I know from past experience.

I dropped the horseshoe like a hot rock, and it clanged as it hit the floor.

"Larry, this bus isn't going to hold up long, not if there are enough of them."

His voice rasped as he bent over the seat where he'd laid Jimmy. "Yeah, hang on. Jimmy's hurt. It's bad, Skye."

More thuds from outside. The scraping of pitchfork claws along the side of the bus.

I peered at Jimmy. The gashes in his sides no longer bled, but they filled with some tar-like stuff.

"Larry, I hate to say this, but I have a gut feeling he's been poisoned by those things."

Larry pulled off his hat and threw it to the floor. His face twisted in a mess of emotions. I couldn't tell if he was about to scream at me or burst into tears. He ran a hand over his sweaty face and back over his bristly iron grey hair. "What am I s'posed to do, girl?"

The bus rocked; Judging by the subsequent howls, I guessed the pukwudgies hurled themselves against the side.

I shook my head. "I don't know. We can't do anything. Just drive, get us out of here."

Larry nodded, took a breath, picked up his hat, and threw himself into the driver's seat.

A pukwudgie crouched on the hood of the bus, smoke rising from its feet. Its eyes glowed bright yellow and it gnashed its teeth at us.

Larry gave it the finger as he started the engine.

The pukwudgie on the hood threw itself at the window, shoulder first. The resulting star pattern in the glass almost reached the edges of the pane.

Larry laid on the horn and stomped on the accelerator pedal. I grabbed onto the back of a seat and hung on as the *GhostBus* lurched forward.

The shriek of claws on steel made me look. Yellow eyes peered in most of the windows. In the red Christmas lights, their sharp teeth gleamed as though already bloody.

Claws clattered and scraped on the metal roof. The pukwudgies howled like cats, and even inside, I heard their chant.

The bus wagged from one side to the other as Larry threw the wheel back and forth to shake them. I saw one or two tumble past the back window, but even more climbed up to peer in the sides.

I fell into a seat and yelled, "Faster, Larry!"

The engine roared and the bus tilted in a turn so tight the tires skidded and the contents of the bus further back shifted to one side. I held on as though my life depended on it. When the wheels bounced and the bus swayed the other direction, I let out a breath I didn't know I'd been holding.

A crash right next to my head preceded a hail of glass as a taloned arm reached in to grab my shoulder, pinning me to the seat. Desperate for a weapon, I spied Larry's shovel on the floor across the aisle.

Claws bit into my denim jacket; my skin burned where the tips scratched me.

"Hard right, Larry, hard right!"

Larry glanced back and then whipped the wheel to the right.

The rusty old shovel slid across the floor and I flipped it up with the toe of my boot, caught it by the shaft and used it like a spear to pierce the pukwudgie's meaty shoulder. It spasmed and fell off the bus, making shreds of my jacket and scratching my skin.

My shoulder burned. My hand throbbed from the impact. Dazed, I went to let go of the shovel and realized it had been torn from my grasp as the monster fell away from the bus.

Well, shit.

Another set of claws grasped at the edge of the window. I cast around and couldn't spot the horseshoe, so I grabbed the first thing —a heavy fire extinguisher—and bashed at its fingers. Its howl and withdrawn fingers made me whoop in victory.

Larry called back to me, his voice hoarse. "We're almost to the gatehouse!"

There came a pounding on the roof, a furious drumbeat of fists rang the bus like a bell.

I scanned the ceiling. "Does it think it can beat its way through?"

Larry cleared his throat. "Well, just so long as it don't smash through the--"

Glass rained down from the shattered skylight; a spiny black mass with incandescent yellow eyes and needle-sharp teeth followed. It growled deep in its chest and bristled as it faced me.

My eyes fixed on the monster as I shouted, "Company, Larry!"

Larry hollered, "Heads up, Skye! Don't miss!"

I spared a glance just in time to catch Larry's heavy pistol. As I looked up, the monster shredded seat cushions and spit black foam as it charged me.

I fumbled with the safety, fired, and missed. It shrieked and reared up over me, tangled in the red Christmas tree lights.

I fired again, point blank.

It stopped and let out some kind of sigh and crumpled to the floor, twitching. I screamed and kicked at the body to get it away from me.

"Great shot, girl! Hang on, we're blowin' the gate."

I grabbed onto the pole next to the driver's seat rather than trust the broken window of my other seat. And I sure wasn't going past the dead or dying pukwudgie.

Out the front window, I saw eyes peer over the fender on one side. Long scratches in the hood's enamel told the story of several other fallen pukas.

The headlights caught a pair of stone pillars to our left, bearing an engraved wooden sign that read, "Thank you for visiting Indy Parks!"

Larry veered the bus to the left. Claws screeched on the hood as the pukwudgie scrabbled for a hold to climb higher.

Larry floored the pedal and let out a long howl of his own.

The bus shook as the wheels on the left side left the pavement. Headlights caught the sign full on, and just as I thought we'd slam into the stone pillars head on, Larry threw the wheel to the right and the *GhostBus* bounced off the sign, hard. The impact scraped the pukwudgie off the fender; I glanced back, and eyes in the windows all along that side blinked out in rapid succession.

Out the back window, I saw the park ranger stand in a pool of light, arms flailing in the air, mouth hanging open in dismay.

It wasn't funny, I know, but I laughed, and joined Larry in his war whoop.

My blood sang in my veins and pounded in my ears. My head spun with adrenaline, and all I could think about was the thrill of getting away from the pukwudgies in one piece. And then my nose brought me back down to earth; I gagged on a scent somewhere between rank B.O. and a camp toilet.

I peered down the aisle of the bus. Still tangled in red Christmas lights, the spiny body of the puka lay in a pool of its own blood. It seemed so much smaller now, curled up on its side, not breathing.

"Uh, Larry, what do we do about the intruder?"

"Huh? Well hey, there's a silver linin' to that nightmare, I guess."

"Silver lining? It's stinking up the place. And we're driving around with a dead body. How's that a good thing?"

Larry glanced back at me to flash me a grin. "Came here for solid evidence, and looks like I got me some!"

I groaned. I had no love for the monsters that would have preferred to tear me to little pieces, but it seemed wrong. "I don't know, Larry."

"Never mind that now, check on Jimmy, would you?"

I clambered over to the other side of the bus and crouched in front of the seat where Jimmy lay. His breath seemed shallow and fast, each inhale accompanied by a wheeze. He opened an eye when I touched his head, and his tail thumped once.

"It's not good, Larry. I'm sorry."

"Damn it, girl! Don't be sorry! Get on your phone and find me an animal hospital."

Ice formed in the pit of my stomach. My shadow sprayed in all directions around me in the many little lights, but one shadow, over Jimmy, waved its hands with terrible urgency. "I think he needs more than a vet. If that black stuff is poison like I think it is, it's going to take a supernatural cure."

Larry spat rapid-fire curses, and then pulled over on the side of the road and put on the blinkers. He joined me at Jimmy's side. "Can't you do nothin', Skye? I got some whiskey, won't you use your powers to save a poor ol' dog?"

I took a deep breath and let it out. "Wouldn't matter if I did. All I could do is see past fairy glamours and a little into the other world around us. I haven't got healing powers like that."

Larry took off his hat and clutched it in front of him. He stroked Jimmy's head and watched him breathe for a moment. He turned to look at me, eyes pleading. "He's all I've got, Skye. What can I do to help him?"

If anyone ever told me I'd ever cry a tear for Larry Fisher, I'd have laughed in their face. Nevertheless, my vision blurred as my eyes welled up. "Okay Larry, just drive where I tell you. Don't get us pulled over, the dead monster would be tough to explain, and Jimmy needs the time."

"What's your plan?"

"Only one man I can think of who can fix this. We've got to pay a visit to King Bask."

Chapter Eight

I stayed by Jimmy's side as Larry drove through town. In giving him directions, I warred with myself between taking the most direct route to save time and taking back streets to avoid the inevitable attention that the flashy *GhostBus* would draw.

Expedience won out, and horns blared greetings and people shouted out of their cars at us the whole way.

I could only imagine what the outside of the bus looked like after the fight.

Jimmy's wheezy breath became more labored, so I rummaged around and came up with bottled water, which I dribbled on his muzzle. He lapped at the water and thumped his tail. His breath slowed and deepened, and he closed his eyes and sighed.

We pulled up in front of Holliday Park, right at my usual bus stop.

That's when I saw the barrier. "Shit. I forgot there's a big metal gate that rolls shut at night."

"No problemo."

"You're right, we could just hop over it. Okay. You carry Jimmy, and I'll--"

"Screw that. Hold on, we're knockin' on the front door!"

The engine roared and metal ground metal as Larry jammed it into gear and stomped on the pedal.

A stop sign glowed bright in our headlights, and I covered my head with my arms as the *GhostBus* smashed into the heavy metal beam across the entrance. It bent, but didn't break, so Larry put it in reverse, looked behind him, and pulled out into the street.

"Larry! What the hell--"

He threw it back into forward gear and the tires squealed on pavement as I was thrown back against my seat.

This time, the gate crashed wide open and we entered the park.

A half dozen rotund park rangers appeared in Larry's headlights, each with a long black clublike flashlight.

"What the hell are those guys doin' out at night?"

The men stood their ground, flashlights held across their bodies to form a living wall. Their body language couldn't have been clearer if Gandalf himself stood there shouting, "You shall not pass!"

Larry hit the brakes and the *GhostBus* squealed to a halt.

I squinted and unfocused my eyes, trying to force my eyes to see what I knew had to be there. All I got from my efforts was a dull ache between my temples. "Doubt they're what they seem. Those have to be the Transit King's goons."

"Skye, I know you want to be good, but I can't play games here. Have a swig." He threw a small black and silver object at me. I caught a leather-clad pocket flask. Liquid sloshed inside; I told myself, just a little sip couldn't hurt.

I got as far as unscrewing the cap when the Transit King's voice rose from memories of my worst day to accuse me. *Oathbreaker!*

I screwed the cap back on and fought tears. *If I can't keep a promise to myself, how can anyone else ever trust me?* "I c-can't, Larry."

"Just do it, girl. I mean it. If that dog dies, I don't know what I'll do."

I met his eyes and shook my head. "No. We've done it your way so far, now we're doing it mine."

I tossed the flask back to him and stood at the door. His eyes smoldered with anger under that cowboy hat, but he pulled the door open for me.

I stepped out and raised my hands. "Asylum! Lady MacLeod begs asylum!"

One beefy man approached and pointed his stick at my hand, which still held Larry's revolver. I hated to give it up, but diplomacy demanded it. I tossed it back in the bus, where it landed with a clang. Larry started to step down after me, but I shook my head and mouthed, "Not yet."

I got a glimpse at the outside of the *GhostBus*. Scratches and streamers of black ichor ran down its sides. A long, thick crease ran from nose to tail where the gate dragged along the side. And this was the right-hand side. The other had to be far worse after scraping the pukas off.

Maybe my eyes played tricks on me, or maybe it was Minnie playing games to tell me something, but I'd swear I saw a shadow slide off the top of the bus and into the deeper shadow of the park. Movement from the ranger in my peripheral vision gave me the impression of goggle eyes and slick greenish skin and the glint of sharp metal in the headlights.

The "ranger" who'd stepped forward approached me, making a gurgling, burping noise. He said nothing, but gestured for me to put my hands out.

"I'll come without trouble."

The guard shook his head no, and repeated the gesture.

I glanced up at Larry, and did as the guard wanted. Not looking, I felt wet flappy hands tie my wrists with a thin cord. It wasn't comfortable, but it didn't hurt, either.

Larry stepped out of the bus, Jimmy in his arms. The false ranger looked him up and down and held out his hands the way he had for me.

"I can't. I got a sick dog here we're bringin' to King Bask."

The rangers burbled and grumbled as they conferred in a huddle. They moved to surround us, and the beefy ranger motioned for us to follow.

As we walked, I heard more footsteps than accounted for by the people I could see. I caught glimpses of green-gray-skinned things walking upright to our right and left. The swampy smell of watery decay wafted through the night air. My shoulders tingled as though a bullseye hung on my back. The cord itched.

The guards' flashlights lit up a tall sign advertising renovation on the artistic but fake ruins that served as the city park's centerpiece. The money thermometer almost met the top, only a few thousand shy of its goal. We skirted the caution tape that surrounded the monument I knew to be a cover for the fairy castle that served as Bask's residence. I'd spent a few hours in the fetid dungeons under that castle.

It bothered me that no matter how I squinted my eyes, no matter the games I played with my peripheral vision, I failed to see through the illusion surrounding the castle.

The guards stopped at an unremarkable stretch of fencing. One whistled and we waited.

After a few moments, the fence bowed down, and a drawbridge led into an impossible hole in space. My eyes strained when I peered into it, my brain fighting me, struggling to look away, anywhere else.

To my left, Larry let out a low whistle of his own.

As we were prodded onto the drawbridge, the world sort of did a flip-flop, turning inside-out as we marched into the castle that hadn't been there before. I peeked the way we'd come, and found a stone archway framing the grassy lawn of Holliday Park. A statue gave me a blank look, eyes focused somewhere below and behind me.

Inside, the guards showed their true faces as the frogmen I expected to see, wielding pikes and carrying flaming torches. Their bulbous eyes rolled in their sockets as they took up positions to block our exit. There had to be a dozen or more all around us. They left the side facing into the castle proper open.

"Raise the gate, ye great damned fools!"

I turned around to see my friend, Bask, the Transit King, red-faced and waving his arms, glittering silver crown askew, tufts of his gray hair sticking out above and below.

He marched up to me, raised to his full four feet of height, peered up and shook a finger at me. "Skye MacLeod, ye excel at mucking up the works. What did I ever do to ye?"

Behind me, the clank of chains and groan of wood and metal signaled the closing of the drawbridge, shutting us in.

I drew breath. "Me? I came here to ask your help. See, Jimmy the dog--"

He kicked my shin. It hurt, and I yelped. "Shut it! Yer boyfriend bashed in me gate with his poor excuse fer a bus, an' led an army of ragin' pukas to me doorstep!"

"Oh, no. Larry's not my--"

"I said, shut it, ye daft girl! D'ye ever think about anything before ye do it? Are ye back on the sauce, mebbe?"

I shook my head. "No, I'm still dry, but--"

"Shut. It. Ye meddled with creatures of which ye have no ken, riled 'em up, an' now they're mine ta deal with! I've got enough going on, things bigger than this. Ye've nae idea!" He huffed and wheezed, but his eyes blazed with an anger I hadn't seen since I crossed him at Big Con.

"Listen to me! Please. It's urgent, and you're the only one I can turn to."

He threw his hands in the air and turned his back on me to stomp a few paces away before turning back to face me. His eyes narrowed and he twirled one hand in front of him. "Out wit' it, but be quick. We're about ta be under siege."

Larry spoke up, eyes shifting and guarded. "It's my dog, sir. King sir. Your Highness. Sir."

"He's hurt," I said. "By the pukwudgies. I think it's poison."

Bask took his silver circlet off his head and wrung it in his hands, brows low over his stormy eyes. "Oh, it's a wee sick doggie, is it? Why o' course, I'll drop everythin'! My men kin handle a few hundred ancient, bloodthirsty bein's fer me while I tend to yer pup. No problem at all!"

I folded my arms. "Sarcasm isn't pretty when you do it, Bask."

He jammed the crown back on his head and stomped up to me. "That's *King* Bask ta you, ye idiot fairykin!"

"Please," I said. "Can I have it as a favor, for old times' sake?"

He shook his head, and a lock of hair fell between his eyes. "Nae. I can nae. Not e'en fer *old times* sake', Skye. Ye may be kin ta me, and we might be friends, but ye broke yer promise to me once, an' I can nae trade favors with ye again."

I can't say I didn't expect this, but it still hurt my heart to hear it. "I hoped we'd be square, you know, when I turned over the Fairy Hilt to you for safekeeping?"

He chewed his lower lip a moment. His voice lowered and softened just a touch. "T'was a gracious gesture, to be sure. But whatever else may happen, I can nae engage in that sort of contract with ye again. There be no bindin' to wrap power around, ye see. No, I can nae. That is final, Skye."

Larry's voice cracked as he jumped in. "Then I offer a favor for a favor. Heal Jimmy, and I'll be in your debt, okay?"

The Transit King took his eyes off me and approached Larry. "Larry Fisher, is it? By yer reputation alone, I should nae e'en believe the dog is sick. If I search yer pockets, will I find a weapon?"

Larry glanced at me, then back at Bask, and nodded. "Yes. A handgun. Loaded. Couple shots left. It's yours, too, if you help him. Please, he's my only friend in the world."

Bask peered up at Larry. "A great tall one ye are to be cryin' o'er an animal. Will ye give me yer bus, too?"

Larry didn't hesitate. "Yes."

"An yer silly cowboy hat off yer head?"

Larry's mouth puckered as though to spit, but his Adam's apple bobbed and he said. "Whatever you want."

Bask grinned. "Now ye get the spirit o' the bargain. Put the pup down on yon bench, an' we'll see what I kin do, shall we?"

Chapter Nine

A high keening wail drifted over the wall, joined by five, ten, a hundred other voices.

The frogmen whistled, burped, and flapped around the courtyard, and were soon joined by maybe twice their number, carrying various medieval weapons. Several wheeled a wooden staircase up to the ramparts, and others ran up to take posts along the wall.

Bask stroked his scraggly beard and muttered over Jimmy. "Skye, ha' ye any booze on ye?"

"No. Told you, I'm on the wagon."

"I've got some sippin' whiskey," said Larry, offering his flask.

After asking Larry to open it first, Bask took the flask from him. I noted that he held the steel container by its leather covering. Bask snapped his fingers and barked an order, and soon a frogman ran up with a stone goblet. The aroma of the bourbon reached my nose as the little king poured a few ounces into the goblet. He returned the flask to Larry. Larry took a swig.

I can't think of when I've needed a drink more than that moment, but I said nothing. Larry caught me watching him and offered me a drink.

My thoughts warred within me. *You're being treated as an Oathbreaker either way, what's it matter?* My fingers twitched and I raised my hand to waist level. I licked my lips.

I shook my head, dropped my hand to my side, and sighed. "No. Better not. But thanks anyway."

Larry shrugged and tipped it back once more before capping it and sticking the flask back in his jacket pocket.

Bask crumbled something into the goblet and mumbled incoherent words. His eyes fixed on Jimmy, whose breathing had slowed to the point I feared he was already dead. But Larry spoke Jimmy's name, and the dog's eye popped open and his tail gave a weak twitch.

"Ye could nae have been later," said Bask, as he snapped his fingers, producing a spark that fell in the goblet. The contents flared up in an almost invisible blue flame, which he poured on the dog's wounds.

Larry shouted, and he leaped to stop Bask, but I blocked him.

"Larry, stop! He's Jimmy's only hope. Don't get in the way."

The flames licked the wounds, changing from dim blue to a bright red. The dog's fur failed to catch fire, and the black of the wounds seemed to feed the flames like wax in a candle.

A voice spoke inches from my left ear. "Neat trick!"

Long habit kept me from freaking out; I turned my head and smiled at my little shadow, perched on my shoulder. "Minnie!"

"Good to see you in the flesh, Biggun!"

I glanced at Larry, but he had eyes only for the Transit King and his dog. The flames turned purplish and burned lower.

"I might not be 'in the flesh' at all if not for your warnings, earlier. Thanks."

Minnie stretched. "All part of the job, boss."

"I'm flying blind, sis, and I can't take much more of it. What else am I missing?"

She made a zipping motion across her lips and then held a finger up, but said aloud, "Oh, the usual. Nothing worse than what you've seen, at least. You sure know how to make friends where ever you go, eh Skye?"

I made a rude noise.

"Skye, I ken ye dinnae get as much chance ta chat with yer other half anymore, but could you do me a favor?"

I turned back to Bask. "Huh? Sure, what?"

"Shut it! I can't hear meself think, an' this is the important part."

So, I shut it.

Bask took Larry's hands and laid them on Jimmy's head. "Hold the pup still, ye ken? No matter what."

Larry nodded.

The Transit King took the hat from Larry's head and put it on his own, covering his crown and resting on his ears. If not for the darkness in his eyes, I'd have called the little king comical.

Bask passed his hands once over Jimmy's body, without touching. As he passed his hands over again, Jimmy twitched and shuddered. A third time, and Jimmy disappeared inside a cocoon of pinkish light.

Larry struggled to hold on. "You sure this is right? He's bitin' at me!"

Bask's jaw set, his eyes nearly crossed in concentration as he seemed to hold the expanding bubble of light in place. "Ye want a second opinion?"

"No. Just don't hurt him."

The fairy lord grimaced with some invisible effort. "Ta get better, sometimes it's got ta hurt."

I could hardly look at the place where Jimmy had been, so bright was the light. Somewhere inside that cotton candy sun, Jimmy bayed and howled. Larry grunted and cursed. The Transit King spoke rough words that sounded Gaelic to my ears.

And then it all stopped, and the light vanished.

I leaned in to see what had happened. Raw pink strips of Jimmy's flesh showed through the slashes in his fur coat, but no black goop and no wound could be seen.

Jimmy remained asleep, but his ribcage rose and fell in deeper, stronger breaths.

Larry, meanwhile, had an ashen look about him; he looked sick or terrified. "It worked."

Bask grabbed a handful of my coat and leaned on me. "T'weren't nothin'."

Larry rubbed his face. "I suppose I owe you."

"Ye *suppose*? That were the bargain. But here," said the Transit King, as he threw Larry's hat back to him.

"Thought you wanted this. What about my bus?"

"I ha' all the buses I need. Ha' ye ne'er heard of the Transit King?"

"But, why'd you ask, then?"

Bask laughed. "Care ta explain fer me, Lady Skye?"

"It was a test. He asked for what he thought you prized most, a sort of down payment on future favors he might ask instead. A show of good faith."

Larry beat his hat against his leg before replacing it on his own head. "So what do I owe you? I haven't got all that much."

T.K. nudged me, so I went on. "Don't worry, he'll ask when he figures it out. Could be anything, though."

Larry's throat bobbed. "Anything?"

I nodded at the same time as Minnie and Bask.

Larry peered at the sleeping dog and said. "I reckon it's worth it."

Bask snorted and echoed Larry's accent. "I reckon."

Shouts from the ramparts drew our attention. The pikes and clubs of the frogmen rose and fell, and the tips of spines and claws appeared for moments, and then vanished.

"Guess they're not afraid of water," I said.

"Guess yer right. Tis the light they fear, an' bein' seen by bunches o' mortals. This ain't my fight, lass. Ye ken that? It's yours, and ye brought it ta me."

I nodded. "But what can we do? Lower the gate so I can wrestle them with my bare hands, while Larry takes out a few with his gun?"

Bask chuckled. "T'would be a brave sacrifice fer yer ol' Transit King, but nae. There'll be enough death and destruction by and by. If I get ye unharmed ta that bus of yours, can ye do me the favor of leadin' the beasties elsewhere?"

"But where? Once we stop, we're as good as dead."

"Nae, don't think like that. Ye'll think o' somethin'. Ye always do, don't ye, Skye?"

I looked at Larry, who shrugged. "Guess the odds must be okay, or he wouldn't risk his investment, right?"

I shook my finger at Bask. "That's right. What's your percentage?"

Bask shrugged. "Notice I'm askin' as a friend, not callin' in my favor from yon cowboy. Stay if ye must, but froggy an' puka deaths'll be on yer head."

He might as well have twisted a knife in my gut. "More deaths, you mean."

"Yes, more. Mebbe not as many as ye think, and mebbe not as permanent."

Minnie shifted on my shoulder. "What's that supposed to mean?"

Bask seemed to notice her for the first time. "Eh, never ye mind, wee lass. Just that these pukas are tougher ta kill than a slap wit' an iron poker."

Larry snorted. "Seemed to work pretty good earlier."

Bask waved his arms and glared at Larry. "Oh, so who's the expert on pukas now? Yer in great trouble, Mister Fisher, an' ye should listen ta those who know what they're talkin' about!"

Larry nodded. "I listen. Bright light bad. Crowds of people bad. So we gotta get through the night, daytime's our friend. What else? Don't feed them after midnight? Don't get them wet?"

I tried not to, but I laughed.

The little guy whirled on me. "Ye think it's funny, O Rogue Knight MacLeod? I warn ye this: lay low, an' keep out o' the comin' days' events or ye'll get squashed like a bug. E'en if ye did work for me, I'd be keepin' you out o' this one."

I squatted so I could meet his eye level. "Yeah? You're the third supernatural being to warn me off today, and I was already keeping to my mortal life as best I can. Tell me what's going on. I can't avoid things I don't know anything about!"

King Bask stroked his beard and searched my eyes with his. "The third? Who else?"

I stood up and crossed my arms. "That's all you get for free, your Majesty."

Bask let loose a stream of Gaelic words I suspected might be quite vulgar. He took a deep breath and spoke his next words with care. "Ye dinna want in this game, Skye. The stakes are too high. If the other players be pushin' ye, it be more serious than I thought. Who?"

Screams came from the ramparts, and one of the frogmen fell. A pukwudgie clambered over the wall and leaped. Flaps appeared between its hands and feet, like a giant flying squirrel, and it glided to the courtyard floor. It took four frogmen to wrestle it to the ground.

Minnie whispered in my ear, "Bad time to make T.K. mad, Biggun."

I sighed. "Find me tomorrow. I know you can. If I don't see you, I'll hop a bus and we'll talk when it's quieter, okay?"

Bask nodded. "Fair enough. Off wit' ye then."

Before I could ask another question, he snapped his fingers and a bus stop sign appeared between Larry and me.

The Transit King patted my shoulder. A warmth spread through me where the pukwudgie's claws had pierced my jacket.

To Larry, he said, "Grab yer pup. Bus is comin'."

"King Bask," I said, drawing breath. "You promised I could have the Fairy Hilt back in times of need. You just got done telling me how dangerous it's getting to be."

T.K. shook his head. "Nae, don't ask. Not yet. 'Tis not time. Ye could wreak greater mayhem with that weapon than ye intend. The balance is too delicate yet, lass."

I frowned, but nodded at him.

The distant roar of an engine echoed, as though from an unseen TV.

Larry picked up his dog in his arms. Jimmy kicked the air and chuffed in his sleep, then licked Larry's face.

Something like a heat haze made the air shimmer between us and the rest of the courtyard. Frogmen appeared to bulge and squish as though seen through a moving funhouse mirror. My head ached in the same way it had as we passed into the castle.

Larry held onto his hat as a wind picked up, and the sound of squealing brakes accompanied a transparent *GhostBus* pulling up at the stop. "What the F--"

He was cut off by the slam of the door opening. Out marched three frogmen, who stood aside and saluted as a ten-foot-tall gorilla squeezed out of the door, nearly popping the buttons off of his IndyGo bus uniform in the process. His namebadge read, "Joe."

"Jesus," breathed Larry.

Minnie hid in my hair.

I took a step back.

The Transit King saluted Joe, who grunted and handed the keys to a stunned Larry.

"Now step quickly, lad, I can't hold this stitch in space long. Ne'er mind Joe, he's a pussycat."

Larry transferred the sleeping Jimmy from his arms to mine. He took the keys from Joe. Joe nodded and stepped aside, gesturing for us to board the wavering bus.

Larry began to waver, too, as he took the first step up into his *GhostBus*. I followed, and with the first step, the rest of the castle, Bask included, warped and stretched and wobbled, while the bus and Larry solidified, or synchronized with me maybe.

Bask's voice came as from down a long tunnel. "An' Skye? Be careful. Things are nae as they seem."

I wanted to shout back a retort. Something about how if only he'd *tell* me more, maybe I could be even more careful. But the second Larry shut the door and started up the engine, the castle vanished, and the *GhostBus* and everyone in it sat where it had when we burst into Holliday Park.

Minnie vanished off of my shoulder, and a lump congealed in my stomach. Every time I see her, I hope that this time she won't have to go away again.

"Here they come. Set yourself down and hang onto Jimmy!"

Larry didn't have to tell me twice. I laid Jimmy across a seat and sat on the edge with one hand on the dog.

Claws scrabbled at the sides of the bus, and glowing yellow eyes blinked from several windows.

I shouted something incoherent, at Larry.

He threw the bus in reverse and stomped the pedal. Tires squealed, and lights streaked past outside the windows as we backed out onto the city street. A car horn blared as its driver laid on it.

Larry laughed, ground gears, and jammed the shifter home. The acceleration threw me back into my seat, and we took off down the curvy, hilly road.

Chapter Ten

"Skye, where you figure we ought to go?"

I didn't even have to think about it. "Let's head downtown. There's lights and crowds, in case the army of pukas follows us all the way."

"I hear you. Can't drive around forever. But what about King Bask? He wants us to drag them critters away from his place, yeah?"

"Yeah, but they'll stop their attack once we've left. Besides, I don't know about you, but I'm not keen on them catching up to us no matter what T.K. wants."

"Gotcha."

One by one, the pukas peering in the windows dropped off the side of the bus, losing their grip with each twist and turn the road took, and with every pothole the tires bounced out of.

A couple clung on, and I had to bash at claws a couple of times with the fire extinguisher. I also used it to spray one in the face, and it let go and fell behind.

"Hey Larry, do you have a good flashlight?"

"You better believe it. Got a pair of million candle power LED models back there. Look for an aluminum hard shell case."

A couple pairs of yellow eyes followed me as I stepped over the dead puka, holding my breath the whole way. I found the case among a bunch of strapped down plastic storage crates. I took a few quick breaths before holding it again to go back to the front.

"Larry, what are we gonna do with that corpse?"

"Sell it, of course!"

I popped the latches on the case and rummaged around inside. "What? Are you crazy?"

"Naw, it'll be worth a *fortune*! Just gotta find a buyer. Maybe the History Channel? They go in for the alien crap, they ought to jump at a freshly dead pukwudgie."

"Where are you going to keep it until then? Because your bus is a gory mess with its blood back here, and I bet people can smell us coming a block away.

Larry turned us onto a wide, busy street that I guessed was Meridian. "Huh. Maybe we better detour to a self-serve carwash? Maybe a truck stop, they've got those. I've got some fifty-five-gallon trash bags, that oughta hold the body, and it'll get cold enough tonight so it won't spoil."

I stood up, hanging onto a pole up front. "Okay then, let me off."

"Huh? Naw, come on, Skye, I need your help."

"No, Larry. I can't be part of this. If the pukas clinging to the side of the bus get us pulled over, we're spending some time in jail, and I'm too pretty for that."

Larry snorted. "Okay, then what's your plan, darlin'?"

"Turn right up here, we can get to the canal. I know a bridge we can stow the body under. You want to come back and get it tomorrow, that's not my problem. But if you want to get away tonight, we'd better go downtown right after that."

"What about the pukwudgies I see in my side mirrors?"

"Leave them to me."

I found the rather substantial flashlights Larry'd mentioned, each weighing a few pounds. Their painted steel casing made my fingers tingle with a disturbing electricity, but the rubber grips made holding them bearable.

I switched one on. It was as though the sun had risen, and I held it in my hand. The interior of the *GhostBus* lit like daylight. I focused the beam on the windows one at a time, reflections off the glass bouncing off the seats, the dead puka, and into my eyes.

I admit, I grinned a little as my plan was rewarded by the screech of claws accompanied by piteous screams.

"Shut that damn thing off, I can't see to drive!"

I flicked the switch, and the inside of the bus plunged into darkness. My eyes took a bit to adjust, but Larry found the canal and pulled up to the pedestrian bridge I'd had in mind.

Jimmy whimpered in his sleep, so I scratched his ears while Larry hurried to the back. I switched the flashlight back on to help him see. I noticed a curious thing as I did: wherever the beam touched puka blood, it turned to steam and vanished without a trace. Even a streak of blood on Larry's jeans evaporated in the intense light without staining.

Just in case, I had Larry open the windows. I got out and circled the bus but found no more pukwudgies clinging to its sides.

Larry emerged with a black bundle, cursing.

"Had to ruin a good sleeping bag. Damn quills kept poking through the trash bag."

I shut off the million-candle-power flashlight and showed him the hiding space under the bridge using only the nearby streetlights to guide us.

I hoped the gas station's security cameras didn't aim this way, or there could still be trouble if someone found the body. At the very least, Larry would have some explaining to do, as the lettering on the *GhostBus* could probably be spotted from a couple blocks away.

Larry and I cleaned up the blood with the flashlights, and then we resumed our path toward downtown.

It grew cold in the bus, so I shut the windows one at a time as Larry drove. I cleaned my coat with the light, cupping my hand. I wasn't sure if the heat I felt was from the light or from the metal on my fairy-sensitive skin.

The streets passed by at a rapid pace. I checked the time on my phone and found it past eleven. I rubbed my eyes and yawned.

Something wet and warm slapped me in the face. I let out a cry, but as I moved my hands from my eyes, Jimmy's doggy face seemed to smile into mine as he licked my nose once more.

"Larry, somebody's awake. And he's got doggy breath."

The bus swerved as Larry threw a glance over his shoulder. He grinned, then faced forward and straightened out the wheel. "Hey boy! Welcome back!"

Jimmy's tail thumped the back of the seat, and he barked twice. I thought he'd jump down and trot up to visit his master, but Jimmy stayed put; a mark of smarts or training, I supposed.

I ruffled his fur, and he yelped. I jerked my hand away as though I'd been burned, then realized I'd touched one of his newly healed wounds. "He's still tender, but he looks happy."

Larry sat up straighter and began to sing some country song I didn't know, slapping the wheel and whistling to accompany himself.

Jimmy's tail thumped out a beat in time with Larry's song.

"Jimmy's really good for you."

"Yeah, you've got no idea, darlin'. When you got no one else, a dog'll save you from the darkest times. He don't judge, he don't hold the past against you. Nothin' purer than the love of a dog, Skye."

I scratched Jimmy's head, and he licked my hand and barked.

The lights outside the bus grew closer together, and I saw the purple-lit Scottish Rite Cathedral go by on one side. I peered out the other side to see the enormous Indiana War Memorial building, with its pillars and stern robed statues staring down at me in disapproval. The eyes of "Courage" stared right past me, hooded under his domed helmet. The shadows on the face of "Peace" made her seem to sneer.

Larry called back to me. "Got any good ideas on where to park?"

"Pretty much anywhere, this time of night. If you want out of sight, you could stow it in a parking garage. They're all pretty well lit."

"Doubt they'd let me park this thing in a garage. What else you got?"

"There's a big lot over by the baseball field. Hang a right up here."

After some wrong turns, I guided Larry to Victory field. The halogen-lit lot might as well have been daytime, so we decided the *GhostBus* was safer here than anywhere. Larry pocketed the parking pass and we headed off on foot, with Jimmy trotting along happily between us.

I didn't like leaving the powerful lighting of the parking lot; by comparison, the rest of downtown appeared dim and gloomy, and I did all the tricks I knew to try to catch glowing yellow eyes in the shadows. All I ended up with was a glimpse of Minnie, riding Jimmy like a golden horse.

"Guess you're callin' the shots, darlin'. What's next?"

"I'm making it up as I go along. Tougher to outguess me that way."

"Huh. Pretty smart."

"Not really, I'm just out of ideas."

"I reckon we need to sit down and regroup. Got a good place? Someplace safe?"

I laughed. "Who knows what's safe now? But yeah, I've got an idea. Come on."

Heath's my favorite. Well, one of them anyway. He's got a brewpub right on Monument Circle, and he's always got a seat waiting for me. Maybe it wasn't the best idea in the world for me to think of his place as home, while I'm trying to stay on the wagon, but Heath knows better than to tempt me with his beer. He respects my decision, even if he's sad not to have me for a taste tester anymore.

Well, maybe someday. But not now, not until I *know* I don't need to drink, that I'm special without drinking.

So, I led Larry into the pub, and we pulled up stools at the bar.

"Skye! Have I got a ginger ale for you!" Greg Heath grinned at me from the far end of the bar, where he filled pints to hand to one of his wait staff.

"Thank you kindly, barkeep! Good to see you."

Heath made his way over to us and produced a swing-top bottle from somewhere under the bar, popped it open, and poured the contents over some crushed ice in a pint glass.

As he slid the glass up to me, the bubbles and the sharp sting of ginger scent tickled my nose. "I feel like a kid, having ginger ale."

Heath tsked. "Just try it. 'Bout time I got some family friendly beverages in here. You might say you inspired it. Who's your friend?"

Larry stuck out a hand. "Larry Fisher, pleased to meet you."

Heath visibly hesitated, his eyes meeting mine before taking Larry's hand to shake it. "Funny. Must be some other guy with your name? But few of my other customers had a run in with a Larry Fisher a year or so back."

"Naw. I'm that guy. I was, anyway. Learned a thing or two since then. Skye's keepin' me out of trouble."

I shook my head. "Noooo. That's not my job. That's Jimmy's responsibility."

Heath leaned over to see Jimmy sitting at Larry's feet, tongue lolling out of his mouth.

Heath looked Larry in the eye. "Just don't make trouble in my place, and don't mess with Skye. Now, what'll you have?"

Larry opened his mouth and drew in breath, then sort of deflated in a gust of laughter. "I like a guy who's to the point. What's your specialty?"

Heath swept a hand to take in a dozen taps. "All kinds of beer and a couple ciders." I must have made some kind of mournful noise, because he added, "Sorry, Skye. Really, try the ginger ale. I made it myself."

Larry touched the edge of his hat. "Surprise me, Mister Heath."

Heath fetched a glass and filled it with a brown beer. "This one's some of the last of the Heather Honey stuff we had over the summer. Way more popular than I'd guessed."

Ohhh, my favorite! I groaned aloud, to my embarrassment, but before Heath could urge me a third time, I sipped his ginger ale.

Ginger filled my mouth and spread out through my sinuses and warmed my stomach. It was as though Heath had supersaturated the liquid with ginger essence, maybe pounds of it per ounce, and only by tasting it could it explode outward to be free.

"Skye? Skye? Yo, Skye!"

My cheeks ached, and I realized I'd been grinning while I went off to the magical land of Gingerness. "Oh. Oh God. Heath. Ginger. Oh."

Heath touched the end of his Roman nose and winked. "See? Who needs booze?"

I raised my hand. "You know what this needs? A good slug of vodka."

Heath shook his head and wandered off to help other customers.

Larry downed half his pint of beer in one long drink. He wiped his mouth on his sleeve and burped. "Not bad. You think he's got any Bud?"

I shoved Larry hard enough that he had to grab onto the bar to keep from falling off his stool. "Hey, what gives?"

"Philistine!" I said, sipping more liquid ginger heaven. "Don't let Heath hear you say that word, or you might get yourself banned. Actually, go ahead, do it. That way I can keep my favorite place to myself."

"Aw Skye, I thought we were friends now."

I met his eyes and said, "I liked you better when you were sucking up, to make up for getting me possessed and all."

Larry's grin had an oily charm about it. "Darlin', if that's what it takes to be your friend--"

I held up a hand. "Stop right there."

He spread his hands, palms up. "Hey, hey. I know you got a girlfriend. I just ain't got many friends, and you saved my dog, maybe my life."

I nodded. "That's true. On the other hand, you started a war that I'm being sucked into. I'd been avoiding those for a while."

"I figure, some folks just have a callin', and maybe that's yours, Skye. Lady MacLeod, warrior princess."

I groaned and sipped at my ginger ale.

A shot glass of beer appeared between us. Heath smiled from behind the bar. "Figured your little friend didn't go dry, maybe she'd like something. On the house."

"How do you know--"

Heath waved a hand at me. "Figure she's got to. It's been a hotbed of weirdness today, she's got to be around.

"What? Weirdness? What do you mean?"

"Those big football player guys you hung out with at Big Con? They were here lookin' for you. Said it was important they see you."

Larry downed the other half of his beer. "Football guys?"
I sighed and scanned the room. "Trolls, Larry. Trolls."

Chapter Eleven

When I looked back at the bar, the shot glass was empty. *Wish I could join you, Minniekins. Oh how I wish.*

"Trolls? You're kiddin'."

I shook my head. "Come on Larry. You're a professional ghost hunter. You've hung out with demons. You just survived a couple of pukwudgie attacks. And you draw the line at trolls?"

He snorted. "I know what I seen, but trolls sounds, oh, I don't know, kinda too *Tolkien* for real life."

"Thought you'd seen the news. Big one. Maybe a hundred feet from where we sit, three months ago. Throwing motorcycles like toys."

Larry turned his head to give the door a nervous glance. "Yeah, there's that. But still."

I glanced at my phone. "Going on midnight, want to go see what they want?"

Larry guffawed. "Good one."

I shrugged. "I know how these things go. They're gonna catch up with me eventually, so I might as well get it over with."

Larry squinted at me. "You're serious. And what'll you do if they want to eat you for a late-night snack?"

I shook my head. "Never happen."

He stared at me. "Yeah? Doubt that flashlight'll hold 'em off long. What makes you so sure?"

"I killed their god."

Larry made a show of taking off his hat and bowing to me from his seat. "If it's all the same to you, I'm bushed. Thinkin' about gettin' a hotel for the night. Join me?"

"Larry--"

"Two beds, darlin'."

"Yeah, no. If I sleep tonight, it'll be snuggled up to my boo back home."

"Heh, the energy of youth. I'm done with all-nighters myself. You have fun. Catch up with you tomorrow, I'm sure."

"Happy Thanksgiving to you, too, Larry."

I headed for the door, but Heath touched my elbow to stop me. "Anything wrong, Skye?" His eyes jerked toward Larry and back to me.

I shook my head and smiled. "No. Well, yes. But not like you think. There's some big stuff going down, maybe within the next few days, and as much as I'm trying to stay out of it, as much I keep being *told* to stay out of it, I'm being pulled in anyway."

He nodded. "But no booze, hmm?"

I shrugged. "It'd help a lot not to fumble around in the dark, but I've got promises to keep."

"Miles to go before you sleep," he said with a crooked smile.

I hugged him and gave him a peck on the cheek. "Exactly. Maybe I'll have a beer with you when this is all over."

Heath nodded. "Look forward to it. Keep strong, Skye."

I turned and stepped out onto the circle. I tightened my scarf and buttoned my coat higher against a sudden wind.

A bent old woman stood feeding pigeons on the edge of the sidewalk. The birds surrounded her in a twitchy little pool, pecking at the crumbs she scattered.

She met my eyes, and I recognized Mother Wren.

I waded through the pigeons to confront her. "Are you following me?"

"Fie on the manners of the youth. The Knight addresses a Queen poorly. Her King moves her into check, and she speaks bold words that shall surely get her captured."

"Stop it with the riddles, okay? I'm not here because of the Transit King, or anyone else. More like despite. And I'll tell you what, crazy bird lady, the more you 'lords and ladies' tell me to get out of the game, the more I'm inclined to get in on it. Or mess it up on purpose. You hear me? Your majesty, that is."

Wren's eyes blazed. "The stone-hearted Knight shall come into her own inheritance, that is for certain, but she shall lose much that she had. She shall need to choose her allies wisely. Pawns will be taken, of course, but so shall perhaps another knight, a bishop, or even a rook, before royalty falls."

I balled my fists. "I have no clue what you're trying to tell me."

She laughed, a rich, warm sound. "All has been paved over with stone, all has been hidden under buildings, shoved down in the deeps. But some things stand tall and need only the right push to open a door that Mother Wren once helped shut. One that perhaps should stay closed, but maybe it matters not. Which way shall the Knight turn the key, what face shall she choose in the end? That is the riddle."

I stood there, turning her cryptic words over and over in my head, running my mind in circles, and something caught at the edge, like a glimpse of a forgotten dream. Just a wisp, a fragment, dissolving even as I tried to hold onto it, spiraling away from me. Spiraling and whirling, chasing its comet tail back into forgetfulness.

And when I came out of my daydream, the air filled with fat pigeons, circling me like a feathery tornado, then they scattered, and I stood alone.

Almost alone. A couple of stocky guys in Colts jerseys blotted out the streetlights around the Monument.

"Brick and Limestone, I presume?"

"Har," said one.

"Har," said the other.

It occurred to me that I hadn't learned any of the trolls' proper names. To my credit, they hadn't ever introduced themselves with, but seemed happy enough to accept the nicknames I gave them.

"Let's get this over with," I said, and the three of us walked around the Circle together.

I found it strange to look upon the trolls in their human glamour. I knew them to be a couple feet taller and broader than they seemed, and made of living stone, rather than the craggy flesh they presented to me. I did feel better when I managed to catch Brick in my peripheral vision, his red-mortared skin as I remembered it. It comforted me somehow, though I couldn't have told you why.

"Look guys," I said, as we made our second counter-clockwise circuit of the bricks of Monument Circle. "If you don't know where you're going, just say so."

"Har," said Brick. "You fink this is a game, but fings have rules."

"One more time 'round, fairykin."

I sighed and went along with the ritual, and then halfway around the last lap, things around me flickered and changed. I looked at Limestone and could see two aspects to him, as though one eye saw the football dude, and the other saw a hulking troll made of blocks of khaki stone that had earned him the nickname.

I looked around the Circle. Bluish energies crackled up and down the wires that connected the top of the Monument to the ground, as though the World's Largest Christmas Tree had been lit already. Buildings wavered like mirages all around us. The bricks at our feet glowed with a pulsing internal light. "What's going on, guys?"

"Oy, look who's so smart now?"

"Har. Third time's a charm, Lady."

As we finished the third time around, a bright archway opened at the base of the monument, right where repairs had been underway in the mundane world. Right where the Chained Lord had burst from his underground prison to stomp through downtown Indianapolis, leaving destruction and mayhem in his wake.

Brick steadied me as I tripped over some rubble at the entrance. "Yeh watch yer step, yeh hear? No call bringin' you in wif a busted crown, eh?"

"Har," said Limestone.

"Why *are* you guys bringing me in, anyway?"

Limestone led the way down a spiraling stone stair. "That's jumpin' ahead, mum, but yer got nuffin to fear from us."

"Yeh," agreed Brick. "Nuffin but us trolls down here. We drove back the gobbos fer now, the lousy stinkin' sewer rats."

"What do you trolls have against the goblins?"

Both of my rocky companions seemed like nothing but trolls now. They made a grating, grinding noise in unison.

Brick said, "Yer been topside too much, Lady. Gobbos leak through cracks, break the stone, gnaw at yer ankles."

"Sneakin'," added Limestone. "Don't ferget the sneakin' an' stealin' and messin' wiff stuff what they ought not to."

"So, basically, you just don't like them."

Brick snorted. "Yer bet, and yer gots ta watch fer the Kelpie."

"Oy, the Kelpie," agreed Brick."

I was about to ask about the Kelpie, but we'd reached a landing. I recognized the chamber where the King Below had been chained; for hundreds of years, the Troll Father brooded below the Monument, dreaming of escape from his chains.

And I'd given it to him.

And then I'd had to kill him.

I shuddered, images of the monster's rampage playing through my head as though it had been yesterday and not several months ago.

The iron rings on the walls didn't seem strong enough to hold that creature, the room itself too small to contain the titanic beast.

The inky dark of the room had been pushed back by a half dozen flickering torches. In place of the Chained Lord himself, sat an enormous throne, its seat big enough for a troll-sized butt.

Around the perimeter, and at the archway I'd entered the last time, stood gargoyles, winged things with wicked tusks. Their eyes followed me, their heads turned, as I crossed to touch the throne.

"Ye like it?" asked Brick.

"Love what you've done with the place, boys. It could still use something. Some nice paintings, maybe? Draperies? A window would be quite nice."

"Har," said Brick.

"Har," agreed Limestone.

I turned to see more trolls filing into the room. Small ones, barely bigger than my Minnie, scurried under the feet of bigger ones, which ranged from Jimmy-sized on up to eight or so feet tall. There were more made of brick, limestone, granite, and others that might take a geologist to name. I rather liked the look of one made of silvered-black hematite. Their stone bones ground a millstone chorus as they formed ranks facing the throne.

Brick nudged me with an elbow. "Oy, haff a seat, Lady MacLeod."

"What, on the throne?"

"Yeh. What you fink it's fer, anyway?"

"Uh?"

Limestone offered a hand. "Here, I'll help yer up."

"But--"

"Yeh got ta speak. Yer our guest, hey?"

Not sure what else to do, I let Limestone help me up into the throne of stone. I expected it to be cold and hard, but found it covered with a black velvet cushion I hadn't seen from below.

I sat, peering down at the stony faces, gemlike eyes glittering in the torchlight. A piney scent filled the air, and all the grinding of stone upon stone stopped. It was as though every troll held his breath, waiting for me to speak.

I realized I'd been holding my own breath, so I let it out, then took a few deep breaths before I spoke. "Thank you for this welcome, gentlemen."

"An' ladies!" said Limestone.

I scanned the room. The stony faces gave up no clue of gender, unless gruff was a gender. "Really?"

"Oy! Limestone's a lady."

"Am not. Yer a lady."

"Not neither."

I cleared my throat. "Gentletrolls. I don't know why I'm here. Can someone tell me?"

Hematite stepped forward, face shiny and soft-looking. "For the coronation, of course, Lady MacLeod." He, or maybe she, held a stone box. It had a keyhole, and now that I looked closer, the stone seemed to be the same color as the icy key the gargoyle had dropped for me.

Without thinking, I took the key out of my purse and fit it in the lock. I turned the key, and the lid creaked open. Too late, I thought of Mother Wren's words.

Inside, on a velvet pillow, lay a silver circlet, not unlike the one Bask wore. It was inlaid with gems of every color of the rainbow.

I'd have admired how appropriate those colors were for me, except panic rose inside me. "Wait, what?"

"You haff to be our Queen," said Brick. "Yer killed the Chained Lord, an' now we got no leader."

I shook my head. "But that's crazy. I'm the last one you should want to lead you."

Limestone said, "Yer smart enuff ta beat 'im who held us down fer hunnerds of years, yeh? Yer tough enuff to take 'im on, yer must have a little troll blood, hey?"

I pinched my skin. "I doubt it. I'm flesh, not stone."

Brick and Limestone exchanged a look. Brick shrugged. "Oy, nobody's perfect. Har."

Limestone agreed. "Har."

The room erupted in "hars" and then fell silent.

Hematite held up the crown, and the light caught in its gems, scattering little multicolored beams on the faces around me, like a disco ball.

"What if I don't accept?" I said, folding my arms.

"Then yer doomin' us to troll dust."

"Yer, troll dust."

"Why?"

"Gobbos an' their Kelpie grindin' us from below. Yer Transit King keepin' us down from above. Crows peckin' at our eyes 'cause of their Mother. Winter's winds wearin' us down. Trolls need yeh, Lady MacLeod."

"So, what, you want me to live down here with you all? I don't even have my powers. I'm not even sure how I see things like I do right now."

Brick straightened up and his eyes glittered as they met mine. "Nah, yer can live as yer please. Nuffin' keeps yeh here. Just be our Queen, push back against the other Lords and Ladies what push us around."

"Queen Skye," said Limestone.

"Queen Skye," echoed Brick.

"Queen Skye!" said Hematite, and the gargoyles, and every other troll in the room, over and over. The room rang with the chant. My ears throbbed and my head spun.

I couldn't take any more. "Stop!"

As one, the trolls fell silent.

"If I take this, will you swear, every one, to do no harm, unless it's to defend yourselves?"

The trolls nodded in unison.

"Do you also swear to keep me and my friends safe from harm?"

The trolls so swore.

"Do you all promise to respect my privacy, my life aboveground as my own?"

A chorus of "yehs" answered my question.

"I'll accept this honor on one final condition."

"Anyfing," said Brick.

"If I find a worthy replacement, I may abdicate my throne anytime I wish."

"But, yer Ladyship--"

"I don't have to accept at all," I said, wondering how far troll hospitality extended if I refused their highest honor.

Brick and Limestone conferred with Hematite, and whispers flowed around the room.

After a few minutes, Hematite approached the throne. So tall was she (I decided she must be a girl troll) that we looked eye to eye even as I sat with my feet dangling.

She said, "Lady MacLeod, on behalf of the Undercity, I declare thee to be Her Majesty, Skye the First, Queen of Trolls."

Then the shiny troll placed the circlet upon my head. Its chill sunk into my forehead, and it sat heavier than I expected.

With the sound of an avalanche, the trolls broke out in applause and gravelly cheers, chanting my name again.

The room spun around me, and my vision dimmed. My breaths came quick and short. I hate to admit it, but I nearly passed out.

When I refocused, stony hands touched my backside, bottom, shoulders, legs and arms. My new subjects crowd-surfed me across the chamber and down the hallway, out into the brickwork labyrinth of their underground realm. The trolls' march seemed to descend in some sort of switchback corridors, staircases, and such, lower and lower into the earth.

Chapter Twelve

Crowd-surfing turns out not to be as fun as you'd think after ten minutes or so of hands all over you. Especially when those hands are made of minerals, living or no. "Hey guys, where are we going?"

The repeated chant of "Troll Queen Skye!" was their only reply.

A carpet of trolls, big and small, flooded out into a vast domed space, with stone tables arranged in a circle around a central fire pit. Dozens of torches in sconces ringed the chamber. Smoke rose up and disappeared through a hole at the top of the dome.

Gargoyles rolled in a great wooden barrel and set it on its side atop one of the tables. Bricks on either side served as chocks to keep it from rolling.

The moshing trolls set me on my feet before the barrel, where a hunched, gravely troll flecked with gold or iron pyrite drove a tap into the wood. Foamy liquid gushed forth, and tankards passed to the troll quickly filled with it. Little trolls, the size of my hand, scuttled up to lick at the spillage on the floor.

The aroma of some sort of beer filled the dank air with a warm, earthy, sweet scent; my mouth watered. Not even Heath's beer had drawn me like the scent of this otherworldly brew.

Pyrite himself handed me a stone mug. It was difficult to tell on his craggy face, but I read his expression as a wide grin.

Brick and Limestone struggled through the throng of trolls, then cleared a path for me to a seat at a nearby table.

The trolls filled in the seats at the table, until there was a ring of a few hundred of them, each with a tankard in front of them.

"I fink it's time for a toast or somefing, yer majesty," said Brick, murmuring in my ear.

Oh crap. I'm expected to drink.

All eyes focused on me, hands and claws curled around the tankards. It occurred to me how much stock fairy folk, including trolls, put in manners and etiquette. And as their Queen, they expected a toast.

I checked my phone; the screen told me we were well into the midnight hour now.

Thanksgiving Day.

I stood, holding up my tankard.

A few hundred tankards raised in the air as one.

"Uh," I started, flustered. "Thank you for this honor. Only a few months ago, we fought on different sides of a war. And I'll admit it, I started that war, but it was in an attempt to stop a worse tragedy. And I botched it. You trolls were worthy adversaries, but also sterling hosts. Even when the Chained Lord had me hauled in to talk with him, Brick and Limestone here were kind and gentle, when they could have been rough or nasty. You have honor, and I respect that."

The trolls cheered and thumped their mugs on the tables twice, spilling beer. I sensed impatience.

How am I getting out of this without breaking my own promise or insulting people who just made me their Queen?

I took a breath and went on. "In my world, the human world above, this new day is a day of thanksgiving, going back to a shared table between the people who lived here and the newcomers from Europe. Let us drink, and let us work for peace, rather than war during my reign."

Grumblings echoed around the great chamber, and for a moment, I thought they wouldn't accept my toast.

Maybe they were waiting for something. "Cheers and thank you all."

I raised the mug to my lips and let only the tiniest sip into my mouth, though I mimed drinking deep, the beer flowing over my face and spilling down my front.

The trolls all tipped back their mugs and silence reigned for a half a minute.

Even that tiny sip was a bit of heaven to my tongue. I felt a twinge of guilt but consoled myself as I swallowed it by remembering that it'd take a whole lot more than that to make me tipsy. Just a tablespoon of troll brew couldn't impair my judgment.

Each time I raised the tankard of troll beer to my lips. I spilled a little more down my front, and each time I set the mug down, I did my best to slosh some out onto the table. Tiny helper trolls were more than happy to "clean up" my spillage. Soon, I had a tabletop court of a dozen fist-sized subjects paying me respects and toasting my name.

It was adorable.

The little sips I allowed in with each pretend swig piqued my curiosity. Some sort of spice, underneath the sweetness and earthy character eluded me; I needed to know, so maybe I could tell Heath a new secret ingredient to try.

I called out to the beer-barrel troll, who I nicknamed Pyrite, and asked him what made the beer so special.

His grin widened and parted to show me a mouth full of crooked yellow teeth. His words whistled through gaps as he spoke. "S--simple fing, Queen S-skye, this-s batch was-s infus-sed with Gobbo blood!"

I shoved my flagon away from me so hard that it tipped over. Tiny gleeful trollings fought over the widening foamy puddle of beer. "*What did you say?*"

I must have raised my voice too loud, or perhaps that horrified response came out too shrill, because the trolls froze in place.

Pyrite's grin disappeared. "It's-s a s-special res-serve--"

"As in, I drank actual blood from living, intelligent creatures?" The pitch of my words continued up the scale as my skin began to crawl.

"Naw, naw, yer gots it all wrong, yer majesty," said Brick.

I took in a deep breath and let it out. "Oh thank God! I thought for a moment--"

"Yeh," agreed Limestone. "Them gobbos ain't intelligent nohow. Whatcher take us fer, savages?"

I stared at the three trolls in front of me, their gemlike eyes seeming more alien than ever. The silence drew out for half a dozen heartbeats.

Pyrite's face split in two, his snaggly teeth displayed once again. "Har!"

Brick followed suit. "Har!"

Limestone slapped a knee with a stony smack. "Har! Good one, yeh?"

The room erupted in a chorus of "hars" and I felt my face grow warm. *They made a joke, and at my expense!*

"Har, har," I said. "Very funny."

"See," said Brick, "I told yer she had a funny bone."

And that's when it began to rain goblins.

They swung in on ropes, knocking even some of the bigger trolls down, leading with a double kick from their oversized feet. They hacked with pick-axes and blinded the trolls with black globs of mud or maybe tar, or perhaps something worse. I prefer not to speculate about the liquid that accompanied their blitz, spraying all around the room.

The hall erupted in troll roars and squeaky goblin war cries. Some of the torches winked out, and the bonfire erupted with gouts of greasy, sooty smoke that spread out to cover the room.

Annabelle's fire safety lectures echoed in my head, so I dropped to the floor, under the ceiling of smoke. That alone probably saved me from getting a lungful.

For the second time tonight, hands touched me all over, only this time, the hands were cold and fleshy, and little sharp claws scratched at my clothing.

I let out a cry, and Brick and Limestone swatted their hands at my goblin assailants. The little creatures, smaller than pukwudgies, seemed to blur as they dodged, and they made wet, rude noises at my defenders.

Then Brick let out a gasp and cried out and I had to dive out of his way as he fell. With another cry, Pyrite fell next to me. Limestone fell across the other two, whose inert bodies saved me from being crushed under a quarter ton of rocky troll.

I crawled out from under, only to see more of my trolls falling like dominoes all around the darkening hall.

Goblins piled onto me, weighing me down, slowing my movements. As more and more of them joined in, my breath was pressed out of me and I cried for help. Some muddy, slippery hands stuffed something into my mouth, and my nose filled with a chemical tang that stank of portable toilets. I gagged and coughed and doubled my struggles, but the room darkened further, narrowing down to a tunnel.

My head spun and I lost all sense of up or down. A few of my tabletop court rolled up and unfolded, bashing at the slimy bodies on top of me, but soon they too were overwhelmed by goblins.

As I faded to black, the solid black eyes and needle teeth of one of the goblins filled my view, and I heard the words, "Hur hur hur hur, we gots 'er, boyos!"

* * *

When I woke, I wished I hadn't. Someone had driven a spike made of ice through my forehead, my mouth filled with a paste with the consistency of peanut butter and flavor of rancid fish. My arms and legs pinned to my sides, I found no lights to form any frame of reference.

So naturally, I thought I was hung over, cocooned up in my sheets again. I struggled to clear my mouth of the stickiness to call for Annabelle to help untangle me, but all that came out was, "Merble, meff doo did gigan! Helmph!"

But then more memories edged in, and I remembered I hadn't had a drink in a couple of months.

Let me tell you, nothing could have pissed me off more at that moment. Hangovers are bad enough, but undeserved hangovers are the worst. I wiggled and struggled in my cocoon, spat and cursed and rolled.

And fell.

And hit the dirt. I know it was dirt because I got a mouthful, which must be where the pastiness had come from in the first place.

I lay there breathing hard and fighting back angry tears.

The universe split in half, on a vertical line made of pure pain. Then the crack in the universe formed a right angle and the white light that hurt so much *widened* to the tune of a tortured metal scream.

Someone stood over me. Someone in filthy blue jeans and matching shirt, and a fluorescent yellow vest with silvery reflective stripes. A pot-bellied someone wearing a yellow helmet with a flashlight embedded in it. A grey-faced, bug-eyed someone wearing safety goggles, thick elbow-length work gloves, and a deep frown.

What I liked the most about this person was that they blocked some fraction of the agonizing brilliance that the open doorway inflicted upon my pounding head.

"Urgle, bleff," I said, spitting out dirt.

The Indy DPW worker snapped their fingers (I honestly could not tell their gender) and croaked or burped and with a sharp *snap* the lights in my room flicked on.

I think I passed out, because the next thing I knew, I was sitting up, my hands and feet bound to an elderly wooden chair that threatened to fall apart under me.

The DPW worker raised a canteen to my lips and tipped it back. I let it dribble down my face so I could get a whiff before I let it into my mouth. My nose filled with water and I sneezed.

Patient, the DPW worker tipped the canteen up again, let me fill my mouth, swish, and spit. Then she, or he, let me drink.

I'm sure it was the condition I was in, but this cold clear water beat Heath's ginger ale and the troll brew hands down.

The worker withdrew the canteen and drank, keeping eye contact as they did. Once they wiped their mouth, they scraped another wooden chair up close to mine and sat.

At first, I thought the person gargled their water, but this was their speaking voice. "Poorrah faiwykin, thinks she's queen of the trawls."

A weight on my head told me my crown hadn't been taken from me. It took a couple of tries to find my own voice. I coughed and said, "You know what? It wasn't my idea."

"Poorrah thing. Sad how the mighty race of trawls has fallen to such desperation."

"Listen, bub," I said, "I don't know who you are, but if my army of trolls doesn't impress you—and those guys could push over a building given enough time—then know that I've got some powerful friends."

"Hur hur hur," laughed the DPW worker, echoing the goblins who'd taken me. "Poorah thing. Do you think some enslaved frogkin and surface-crawling machines are a threat? Maybe you think that little king would risk himself for you?"

"Not just him. Not just fairy folk, either."

"Oochie coochie, such language!" My captor pinched and slapped my cheek. "Such a tender young thing."

I'd had it. My hangover receded as my rage built. "Look gopher-face, this is your last chance. Tell me who you are, let me go, and maybe we can work this out like civilized folk."

"Hur hur hur hur! Poorah Skye, scion of a failed line, with your blood so very thin, your powers come from a bottle. You've got nothing, and we both know it. I'll tell you this: I'll tell you my name."

The DPW worker stood, and their nose and mouth became a snout full of an impossible number of teeth. The creature's skin rough and mud colored, its arms shrank and toughened, fingers curling into claws. The chair smashed to pieces as its long, heavy tail thrashed.

This gator-person before me opened its jaws and I stared down its throat as it hissed. "I am called the Kelpie, and now, at long last, it's my time to rise up."

Chapter Thirteen

"You're 'the Kelpie'? So, you're some kind of Fairy Lady. Or Lord?"

"Phaugh! Stop using that *word*. I am a pow-ah to be reckoned with, d'ya understand what I'm saying? Goblin kingdoms have rallied around me, and now we rise up against centuries of trawl oppression!"

I cleared my throat and sat up as straight and regal as a girl could, tied to a chair, covered in drying muck. "You're addressing the Troll Queen. Those guys love me. We don't have to have a war, Kelpie. We can talk things out."

The Kelpie waited a moment, then said, "Hur, hur, you're bluffing. Trawls are savages. Why shouldn't we have a war?"

To my surprise, my throat held a lump as I said, "If we skip the war, then everybody lives."

The Kelpie reared back and opened its alligator maw and gargled out a long, horrible laugh. "Oh, oh, I can't believe mah ears! Hur, hur, you really are just a child. Force is the only way to get through to the trawls."

I shook my head, and my muddy hair trailed along my neck like a handful of earthworms. "No. I had conditions to take on this crown. One was to do no harm except in defense. And they accepted, and my oath to them sealed it."

The Kelpie put its snout up to my nose. Its foul breath threatened to singe my nose hairs. I tried not to breathe.

Eyes narrowing, the Kelpie said, "An oath? How is this possible? Even the Lord of the Lines named you Oathbreaker."

That stopped me. Why *had* the trolls taken my oath?

Maybe my captor smelled the warring emotions inside me, maybe I gave it away in my eyes, or maybe it was just the long pause told the tale; the Kelpie hissed like water spilled on a hot stove. "Poor-haps you lie to me, even now, hmm? Useless piece of trash."

I sighed. "Fine. You don't believe me. I'm an Oathbreaker to you? I made my peace with King Bask, and I've made my peace with the trolls; though you call them savages, they have better manners. Even the Chained Lord didn't drag me through mud. Even Queen Howl never stooped to name-calling."

What I didn't say: *I've killed better than you.* Drunk Skye probably would have. Drunk Skye would probably have ended up as a tasty meat snack in the alligator jaws that snapped inches from my face.

Turns out, subtext works sometimes. The Kelpie backed off, gripping the chamber's doorknob with one gauntleted hand and said, "Whatever your words are worth, Oathbreaker, you and that crown should fetch a pretty ransom from the trawls. Sleep well."

The door opened with a metallic squeal, then closed with a solid clang after the Kelpie slid out.

And with a loud click, all light died, and I was alone. The thick black night of my prison soaked into my heart, and I despaired. How would anyone know how to find me? *I* didn't even have much clue. Given the smells and reputation of the Kelpie and goblins, the sewers seemed more likely than anywhere else. I thought about my phone, but I hadn't seen my purse since the battle in the Trolls' Great Hall.

But without a phone, I hadn't a hope in the world of calling for help. The crown lay cold upon my brow, useless to get me out of this predicament. In fact, as the Kelpie said, I'd already proven a liability to the trolls; they chose to follow me, and now I was already being used against them.

All in all, it'd been a pretty lousy day, and I just wanted to be home, curled up in bed with my Annabelle. After a hot shower and a vigorous scrubbing.

The subterranean chill soaked deeper into my skin, and the aches and nausea of my false hangover returned.

After a few minutes of this wallowing, there came a squeaky voice from somewhere below me. "Thought they'd never leave!"

"Minniekins?"

"Yep, it's me, Biggun!"

"Can you untie me, please? I can't feel my feet."

Tiny fingers picked at the knots at my wrists. "Already on it, sis! But I dunno if it'll do a lot of good. We're both kinda stuck in here."

"One thing at a time, Minnie dear."

Soon, she had my hands free, and it was quicker work for me to undo my own legs. I stood and stretched, and my hand whanged into a metal light fixture hanging from the ceiling. I felt the wind of its passing as it swung a pendulum's arc back and forth.

"Shhh," said Minnie. "There are a couple guards outside. Doubt they can hear us talk, but clatter like that? Not good."

"I know, I know. I can't see. Let me check the door."

I might as well have touched a whistling teakettle. The iron of the door scalded me, and I jerked my hand back, sucking on my fingers despite the grime on them. "Crapburgers, Minnie, iron burns me again."

Her tone was gentle, even if her words came saturated in sarcasm. "You think?"

"Huh? What did I miss?"

She cleared her throat, and her hands tugged at the fabric of my jeans and coat as she scaled me to perch on my shoulder. "Well, first off, we're having this lovely little chat."

In the dark, light dawned in my head as I realized the obvious. "Oh! Right, so I'm actually in the fairy realm?"

Minnie made drawn out sound of indecision, then said, "Hmmm, not exactly. To me, it's like when you're drunk, you're neither here nor there, but both places at once. Not sure how you're doing it. Maybe it's the place?"

I shrugged, knowing she'd feel it.

"Then again," said Minnie, her words careful and slow, "under all that sewage, you smell like beer, Skye. A lot of it."

"Long story, sis. Let's say what spilled on me didn't make it into my mouth. Etiquette demanded it."

"Trolls," said Minnie.

"Trolls," I agreed.

"So, uh, Queen Skye?"

Glad for the dark, I felt my face warm from embarrassment. "Tell you later. How about this door?"

"Don't look at me. If it burns you, it'd fry ya little ol' girl. Maybe if we had some light?"

I searched my coat and came out with Larry's flashlight. I flicked it on, and the super intense beam startled both Minnie and me.

"Holy crap, Skye, a little warning next time, okay? I think I see why the pukas hated that so much!"

I aimed the beam up. It turned out to be a *long* way up. Maybe several stories up. The actual ceiling was lost among a network of pipes overhead. I looked around my prison and found that it contained a few dilapidated chairs, a workbench (where I must have fallen from), some heavy hooks on the walls, and still more vertical pipes and electrical conduit.

The single door was bolted to the concrete wall, and it seemed to be made to withstand an explosion. It had brackets for barring from the inside, but the bar was nowhere to be found.

Minnie whistled. "Nice digs you got here, Biggun!"

I slumped back into the chair, which groaned and snapped in a way that made me decide to sit quite still. "So what do we do, scream bloody murder and try to overpower the guards?"

Minnie shook her head. "Nah, goblins are smarter than that, and you don't really want to fight them unarmed."

I waved the flashlight around. Its beam passed near Minnie, and she ducked. I said, "Could we use this to blind them and run?"

Minnie tsked. "We-ll they don't really see daylight much. So maybe. But they'll yell for help, and we won't get far."

I crossed my arms and played the beam along the pipes above us. "I dunno, Minnie. Maybe we just have to wait for Gatorface to come back so you can make a break for it and bring back help."

Minnie frowned. "That's no good. Could be hours, could be a day or more. The Kelpie doesn't seem real concerned with hospitality. Okay, tell you what, give me a boost."

I stood from the chair and crouched in front of her. "Sis, I'm tall, but not *that* tall!"

"I just want a head start. Stand on the workbench and reach me up to that conduit."

"Minnie, it's metal, too."

She smiled. "Yeah, but aluminum doesn't hurt, right?"

I followed the conduit's path up. "What if you fall?"

"Then you'll catch me!"

"Minnie—"

"I'll be *fine*! But hey, if you want to help, find me some string to use to rappel up and catch myself if need be. You know, like the guys who climb telephone poles?"

I propped the flashlight against a wall so that the beam still faced upward. Then, I pulled the laces out of one of my boots and handed it to her. "They're just decorative anyway."

"Perfect!" Minnie tied a solid loop around her waist and coiled the loose end over one arm. "Upsy-daisy!"

I picked up my little alter-ego with both hands and placed her on the workbench. I climbed up after her, and then picked her up and held her as high as I could reach. She threaded the shoelace around the aluminum conduit and planted her feet on the wall. I let go of her, but I kept my hands close.

Good thing I did, because she slipped trying to tie another knot, and I had to catch her.

"This isn't such a great idea, Minniekins."

"Aww Skye, stop it, I got this," she said, already pulling herself back up with the shoelace.

She took a step, slid the string, then took another step. Her speed picked up as she found a rhythm, and soon all I could do was watch from below as she scaled the wall.

"Ugh this place is filthy. I'm gonna be as gross as you before I get out of here!"

"What? Hey!"

Minnie giggled from at least a story up, harder to see now unless I moved the flashlight. I didn't want to disorient her while she climbed, so I left it where it was.

I fretted but kept quiet. The step-slide-step sounds came to my ear fainter and fainter, and I called out, "Do you need more light?"

"N-no, I'm okay for now."

"What's wrong?"

"Mmph. Nothing, Skye. Just climbing 'round a big steel pipe to get on top. It's insulated, but there're bare patches I'd rather not touch. Hang on a bit."

I held my breath, imagining my Minnie falling from so high up. I didn't even know where exactly she was, so I'd have to be ready to try to catch her if she did fall.

Minnie cheered. "Paydirt!"

I took a deep breath and let it out in a gust. "What did you find?"

"A hole in the firewall! I think I can just wiggle through by squeezing back the insulation."

"Be careful, Minnie. I can handle the Kelpie if I have to."

"Shut up, Skye! I'll see you soon!"

And then the chamber fell silent, and it was just me and the flashlight. I decided to conserve batteries and shut it off and pocketed it. I tried pacing in the dark, but I kept having to steady myself, and it only took accidentally touching the steel fire door once to convince me that wasn't the best idea. I found the workbench and lay back down on it, closed my eyes, and struggled with anxious thoughts.

I must have dropped off to sleep, because I woke to the door opening, light flooding in again. Somehow knowing my flashlight was still brighter comforted me.

A squad of globby, muddy, two-foot-tall goblins carried in a couple of wooden bowls and set them down just inside. I lay stone still on the workbench, playing possum, peeking at them through one squinting eye.

Their eyes gleamed in the dark. One of them said, "That's her awright! Hafta keep an eye on that one, she's trouble."

Several escape plans crossed my mind, but I decided I'd try talking. I sat up, slowly, and pretended to yawn. I peered down at the bowls, one containing a lumpy brown goop and a wooden spoon, the other clear water. "Waiter, I asked for the chef salad, not the soup."

I got a chorus of "hur hur hur" out of the goblins, but they backed toward the door.

I held out my hands so they could see they were empty and said, "No, it's okay. I'm just bored. I could use some company.

"Comp'ny ain't our jobs, Lady."

"Look, I'm not an ogre. I'm not even a troll. I just want to chat."

The first goblin snorted. "Yer as mucha trawl as you lot get. Gotcher fancy trawl crown on yer trawl-lovin' head, yeh?"

I touched the crown and nodded. "They chose me, I didn't choose them. Crazy, if you ask me, since I killed the Chained Lord."

The goblins laughed together. "Hur hur hur, that were a good one! But trawls'd been chained by His Monstrousness, an' now they're all on the rampage."

"Eatin' up respectable goblins!"

They all nodded.

Still touching my circlet, I said, "And who do you suppose could do something about that, hmm?"

They gabbled amongst themselves while giving me the side-eye.

I squinted at the first little goblin. "I remember you in particular. You did me a favor once, you showed me the way out of the troll's warrens after I freed the Chained Lord."

The other three goblins regarded the first with skepticism.

"Yer think I gave a hoot about yer?"

"Maybe not, but I'm grateful. Just sayin', it's good to have the Queen of the Trolls thinking kindly of you. Especially when she doesn't want war with your people."

The goblins squinted at me. "That a threat? 'Cause Kelpie says we kicked trawl buttocks a few hours back."

I shrugged. "That you did, and here I am. But no, it's not a threat."

"War's comin', mum, an' nobody can stop it."

"How do you know that?"

"Errybody knows. Been comin' fer months. Armies gatherin' downside an' upside. Winner take all."

"No. I won't accept it. Maybe there's still time."

The goblins laughed as they filed out. "Hur, hur. You got 'til tomorrow, yer majesty."

Chapter Fourteen

Before the door could shut, there came a sound that filled me with hope and fear: A dog barked and growled, somewhere down the hallway.

I moved fast. I switched on the million-candle flashlight and stuck it high in the crack of the door to stop it closing. The goblins outside screeched and called for help.

The barking grew louder, along with the sound of someone yelling.

The sharp report of a pistol rang out.

I pried at the crack, using the flashlight as a short lever, then shoved my elbow in to push it open. I might have sunburn on that arm tomorrow, but I was glad for the thick cloth of my denim jacket to insulate me from the worst.

Another intense beam of light waved around the hall in such a way as to make an unpredictable strobe effect. Here, a goblin ran away, there my first goblin stood his ground with a steak knife, and all around, dust kicked up.

I coughed and choked on the dust, then pulled my t-shirt up over my nose and mouth and squinted through watery eyes. I called to the goblins, "Run! Save yourselves! Run and tell the Kelpie, Skye MacLeod wants peace!"

The first goblin and I locked eyes. He brandished his knife, point toward me. I bowed to the little creature and smiled. "Until we meet again."

"Ain't seen the last of me, tha's fer sure." And then he took off after the others.

Jimmy the dog pounced on me from somewhere behind the brilliant light, and I lost my footing and landed on my bottom, my face full of wet doggy kisses.

"Ain't got no time for that, darlin', let's get outta here," said Larry, flashlight in one hand, pistol in the other.

"Larry, did you kill any?"

"Naw, little bastards are too fast. Scared 'em good, though. Come on, I'll help you up."

I took his hand and pulled myself up.

I grinned at Minnie, who rode upon Jimmy's back.

"See? Found you, Biggun!"

"Scaring is good. Killing is bad. I'm trying to stop a war."

Larry shook his head. "You don't want to get in the middle, do you? Never mind that now; they're comin' back."

He turned and dashed off back down the brick hallway the way they'd come. Jimmy bounded after him. Minnie held on for dear life, giggling.

I followed them, not wanting to spend any more time in that maintenance closet. The dust thinned as we went, and then the hall ended in a big, round, vertical iron hatch like I'd seen before. The thought of the scalding I'd gotten from the steel door reminded me of the red hot burn I'd get from purer iron in whatever state I was in.

"Larry, I can't touch that. Iron burns me here. Minnie, too."

"Well lah dee dah, miss delicate flower. Y'all don't have to, I'll open it."

The hatch protested with a rusty squeal as Larry pulled it wide. A horrible, sulfurous, rancid wave of stink rolled out and washed over us. Jimmy whimpered. I gagged and retched, but only just held down the contents of my stomach.

"Come on, this is the way, darlin'."

I turned my flashlight back toward my cell. Many pairs of eyes, low to the ground, blinked and scattered.

Somewhere deep in the dark, a terrible voice bellowed and raged.

I swallowed and breathed through my shirt. "Okay. Help me through."

Larry ducked and stepped through the round opening, followed by Jimmy. I eyed the iron edges of the portal moving as slow as I dared, treating it like the near-lethal game of Operation it was.

"Do you *want* the little boogers to catch you again, Skye?"

"Imagine this door's made of fire and help me through, Larry."

Once again, I took his hand, and he pulled me over the threshold with an abrupt motion. I'm sure he figured he was being helpful, but I lost my balance for half a second; the back of my flashlight hand brushed the edge of the hatch and the pain blinded me for a moment.

As I sucked on the blistering burn, I heard the hatch clang shut behind me.

"That wasn't so hard, was it?"

I laughed, and wiped tears from my eyes. I peered out into the cylindrical space we stood in. Bricks arched up above the ledge we stood on, and the tunnel stretched out for a long way in either direction, both ending in a curve in the pipe.

Flowing through the center was a little creek of noxious sewage. I retched again.

"Hey at least it ain't tomorrow night. This place'll be full of all the used Thanksgivin' dinners in Indianapolis."

Minnie laughed. Jimmy barked.

"Shut up, Larry, and let's get out of here."

"Huh. Fine. You're welcome, your highness."

"It's 'your majesty' actually."

"Wondered about the tiara. What--"

"I really don't want to talk about it, Larry. How about you pass the time by telling me how you got here."

As we followed the curve of the sewer pipe, fatigue caught up with me. Each step felt a little heavier than the last one. Despite the outrageous output of the flashlights, my vision dimmed. "Larry, please tell me it's not much further."

"Eh? What's wrong now?"

"I'm crashing, hard."

"Well, you're in luck, there's just a ladder to climb and we're out," he said, gesturing at the wall up ahead.

Rusty iron rungs, built into the brickwork, drew a groan from deep inside me. "Oh crap. I can't climb that. It'll burn."

"Well, I can boost Jimmy, but I can't carry your ass out."

I plopped down on the ledge and let the room do a slow roll around me for a minute. I touched the floor under me, and though I shivered as my body heat leeched away into the bricks, I needed to hold onto something firm and real. Everything felt more real than me, as though I might pass right though the bricks if I squeezed hard enough.

I kept my grip firm but light.

"Hey now. Y'all can't just give up."

"I'm exhausted, Larry. I can't even brain right now," I said. Brains. Brains made me think of zombies. Zombies made me think of Ernie. Ernie made me think of the wonderbooze, and how much I wished for some right now. I needed inspiration, not Larry's nagging. Inspiration made me think of Minnie. My little second self is always full of energy and ideas.

I drew breath and opened my eyes. "Minnie--"

But she wasn't on Jimmy. Or at least I couldn't see her. Come to think of it, I hadn't heard her pipe up since we'd passed through the iron hatch.

Larry sighed. "You talkin' to yourself again?"

"She's gone!"

"Never saw her in the first place."

I pulled myself to my feet. "We've got to go back for her!"

Larry shook his head and grabbed a handful of my jacket to stop me. "Naw. No way. If she's on the other side of that door, we'd have to shoot a lot more critters than I've got bullets. They're not fallin' for the same bull rush again."

I struggled out of his grasp, some of the fog burning away, some small amount of strength flowing back along with the hot anger that flowed through me. "You don't understand. She's part of me. I can't just abandon her."

"How'd you even see her? I only followed Jimmy when he wouldn't stop barkin' his fool head off at the hotel. Thought you had to take a drink or somethin'."

"I don't know. How'd you see the goblins?"

"Not too well, to be honest. Just had a feelin' of things in the dark. Like the pukwudgies, but smaller."

"Hmm. Okay, Larry, hit me with the flashlight beam."

He gave me a puzzled look but aimed his high-powered flashlight my way. I remembered to look away just in time, so as not to get blinded by the thing. My shadow sprang up along the corridor behind me, including a little waving figure on my shoulder.

I let out a sigh of relief. "Okay, never mind, she's with me, I just can't see her."

"Sure, whatever you say, darlin'."

I took a few deep breaths of the fetid sewer air and walked up to the iron ladder. I peered up at the heavy iron manhole cover, maybe two Skye-heights above me.

I took a chance and reached out to touch a pinky finger to the rung.

It burned like a hot mug of coffee, but didn't blister, and I didn't smell burned Skye flesh.

"I... I think I can climb after all. But you'd better get the manhole cover."

Larry touched the brim of his hat and scaled the ladder. After a moment, I heard a grating, then pale yellow-orange light from a streetlamp slanted down and fell upon my face. I couldn't have been happier if it'd been sunlight. Hot tears of relief and exhaustion rolled down my filthy cheeks.

Larry backed down the ladder. "Okay, you next, then help pull Jimmy up when I boost, okay?"

I nodded and stared at the rungs; I counted eighteen of them to get to the top, which was also a ring of--to me—piping hot iron.

Larry urged me forward with an impatient look.

I unrolled the crusty sleeves of my denim jacket. The cuffs only covered my palms, not my fingers; I shrugged off the coat and reversed it, like a smock. I put my arms only part way through the sleeves and used them as thin hot pads to grab onto the iron.

The cloth helped, though my hands still tingled as I climbed. I made my way up as quickly as possible to limit my exposure to the dangerous metal.

I reached the top and my head peeked out onto a street that ended at a T, the domed, illuminated Indiana Statehouse rising up before me. A massive bronze statue of a bearded man labeled "Morton" frowned down at me. His bronze guards in Union uniforms looked like they meant business.

I could have kissed the lot of them as I breathed in the cold, clear night air and hoisted myself up. Standing there shivering in the freezing cold, I didn't even care that I looked like an extra from the Walking Dead, covered in mud and worse from head to toe. I reversed my coat and buttoned it against the cold.

Jimmy's muzzle surfaced, and he gave me a friendly bark. I leaned down and grabbed him under his forelegs and hoisted him up. He barked again and circled me, wagging his tail.

Larry appeared next, along with the ominous echo of something howling in the sewer below. Larry shoved the manhole cover back in place with a clang and spat on the pavement. "Might never get the sewage taste out of my mouth."

I shivered and nodded. "Thanks, Larry."

He touched his hat and nodded. "Now let's get you cleaned up."

"What? No, I just want to go home, Larry."

"Bus ain't runnin' this early, and no cab's gonna take you stinkin' like that."

"This early? What time is it?"

Larry checked his phone. "Bout five, looks like. Why?"

"I gotta check in with Annabelle, and my purse is gone. Can I borrow your phone?"

Larry handed me the phone, and I dialed her digits.

She picked up before the second ring. "D'you know what time it is? Who the hell—"

"Belle, it's me. Had to borrow a phone."

"You still out camping with Larry Fisher?"

"Not exactly," I said, afraid of worrying her, but not wanting to hide anything, either. "We ran into some trouble, but I'm okay now. Just filthy."

"Filthy? Skye, what happened?"

"I'm okay, Belle, and I'll get home as soon as I can."

"Want me to come get you?"

"I kinda stink right now, like sewer stink. Literal sewer stink."

"I don't care. I'm on my way to my car. Where should I pick you up?"

"I'm at the Statehouse, looks like. But it's pretty cold. Larry's got a hotel room, he's staying at the--"

Larry took his cue and said, "Pinnacle Place."

"Pinnacle Place. You know, a couple blocks from the Artsgarden?"

"I know the place. Be careful around Larry. I don't trust him."

I watched Larry scratching Jimmy's ears as I talked to my girlfriend. "Can't say I do either, but I had to earlier, and it turned out okay. Can you bring me a change of clothes and another coat? We may have to burn mine. And stand upwind."

"Sure thing, babe."

"Thanks, boo. Love you."

"Love you too, boo."

We hung up, each making a kissing noise.

"Jesus, I think I've got diabetes now."

"Shut up, Larry. I think I'll take you up on that shower, after all."

Chapter Fifteen

"Ain't no party like a troll party, cuz a troll party don't stop till someone gets carted off by goblins!" I grinned and flashed jazz hands at Annabelle, who was having nothing of my attempts to laugh off my abduction and imprisonment.

Annabelle gave me the side-eye and shut off the car. I'd talked the whole trip home, and she'd said little, even if her stormy hazel eyes spoke volumes. "Skye, I'm glad it turned out okay, but honey, you're crazy to get wrapped up in all this."

"Seems like I can't avoid it, Belle. I keep getting drawn in by people warning me to stay away."

"Sure you could. You didn't have to go hang with Larry at the park." Annabelle picked up the silver crown from the coffee table where I'd set it. "For the love of-- you didn't have to let the trolls make you their freakin' Queen!"

I sighed and let myself out of her car and stalked up the walk to our half of the duplex apartment. I stopped at the steps and waited for her. In silhouette, her petite form might not seem menacing, but my stomach did a flip-flop, worrying what the oncoming fight would be like.

She stopped, toe to toe with me, reached up her hands to clasp behind my neck and drew my face down to hers.

Her eyes still shrouded in the dark of the wee hours of the night, her breath hot upon my face, she said, "You're too much trouble, Skye. Why do I love you so much?"

"Because I'm cute?"

"Maybe that's it."

She pulled me into a fierce kiss that curled my toes inside the sneakers she'd brought me.

Exhausted as I was, Annabelle's kiss fired up a furnace within me, and I responded with a hungry enthusiasm.

She unlaced her fingers and slid them from behind my neck to cup my face. "Mmmmm. Why your Majesty. Do I please you more than Larry?"

I rubbed her nose with mine, warming both. "Hmm who knows what pleases Larry. I sure don't want to know."

"Well, you showered in his hotel room, so who knows what all went on," she teased.

"Baby, I washed off black greasy goop in that shower. I scrubbed sewage out of my hair. And yet, the very thought of anything happening with Larry Fisher makes me want to hurl. Thanks for coming to rescue me before he got any ideas about me staying the night."

She took my hand and led me up onto the porch. "Well, you're home and safe now. Let's get you to bed."

As she unlocked the door, my foot crunched on some sticks to one side of the doormat. I bent down to sweep them off into the lawn, then I realized what it was.

She had the door open now, the porch light flicked on to reveal the Pukwudgies' twig cowboy hat from Eagle Creek Park.

"Oh crap, Belle. This is bad. So bad."

She looked at me from just inside. "Huh? What's that?"

"A calling card from the pukas. They know where I live somehow. Where *we* live, Belle."

"No way. You said they were little savages. Animals. Monsters."

I flung the thing away from me as though it were poison. "That's what I thought. Looks like they're smarter than that."

And I killed one of them.

Annabelle hustled me inside and shut and bolted the door. "I'm not letting some mutant hobbits drive me out of my house. I've got the fire axe, we've got more fireplace tools... what else can we do to defend the place?"

I held up my hands to slow her down. "Babe, I'm dead on my feet. There's nothing much I'm good for without a nap or a drink, and I'm still not drinking."

"Coffee?"

Weariness saturated my whole being, and the world seemed staticky around the edges, but I nodded. "Maybe. They hate the light, so I think we're safe in the daytime. When's sunrise?"

Annabelle checked her phone. "Weather app says 7:40am. About an hour and a half from now. I'll put on the coffee and we'll keep guard till then."

I grabbed the little fireplace shovel and dropped it. "Dang, that burns."

She peered at me. "What's different?"

I shrugged. "Sometimes it's as if the fairy blood in me takes over and iron burns more than it has been."

"Are you hurt?"

I shook my head. "It was scalding maybe, but not sizzling."

"Well, we've got to arm you somehow."

"Hmph, wish I had the Hilt right about now."

She called to me from the kitchen. "What's up with that, why wouldn't Bask hand it over? It's your family's, right?"

I shrugged, though she couldn't see me. "Dunno. He always thinks he knows best."

"You know he doesn't though."

I closed my eyes to think. Just for a moment. "Yeah, something funny going on with him, Boo."

"Funny?"

"Dunno. He's acting weird."

She chuckled. "Be more specific. There are so many levels of weird in your world, Skye."

And then the door opened and Bask danced in, wearing a lion costume, complete with a yarn tutu. He wouldn't meet my eyes, but he turned on the TV and plopped down on the couch between me and Brick. The troll offered the Fairy King some popcorn. They munched and pointed at the screen.

When I looked, a weather report showed Indianapolis covered in suns. The meteorologist tapped the center of the picture with her finger and the suns converged on that point even as the map expanded out to show the one-mile square of downtown. The suns stuck to various parts of the map. When she got to the Thanksgiving evening forecast, the suns clustered in several spots, each pushing toward the very middle, Monument Circle. The suns went dark and light and dark again.

The weather girl, who was a pukwudgie now, clawed at the screen until it only showed an aerial view of the World's Largest Christmas Tree, the lights strung from the top of the Monument in a giant cone to a circle down below.

One hundred thousand faces peered up at the top of the Monument. Each was a little sun. Their faces flew off their bodies and converged on Lady Victory atop the Monument's spire and the screen filled with light.

"E'er seen anythin' like that, lass?" The Transit King sprayed popcorn around without a care as he spoke.

Brick ate the popcorn one dainty piece at a time, not even crushing any between his enormous stone fingers. "Har. You fink them people lost their heads?"

I blinked at the two of them and said, "I don't get it."

They both laughed. So did the pukwudgie weather girl as goblins crept out from under the couch and made off with the TV.

"Ye got a bit o' drool on ye, lass. Right there," he said pointing at my face. He lit up with light shining from my face, which I knew shined like the sun each of those people in the Circle had. I grabbed my ears to hold on, but Annabelle's words made me fly apart.

"Just go to bed, Skye. I'll yell if the pukwudgies come for us."

I snorted and my eyes flew open. I'd been asleep. "But we're all the sun, and the popcorn's going to be burnt by the solar collector!"

"Yeah, like I said, go to bed. Guess if they wanted us dead, there'd have been more than a twig hat to greet us, hmm?"

"I'm so sorry, Belle. Gimme coffee, I'll try harder."

Annabelle dragged me off the couch and kissed me again. She tasted like sweet coffee. "Go. To. Bed. You've been through enough. I'll get you up for Friendsgiving in a few hours."

"Oh damn. Friendsgiving."

"Shh. Go sleep." She swatted my bottom and pushed me in the direction of the stairs.

I don't recall climbing them. I must have kicked off my shoes, because I found myself otherwise still clothed and laying across our bed. Annabelle kissed my cheek and pulled a comforter over me.

I fell into a deep and thankfully dreamless sleep.

All too soon, Annabelle's hand lay upon my shoulder. I groaned but covered it with my own. "Let's have Friendsgiving tomorrow," I said. "Skye's sleepy."

"Skye must be sleepy if she's talking about herself in third person."

"Mmmph. It's my royal prerogative. We are not amused at getting so little beauty sleep."

"Oh ho, look who's getting too big for her britches?"

"By royal decree, Queen Skye demands your presence."

"What--"

I grabbed onto her hand and pulled her off balance, so that she fell into my arms in bed. I hugged her to me and covered her face with little sleepy kisses.

Annabelle struggled and laughed and tickled me. "Hey! Let go! I've got a quiche in the oven! It's gonna burn!"

I pulled her on top of me and kissed her nose. "Let it burn. Your Queen needs you."

She crossed her eyes and puffed out her cheeks and then bared her teeth. "So does that make me a troll?"

I dissolved into giggles and I couldn't hold onto her anymore. She slipped free and kissed me on the lips. "You know I love you if I kiss you with that morning breath."

I feigned offense. "What? That's just eau de troll. I'm a Troll Queen now, trolls are cool."

Annabelle rolled her eyes and dismissed me with a wave. "Get your royal butt dressed, okay? You've still got your dessert to make."

I sat up and pushed my tangled hair out of my face. "Aww, no one listens when I say we should have turkey pot pies. It'd be easier. It's about friends, not about impressing anyone."

She called back at me, halfway down the stairs. "People are driving in from all over for this, we gotta treat 'em nice, baby."

I made my way to the bathroom and eyed my clothes. I'd only put them on a few hours ago, and while the flannel shirt and jeans might not look slept in, Annabelle would know, and I'd know. And Cassie'd asked me to dress up like a goddess for whatever she had planned for this afternoon.

So, I brushed my teeth and untangled my hair and tied it back, then stripped. On my way back to the bedroom, there came a knock at the door.

Annabelle's voice carried from the kitchen as we said the same thing in unison. "Shit!"

I dashed into the bedroom as the clatter of pots and pans downstairs told me Annabelle had been in the middle of something. No time to decide, I pulled a sky-blue dress from its hanger and pulled it on. The stretchy material clung all over, and the hem fell inches from the floor. I realized I'd forgotten a bra, so I stripped it off again and fumbled in my drawer for one that wouldn't show through so much and wrestled to put it on quickly.

The knock came at the door, louder.

Annabelle yelled, "Coming!"

I yelled, "Hang on, I'm not ready!"

I had a fight with the dress; I tried to push my head out one of the narrow sleeves, then a cold breeze on my back told me the scooped neckline faced the wrong way. I tugged my arms from the sleeves and wormed around inside the snug tube, searching for the correct holes for my hands.

The door opened and Annabelle exclaimed, and another woman's voice carried up the stairs to me.

Finally, I pushed my arms out the right way, stepped into plushie bear-paw slippers, and rushed to the stairs. I had to grab the rail to keep from slipping halfway down.

"Hey Skye," said Blue, standing in the entryway. "Nice dress!"

Annabelle shook her head and excused herself back to the kitchen.

Flushed, I smiled and took more careful steps the rest of the way down to greet her. "You're early. But uh, welcome."

She grinned and tucked her blue locks behind an ear. "Yeah, I know, I'm not even supposed to be here. But I thought I'd drop by before leaving town."

I groaned. "Then you're here on business?"

She shrugged. "Kinda. I heard back from the boss--"

"Let me guess. Rebecca wants you to warn me to keep out of whatever's going down this Friday sometime."

Blue's eyebrows raised. "How the hell did you know that?"

"It's been a running theme. Please tell me she's not coming here herself to take care of whatever it is."

She shook her head. "She can't. But she says interfering would only make things worse. Sort of a vision, I guess? Strange are the ways of that woman."

"Sometimes I think that fedora hides an alien parasite that nests in that pretty red hair of hers."

Blue smirked. "Never seen her without it, right?"

"Right! Did she have anything else to say?"

Blue nodded. "Doesn't make much sense, though."

"Out with it."

"Well, she says not to look when everyone else is looking. Use a mirror if you have to see. She wouldn't elaborate, just said to beware the sunrise at night."

The crazy sun faces from my dream danced in my mind's eye.

Blue took a step toward me. "What? Did I say something?"

I shook my head and the vision faded. "No, but this is getting curiouser and curiouser."

She smiled. "Didn't figure you for a lit fan."

"I like Disney as much as the next girl." I held a poker face, waiting for her reaction.

"What? Damn it, that's not right. You of all people should pick up a book!"

I released the grin I'd been holding back. "Love Lewis Carroll. Do you really think I'm that dense?"

She swatted at my shoulder. "What do I know about you, really? You're almost as terribly mysterious as Rebecca."

I laughed. "Oh that's crazy talk. No one's as mysterious as Rebecca."

"Not just mysterious. *Terribly* mysterious."

Annabelle reappeared, wiping her hands on a dishtowel. "You're welcome to stay for Friendsgiving, Blue, but the house rule is, if you're early, you get put to work."

I smiled at Blue. "Come on, you know you want to hang out with us. I'll show you how to make 'pistachio fluff'."

Blue wrinkled her nose and shook her head. "Thanks, but nope. Chip and Phil are out in the car, and we're heading out to Perionne. But I had to drop by and give you the news since you're not answering your phone."

I swore. "Yeah, it's lost somewhere. The trolls have it, if I'm lucky. If not, maybe something awful is going to happen. Something more awful, I mean."

"Trolls? More awful? See, you're terribly mysterious, but I don't have time for another Hardy Boys mystery on Thanksgiving."

I blinked at her. "You're calling what happened last year--"

"You deal with trauma your way, I'll deal with it mine. Have a great Thanksgiving, Skye, and stay out of trouble. Rebecca's orders."

"She's not the boss of me. Say hey to Chip and Phil for me."

"Oh! That's the other thing. I can't stay, but Phil wonders if he can crash. He's been grumping about how everyone's got family in Perionne but him, and when he heard about your Friendsgiving, he asked if I could--"

"Phil's always welcome here," I said.

Blue grinned. "Thanks, Skye."

Chapter Sixteen

Blue let herself out, and despite the door being open, Phil knocked on the screen door. He held a small box in his hands.

I waved for him to come in.

"Hey Skye! Sorry for the lame contribution, but--"

I pounce-hugged the big guy. "Good to see you. I kinda thought maybe you wouldn't want anything to do with me after Big Con."

"N-no, you know it's not like that. You just suck as an employee. Here's my pitch in thing, sorry."

I took the box he offered. I gasped. "Phil. Are these?"

"Yep. Long's donuts."

"Oh my God, Phil. The box is still warm!" I had it open in an instant and stuffed one of the soft, delectable pastries in my mouth, chewing in sugary bliss.

"Hey, those are for everyone, you know!"

"Mmmfh 'vrrynnn."

Phil chuckled. "And I thought this was a friendly gathering."

Annabelle beckoned from the kitchen. "Hey Phil. Come peel potatoes."

I swallowed to speak. "Peel potatoes? Isn't this supposed to be informal?"

"I want just one thing that says 'Thanksgiving' on the table, and that's mashed potatoes. Real, lumpy, mashed potatoes, with bits of peel and lots of butter."

Phil lit up and made his way around me to join Annabelle. "You have my attention. Got gravy?"

Annabelle nodded. "Guess Frannie's bringing the gravy, along with her stuffing."

I followed them into the kitchen. "All vegan, of course."

Annabelle shrugged. "Can you blame her?"

I shook my head. "No, if I'd gone ghoulish like she did, I wouldn't want any more meat, either. But vegan gravy? And you said buttered potatoes. That's not vegan."

"She's having the vegan stuffing with the veggie gravy. The potatoes are for us."

Annabelle set Phil up with a pile of potatoes and a peeler. She had him save the peels so she could toast them for a snack.

My contribution suddenly seemed lame. I mixed a can of pineapple chunks with pistachio pudding, marshmallows, pecans, and whipped cream, then put the bowl back in the fridge.

While they continued to work and chatter, I snuck back out into the living room and stole another donut. *Oh, heaven. Did I even eat yesterday?*

A knock on the door startled me and I yelled around my mouth full of donut, "Mlll gfff ert!"

I opened the door and swallowed hard. A biker dude in a leather jacket and jeans, face full of scruff, grinned at me. "Holy crap, it's the L.T.!"

My turn to be pounce-hugged, I found my feet lifted from the floor as I was spun around and set back down. He planted a scratchy kiss on my cheek, and bellowed, "The party can start now, the L.T.'s here!"

Annabelle's voice carried from the kitchen. "Oh man, hide the liquor."

"We don't have any liquor, remember?" I poured every drop down the drain or gave the more precious stuff away to Heath in August. Best not to have temptation around.

All except for the airline bottle of Jaegermeister I kept in the back of the spices in the cupboard. I hate the stuff, so there's no temptation there, but just in case of crazy fairy emergency...

The L.T. looked sheepish. "Well damn, I forgot. Did you ever forget? I forgot, I got a bottle of Jameson out on my saddlebag. You know, just in case Gonzo might show."

The thought of Jameson in the house made me question my promise. *The fairies are still making my life hell, aren't they? One little drink at Thanksgiving doesn't count, does it?*

I heard myself say, "It's okay, but you'd better leave it outside, big guy. Share with anyone who wants some, but I'm still struggling."

He slumped and avoided my eyes. "Sorry, Skye, that was my pitch-in item."

I hugged him again. "Stop. It's me who had to quit, not you."

"How's that been goin'?"

I shrugged. "In the past day, I've passed up Heath's new brew, and troll beer. Could have used a drink a few times for professional reasons, too."

"Troll beer? Professional reasons?"

I caught his eye. "Trouble's stirring. Maybe worse than Big Con."

His eyes unfocused a moment, taking that in. Then they met mine again and saluted, "I'm in. Reporting for duty, ma'am."

I lowered his hand with mine and smiled. "There's some big fight coming. A war among the spirit realm people. I keep being told to stay out of it, but my gut says it's going to spill over into our world in a big way, just like Big Con. I don't want you, or anyone else I care about to get hurt."

"I'm in, too," said Phil, from the doorway.

"No, Phil, I can't--"

"Me, too," said Annabelle, slipping out from behind the big guy.

"Belle, no. Thank you all, but no. Not this time. I've got trolls to wrangle, goblins and pukwudgies to fend off, and maybe all the birds in the city involved. I think even T.K. has a stake in this."

The L.T. frowned. "Who's T.K.?"

I waved a hand in the air at about waist height. "The Transit King. He's talking war, too."

"Power vacuum," said the L.T.

Phil nodded. "Yeah, with the Chained Lord gone, that whole landscape changes."

"You been to war, bud?"

Phil shook his head. "No, but I'm a general in Fantasy Free Form."

"That's your video game, right?"

Phil stood up straighter. "It's very realistic."

The L.T. snorted. "You wrote it yourself, right?"

Phil's face reddened. "Our research was very thorough. Anyway, I did my part against the trolls last summer at Big Con."

I held up hands pretending to push them apart, even though they stood across the room from each other. "You did, Phil. Both of you helped. And yeah, you're right, that explains a lot of the crazy talk I've been getting from the Lords and Ladies."

The L.T. frowned again. "Lords and--"

"Fairies," said Annabelle.

"But don't call them that," said Phil.

I laughed. "See? You're all too involved already. Let me handle this one."

The screen door banged as someone let herself in. "Hey! What's going on?"

Frannie placed some crockery on the table, then everyone took turns hugging her.

I smiled at Frannie. "Trying to talk everyone out of getting involved in a fairy war. You know, same ol', same 'ol. So, Jimbo got stuck working after all?"

She nodded, eyes sad. "Poor guy's got a major system down."

The L.T. said, "On Thanksgiving? Can't it wait for tomorrow?"

Frannie shook her head. "I wish, but the university depends on this system, and every hour it's down costs hundreds, if not thousands of dollars in lost research time."

Phil nodded. "Yeah, I know the feeling. Chip and I don't like leaving our game with no one to watch it, but I've got a laptop with me just in case."

Annabelle corralled everyone around. She had the L.T. set the table while Frannie warmed up her dishes in the microwave. The table had a spread of hodge-podge dishes, but it felt like Thanksgiving with so many friends in one place.

Annabelle filled everyone's wine glasses with sparkling grape juice. The L.T. offered Jameson for anyone who wanted it later, but Annabelle shushed him and asked me to make a toast.

Unprepared, I stood up and raised my glass. "I'd rather this glass had something stronger, but I've kept my promise to myself so far. So, here's to keeping promises. Anyone else want to make a toast?"

Frannie stood and raised her glass. "To anyone who has to work today, and anyone who's alone."

She meant Jimbo of course, but Larry came to mind, all by himself in a hotel on Thanksgiving Day. *At least he's got Jimmy for company.*

Annabelle said, "Here's hoping not too many dumbasses set their deck on fire trying to deep-fry a turkey this year."

The L.T. stood and raised his glass and looked at me. "To those who've got your back."

"Hear, hear," said Phil, and everyone tipped back their glasses and drank.

"So," said Frannie, as we passed dishes around and filled our plates. "What's this about a fairy war?"

I groaned. "I wish I'd never said anything."

Frannie peered at me through her brick red bangs. "Oh, really? That bad?"

"Worse," said Annabelle.

The L.T. said, "So what's going down, Skye?"

I shook my head. "I just know the goblins and their leader plan to go to war tomorrow. And I'm pretty sure the trolls and the Transit King and a couple other players are in on it, too."

The L.T. heaped mashed potatoes on his plate. "What other players?"

"Well, there's a sort of fairy sorceress or nature spirit who calls herself Mother Wren. She's like Aquaman, but for birds instead of fish, I think. She's pretty annoying, she speaks in riddles and chess terms. And this Earl Winter guy who might be a badass, or he might just be working for one of the others. He knew a lot about me. Seems to be going around."

Frannie smiled at me with her eyes. "You're famous!"

I washed down a bite of quiche with some sparkling grape juice. "Yeah, yeah. Like I asked for that."

"Not like you shied away from it at Big Con," said Phil.

"What? Just because I was your booth babe--"

"No, I meant going after the troll, then gathering an army to finish the job. You stepped up, Skye. If you hadn't, Ernie's zombies would have overrun the city. No way he'd have kept control."

Before I could refute that, Frannie jumped in. "Really, he wanted to use the Chained Lord like some kind of genie. He'd have been eaten and not only would the troll have gotten loose anyway, but he'd have a limitless army of thralls."

Annabelle put down her fork and touched my shoulder. "As much as I worry about you, your 'mistakes' made things better. You saved so many lives, Skye."

I pushed back from the table and stood. "Tell that to Raven. I gotta get some air."

I tuned out the chorus of protest behind me and pushed out the front door and started walking. Annabelle called after me. I stopped and said, "Please? I just need a minute, otherwise I'm gonna take the L.T. up on that whiskey."

She nodded and disappeared back into the house.

I stalked around the corner and stopped there on the sidewalk and stared straight up into the overcast skies. A few lonely snowflakes floated on the light wind, and I wished I could float away with them. Maybe I'd taken the wrong gig, since the trolls' underground world never saw sky. I envied the wings of Earl Winter and the birds of Mother Wren. Flying away, I could leave these earthbound troubles behind me. I could leave the dead to their graves.

I thought of the puka I'd shot, all bagged up, under the footbridge along the canal. Had anyone found it yet? Was that what the hat on my doorstep was about?

A terrible thought came to me. If the pukwudgies were smart enough to find where I lived and smart enough to leave me a message, then they weren't just monsters. They were *people*, just like the trolls and the goblins.

Oh, sure, I'd killed in self-defense. The puka had it in for us, and so did the others. But although it'd never sat right with me, now I knew what I had to do.

When I let myself back in, everyone sat at the table, their plates empty. I said, "I'm sorry I stormed out. It's just too much.

I'm just Skye, not some superhero. The best that can be said for me is that under my leadership, I only lost one person, But I'm not even responsible enough to take care of my own self, and yet other people followed me, and that poor girl died."

The L.T. said, "But Skye--"

"Yeah, I know. Death's part of war. But I didn't ask for war, and all I want to do now is *stop* a war. One I didn't start, and I don't understand. And you all are ready to jump to help me."

Frannie looked around the room. "What? I didn't volunteer for a war."

I threw my hands in the air. "Good! At least one of you has sense! Maybe we should all just get out of town for a week or two until it blows over. Tell people we care about to stay away from downtown."

"Why downtown?" said the L.T.

I stopped. Why had I said that? "Well, you said it yourself. There's a power vacuum where the Chained Lord was until Big Con. The trolls have the center of the city, which is a focus of all kinds of energies and roads, and it's pretty symbolic, too. Plus, the goblins are already fighting them for it. I saw Mother Wren there. The only missing pieces are the Transit King and Earl Winter."

"Don't forget the pukwudgies," said Annabelle.

Phil, the L.T., and Frannie spoke in unison. "Pukwudgies?"

"They're these little monst—well, they're vicious little fairy people who live in the woods, can't stand bright light, and seem to want Larry and me dead."

Frannie paled, though I wouldn't have thought that possible with her complexion. "Larry? You mean Larry Fisher? What's he got to do with this?"

"It's a long story. He was doing his *GhostBus* show in the area, on the pukwudgies, and he shot one that tried to kill me. They went after him--and me--in force, and we had to run away."

She sniffed. "Let 'em have him, I say. That guy's bad news. The worst."

"Well, I killed one, too."

"Shit, Skye," said the L.T.

I sighed and pinched the bridge of my nose. "I can't ask this, I really can't. But do you know the expression about how good friends help you move, but best friends help you move a body? I could use help, later."

"Why later?"

"A new friend, Raven's sister Cassie, should be on her way over in a bit. Maybe she's got a way to let me have my power back, but without drinking."

The L.T. mimed sucking on something tiny, pinched between his fingers. He gave me a silly grin.

"No, I don't think it's that. Hope not, since it'd defeat the purpose of getting away from judgment-impairing stuff."

"Suit yourself," he said. "You want me to take care of the body for you while you do that?"

"I can help," said Phil, nibbling on one of the donuts he'd brought.

I shook my head. "No, you'll need me to find the spot it's hidden, and where I need it to go. Plus, I've got to be there when it's moved. If you can find a couple shovels, that'd do double duty, since they'll make good weapons against fairies. If need be."

Phil and the L.T. looked at each other, then nodded. The L.T. said, "No problem, boss."

"Stop that, I'm just Skye."

Annabelle hugged me from behind. "But you are the boss. Call me crazy, but I'm starting to see it, too. Believe in yourself, Skye."

"But--"

Phil said, "A good commander has to have that confidence. You did at Big Con."

"But I was half drunk half the time!"

He nodded. "Then find it without drinking. Be that Skye. Just keep your head."

The L.T. pumped a fist and cheered. "Or die trying!"

Silence fell on the room.

Annabelle coughed.

Frannie's eyes popped open wide.

Phil stared at the L.T. "Maybe not the best thing to say."

I stood straighter and put my fists on my hips. "He's not wrong. This isn't some role-playing exercise. I called it a game, but it's not so frivolous when we're all pieces on the board. God, I sound like Mother Wren now. But any of us could die. All of us could. People keep warning me not to get into this, and I've tried. Now you all want in, too. You'd better understand that the pukwudgies and goblins at the very least mean lethal business. Anyone who wants out now, you're probably best off."

No one spoke for a long moment.

"I'm not sure what I can even do, Skye," said Frannie. "I'm no good in a fight, and this is fairy business, not ghost business."

I thought about that for a minute. Frannie and I had the same traumatic history, only instead of spawning a Minnie, she'd split so that most of her soul lived outside her body as a ghost.

"You could do some recon work. See what's going on around Monument Circle?"

She shrugged. "I can try, anyway."

Annabelle glanced at the clock. "Friendsgiving's almost over, for me anyway. Firefighting doesn't take a day off, and propane warriors are all fired up today. But you said the war's tomorrow? That works, I'm off in the morning."

"Phil, I'm without a phone. Can you get everyone's number and help coordinate for me?"

He pulled out an enormous smartphone jacketed in a Star Trooper case. "Got it!"

There was a knock at the door.

Everyone turned to look, as though the pukwudgie horde, or maybe the goblins, might be behind it.

I opened the door to find Cassie smiling at me. I showed her in and introduced her around. Cassie and Annabelle exchanged a long look, and if I was a jealous girlfriend, I might have worried.

"So, you're Raven's sister?" said Phil.

"Well, she was Jessica to her family, but yes."

Phil, the L.T. and Frannie all said they were sorry for her loss. Annabelle hugged Cassie without a word.

My new friend blushed deeply and favored us with a sad smile. "Thanks. Looks like Jess picked her friends well. I feel a warm heart in each of you. I sense your bond, a bunch of heroic friends. I don't think much could stand against you if you put your minds to it."

Needless to say, Cassie made a good impression. She fit right in, like an old friend returning after a time away.

Annabelle broke the cozy silence. "Are you here to take my girl away from me?"

Cassie returned Annabelle's crooked smile. "No, just borrowing her for a spell."

Annabelle giggled. "A spell? Ha, I see what you did there."

Cassie winked and gave Annabelle a cheesy grin. Then she said to me, "Am I interrupting your Friendsgiving, then?"

I shrugged. "If you're hungry, have yourself something to eat, then you're just joining late."

Annabelle excused herself to change for work, while Cassie sat at the table.

Frannie gasped, staring past Cassie.

I didn't see anything where she looked. "What is it, Frannie?"

"I... I don't think I should say."

Cassie turned to regard Frannie. "What's the word for vaguebooking, except in person?"

Frannie shook her head, eyes wide.

Cassie looked over her own shoulder, then back at Frannie. "Come on, what is it? You look like you've seen a ghost."

And then, I knew what she'd say; I felt it as a lead weight in my stomach.

Chapter Seventeen

"It's Raven," Frannie said. "She's here. Standing over you, Cassie."

Cassie bit her lip, then closed her eyes and put her hands on the table, palms flat. "Oh sis, happy Thanksgiving. Thank you for coming to see me. To see us. You know Skye visits you, don't you?"

Frannie's eyes only widened further. "Oh, she knows. And she says thank you for the graveside die rolls and Mountain Dew. But she's here to tell you something."

I swore. "Let me guess. She's the latest to tell me I need to stay out of the fight?"

Frannie shook her head. "No, nothing like that. She says the dead are restless, that you know what needs to be done."

Cassie turned in her chair to study my face.

I bit my lip, and then nodded. "Yeah, tell her I'm already on that one."

Frannie's mouth made an "O" and the room held its collective breath, waiting. She said, "She also says, you have a demon to face."

My eyes locked with Frannie, and I felt certain her skin crawled in exactly the way mine did. "No. That's not possible. No way in hell."

Frannie rubbed her face with her hands. "I hear you, Skye. If that demon came back from wherever Brett banished it, I'm out. No way."

"Ask if she's sure--"

Frannie held up her index finger. "Wait. There's more. She says it's not the demon himself, it's what he left behind."

I looked around the room, as though I could suddenly see into the shadow world to talk directly to Raven's ghost. "What do you mean? There's some demon bits in me, like a splinter? We took care of that, I know we did!"

Cassie touched my hand with hers. Her eyes met mine, and I took a deep breath and calmed myself with an effort of will. I nodded to her, and she smiled.

A tear ran down the side of Frannie's nose. "Raven says, the damage the demon did, it shows on both of us, from where she stands. It's been sewn up, but we each haven't really healed. She says if you can do that, then you can be whole again."

"I can be whole? But what about Minnie? What about *you*?"

Frannie shook her head and I couldn't make out what she said through her tears.

The meaning was clear though. Frannie was too far gone to ever be whole again. And I got the idea that not even Raven knew what might happen with Minnie.

Cassie said, "Frannie, how does Raven say that Skye should do this?"

Frannie shook her head. "She says only Skye knows how. And that I'll figure it out someday, but not yet."

The L.T. punched a wall, hard enough to make each of us jump. He shook his hand but hadn't left a mark. "Damn it, how's this ghost know all this? Why are we just sitting around talking? Can't we *do* something, like right now?"

Phil shifted in his seat. "I know you're all jaded about weird stuff like this, but I'm with the L.T."

Frannie took a breath and looked at Cassie. "Raven's fading."

Cassie stood up and opened her arms wide, eyes closed. "Jess, I love you and I miss you."

I barely heard Frannie's whisper. "She said she loves you too, Cassie. She's gone now."

Cassie slumped and her shoulders shook. I put my arms around her, and we cried on each other in silence.

Annabelle came down the stairs and ran to me. "What happened? What did I miss?"

The L.T. explained. "We had a visit from a ghost."

"Raven," I said, wiping at my face with my sleeve.

Annabelle hugged me, and then kissed me for a long moment.

Both Phil and the L.T. chose that moment to let out a long sigh.

"I hate to go right now, in the middle of this. But I got Phil's number, and you let me know if anything happens, okay?"

I smiled and choked on a laugh. "Aren't you going to tell me to be careful this time?"

She patted my cheek. "You know I want you safe, but I'm on the team, okay? We're out to stop a war, and maybe being careful isn't as important as thinking before you act, you hear me, *your Majesty*?"

I kissed her goodbye and watched her go.

The L.T. whistled. Phil coughed.

I turned around to glare at them. Phil's face burned with embarrassment.

The L.T.'s eyes gleamed as he flashed me a mischievous grin. "Hot stuff, lady."

Frannie smiled. "It's so nice to see you and Annabelle back together."

"Psh. We were broken up for like, five minutes." It was total B.S. on my part, but I didn't like to think about how close it had come to being over between Annabelle and me. How fragile it still felt. The hour or two when I'd lost her had been the end of the world for me. *But no sense going there right now.*

Cassie wiped at her face and sniffed. "I barely know you two, and it's obvious you belong together."

I shrugged. "I might not be able to hold down a job for very long, but I've been doing everything I can to listen to her. She said we lived in different worlds. I've tried to show her what we do share. And now she's jumped on board this crazy train, so I guess I'm doing something right. Maybe. I mean, unless I'm not."

Cassie glanced at her phone. "I'm not sure how long we're going to need, but I've got Thanksgiving dinner with my parents in a few hours. I hate to break up the party, but--"

I stood and slung my bag over a shoulder. "I get it. Let's go. Phil, L.T., Frannie--"

The L.T. saluted. "We've got our orders, boss."

I made an exasperated noise. "Would you please--"

"I'll make sure everyone keeps in touch, but I'll need Cassie's number," said Phil.

Cassie glanced at Phil, then at me; her eyes held a question.

I nodded to her. "That's best. At least until I find my own phone, I'll need your help keeping in touch with the others, Cassie."

She traded digits with Phil. I shrugged on my leather duster, grabbed one last donut for the road, and waved goodbye as I headed for the door.

Frannie caught my arm to stop me. "Skye? What did Annabelle mean by 'your Majesty'?"

I felt my face warm, and pulled the troll crown out of the coffee table drawer to show her. Everyone in the room stared at me, and I stammered out, "W-well, the trolls sort of made me their Queen. You know, because of what happened at Big Con."

Frannie plucked the crown from my fingers and marveled at it sparkling in the sunlight filtering through the curtains of the living room. "Seriously? Because you killed the old Troll Lord?"

I nodded. "Yeah, trolls aren't too bright. Do you think you could hang on to it for me? I don't think I want to carry it around right now. I think I may need it tomorrow night, though."

Frannie stared at me a long moment, then nodded. "Sure. Keep it secret, keep it safe."

"Thanks, Frannie. I gotta go."

Cassie followed me outside. She said, "I mean, we could stay another fifteen or twenty minutes if you like, I just wanted to make sure we have enough time without feeling rushed."

I shook my head. "Nah, it's not that, I just want to get some fresh air and movement. I dunno. Too much I don't understand yet, too much chatter about what might be going on, and too much worrying about whether this is all stupid."

Cassie touched my elbow to stop me. "Skye, everyone's behind you. Even Jess is, and she--oh, I'm so sorry. I mean--"

I took a deep breath and just stared at her a long time. "She's dead. It's the truth. It's a lot easier to have confidence when you're drunkenly barreling headlong into danger.

Stopping to think about trolls and goblins and lethal pukas, well, it's scary."

She nodded. "And the fact that you're scared, but go ahead anyway? That's bravery."

"But is it really even our problem? This risk is for what? So the fairy folks don't kill each other in a war I've been asked to keep out of?"

Cassie bit her lip. "I miss my sister, but I know now that it'd have been a lot worse if you hadn't led her and the others into battle. You know it too, I think."

I sighed and looked up at the sky.

"You'd rather fly away from all this, wouldn't you?"

"What? How'd you know that?"

"I can just see it in you. It's obvious. Come on. Let's go. Maybe you'll learn to fly after all?" She offered me a hand.

I took it.

She led me to her car, and after a couple of false tries, her elderly Beetle coughed to life and we rolled off down the road.

I watched Broad Ripple slide past my window. "So where are we going?"

She smiled and gave me a side-eye. "Oh, just this little patch of ground I know."

"We're going back to Crown Hill, aren't we?"

She shook her head. "Nope! But close!"

She turned on the radio and sang along with pop songs the rest of the way. I can't carry a tune in a suitcase, but I did boogie a little in my seat.

I still wasn't sure she wasn't taking me to Crown Hill, since the roads took us down Michigan Road toward the huge cemetery. But just as we got to the north fence of Crown Hill, Cassie turned left onto a road that followed it, then left again into a church center's parking lot.

"Oh, Cassie. I'm not a churchy girl, not at all."

She smiled. "Hello, witch here? I'm not either, but this place has something for everybody. Including the little patch of ground I mentioned."

She pulled into a spot. We had the whole parking lot to ourselves, but she parked as far from the building as possible. I didn't see anything but a park bench and a small field on the edge of a thinly wooded area.

She hopped out of the car and slammed the door. She waited and motioned for me to come along.

I followed, still not sure what was up. "Are we having a picnic in the grass? It's in the forties. Brr. Besides, I didn't bring anything to eat."

She smiled and took my hand and led me to the park bench and pointed.

The ground resolved into a series of concentric circles of grass and dirt, or a big spiral. No, the pattern was more complex than that, it twisted back on itself in many arcs of various sizes, difficult to take in all at once.

"It's a labyrinth," I said, trying to make sense of the way the path twisted and turned. My eyes kept sliding to the center, where a few paving stones marked the goal.

Cassie must have been watching me, because she said, "It's not a maze to solve, there's only one path. It's not a game, it's a meditative tool. A path to follow like a needle in a groove on a record."

"Oh, my mom had a vinyl record player. I used to watch it turn and turn as the needle made its way to the middle in a long spiral."

She nodded and took in the whole pattern with a sweep of her hand. "But this spirals in and sweeps out and then twists and turns and ends up in the center anyway."

"What do you do when you get to the end? Is there a different way out?"

She shrugged. "Some people reverse their path and come back out, some just step over the lines and walk out."

I frowned. "So what's the point, if it's not a puzzle? How's it help you meditate?"

"Well, it gives your body something to do, to free your mind. For me, it represents the twists and turns and unpredictability of life, the whole idea that it's all just a journey, the destination isn't the real point. It's what comes to you along the way that's important. That's just me though."

I filled my lungs with the chill air and let it out slowly. "So, I just walk around and around?"

"Stay within the dirt. Pretend the grassy parts are walls you can't step over. Just go at whatever pace you like, but don't rush it."

"And how's this going to help with my issues?"

She touched my shoulder and looked up at me. "I don't know that it will for sure, Skye, but it's a good way to get your head in another state without chemical alteration. If it doesn't work, we'll think of something else instead. Okay?"

I nodded. "You know, the last time I tried walking in circles in a special place, I ended up in another dimension."

Her eyes widened. "Wow, really?"

I smiled and shrugged. "I was drunk, and it was a magical place, and I'd seen someone do it already. I'm actually pretty lucky we got back in one piece."

"We?"

"Oh, I had Annabelle with me, back when we first met, last year. That's a long story, full of goblins and spider-squirrels. You probably aren't interested."

"You're kidding me!"

I let my grin loose. "Well, yes and no. It's true all right. I'll tell you the story another time though. You've got dinner to think of."

She rolled her eyes. "You better tell me. Or wait, can you take me there?"

"I can take you to the fairy circle, but without booze, I dunno if I can make it work. I think I'm stalling. Am I?"

Her lips twisted into a wry smile, and she nodded. "Yeah, seems that way. Relax. It'll be okay. I doubt this place is a portal to another world."

Her words made me curious, so I darted my eyes around the field, hoping to catch something in the corner of my eye.

It all still just looked like a field with some dirt trampled in a bunch of arcs and curves.

"Here's where you start," said Cassie, pointing at a longish straight line leading into the twisty path.

"Aren't you going to do it with me?"

She shook her head. "I think it's best to let you do it alone. Less distraction that way, plus I can keep a lookout for spider-squirrels."

"You think--?"

She laughed. "Just go already."

Chapter Eighteen

I put a toe on the path and felt committed to the walk. My leather duster flapped in a light chill breeze, and the sky-blue dress I'd worn seemed too thin and filmy to be enough good against the elements. I wish I'd gone for some thick knee socks or fleece tights underneath.

I took my first step, and then another, thinking of an old Christmas special. I sang aloud, "Put one foot in front of the other..."

"Shhh. Just walk, Skye. I'm not here."

The silly tune continued in my head, but soon I found myself at the very heart of the labyrinth, separated only by a thin strip of grass I could step over without thinking. But the path swung out and switched back and forth over and over, pulling me away from the center. My dress clung to me and my coat warmed up more than I'd expect from just walking. The sun came out from behind a cloud and heated it up even more as I reached the edge of the pattern.

The arc I found myself on spanned half of the circle, and as I trod along it, my steps slowed down, and the static cling became a more tangible thing, my body tingling from head to toe with a sort of force field of static. I wondered if my hair stood up. I caught sight of Cassie, and she seemed much further away than she should be. The light from the sun seemed brighter than it had been since summertime. The cloud cover vanished as though shredded by unseen claws. The moon, which should not be out in the daytime at this time of the month, shone on the horizon as a crescent of watery light.

By the time I reached the end of the long curve, I had begun to sweat, and the air felt close and still. Without missing a step, I shucked off my leather duster and cast it aside. I thought it'd caught fire, in my peripheral vision, but when I turned my head to look, it lay flat in the grass without any damage or special effects.

The path took a sharp inward turn, and then I followed another set of switchbacks that made me forget about my coat. The staticky energy clung to me like a thick bodysuit, and now there was no question, my hair moved like a thing alive on top of my head.

I half expected to see Minnie right about then, as much as my head buzzed with the energies around me. But my focus was on the path ahead, the next step and the step after that. The effort never became exactly difficult, but it had become a sort of wading walk, like in a shallow pool, with the touch of imaginary cobwebs stringing across my face and arms and passing through me on occasion, making me shudder.

The shape of the labyrinth became clearer as I walked it, and when the path took me back outbound again, I wasn't surprised.

My mind wandered as I found it more and more difficult to look past the next step, as my body moved almost without my will directing it. My thoughts drew back to the fairy circle on the hilltop in Holliday Park, and to the goblin market my circling steps had led Annabelle and me. The swirling darkness that had grabbed at us worried me, as I hoped not to visit there today.

From the market and darkness in between, another sort of darkness welled up within me. The world had been distant like this one other time; when the demon had taken my body, I'd been shoved far into the back of my own mind, helpless to do anything but watch.

Cassie's voice reached me. I couldn't make out the words she spoke, and then I realized she sang them in a high, clear voice. "This is my fight song, my take back my life song..."

I would have laughed, but I needed that encouragement, I needed that anchor to reality just then. I don't know if she knew or not, but I gave her silent thanks.

Now the memory of the demon, instead of trapping me in my head, merely surrounded me like a dark, domed space, defined by the perimeter of the labyrinth. It reminded me of something, but what didn't come to me right away.

My feet took me from the inside to that black outer edge, and the flapping of birds' wings and gibbering of something far worse, made my skin crawl even inside the buzzing bee suit of electricity that encased my body and my being.

And then, the dirt path bent around an isthmus of grass and I took a few steps inward and stood on the little island of paving stones at the center. The black dome roiled and boiled outside the circle, and I could not see Cassie at all. It was just me, the labyrinth, and the blackness held at bay by I didn't know what.

A deep voice whispered in my ears. "You need me, Skye."

I clapped my hands to my head to shut the voice out, but as I suspected, the voice came from inside my head. It whispered, "Without me, there'd be no Minnie. Without me, you'd just be plain old Skye, nothing special at all."

"Shut up," I said.

"Oh, you'd have your game, being a pretend vampire with a bunch of other delusional nobodies. But you know it's not real."

"Go away. This is my moment of meditation. You're not wanted here."

Chuckling all around me made the flapping black above and around ripple and boil. "Poor Skye. You crave something more real, but you can't handle it."

I shouted at the darkness. "You're the one that's not real. The demon's gone, destroyed or banished for good. You're just a figment of my imagination."

A pause, then: "Am I? What makes you so sure? And where did the demon come from in the first place but the inside of someone's head. Insecurity, self-loathing, anger, guilt. All these things personified. I am as real as you, Skye."

I took a deep breath and said, "There's a lot more than those things in me. Everyone has all that. But I'm special even without my powers. I've kept off the sauce since Big Con. I've been without my second sight, and mostly without Minnie. Yet, I'm still important enough that the local powers that be are afraid of me meddling in the war that's coming."

"If that is so, then make the darkness leave, if you can."

I crossed my arms. "I don't have to. It's not real, either."

The voice hissed, "It's as real as me. As real as you, Skye."

I smiled. "That's just it, isn't it? The dark's as real as me because it's part of me, and so are *you*. I accept my darkness. I embrace it, but it doesn't define me. I won't let it limit me, either."

The voice fell silent. The boiling blackness slowed to a low simmer. Glints of sunlight peeked through gaps. I thought I could make out the silhouette of Cassie just beyond, back at the start of the labyrinth, her arms raised.

"I'm done here," I said, and the dome shattered into a million shards that boiled off as smoke in the sun.

"Yes!" cried Cassie, pumping her fist.

The chill wind cut through my flimsy goddess dress and I hugged my arms tighter to me. "You saw it too?"

She bounced up and down in place. "No!"

My eyes traced the labyrinth as I considered my options; walk back the way I came, or step over the pattern. "Then what?"

"You weren't there for a second or two after you reached the center. I thought something bad happened. But there you are. You won."

I looked up at her grinning face. "Won? You said this was only a meditation thing. What did I win?"

She picked up my leather duster and threw it to me. It flapped in the breeze like an enormous bat, and then I caught it. She said, "Well, I'd be lying if I said I thought that's all that'd happen for someone of your power, Skye. Especially after what my sister said."

I wrapped my coat around me and opted to step over the lines to get back; I had this gut feeling that reversing my course might undo what I'd just done. Whatever that might be. "So, do I have my powers now?"

"You tell me! Do you see anything special?"

I stood next to her and regarded the arcs and curves of the labyrinth. I looked Cassie herself up and down. I scanned the area around us. "No, it looks like it did before we got here."

"No Minnie?"

I shook my head. "No Minnie."

She sighed. "Well, do you feel better?"

I thought about it. "You know what? I *do* feel better. Like... oh, I don't know, sort of like after you confess a secret to someone? Or maybe the relief after a deadline's passed, for good or bad, and there's no longer anything you can do about it."

She nodded. "Absolution? Amnesty?"

I shook my head. "Not at all. Relief. Resignation."

She poked me. "My A's are more positive than your R's, you know."

I met her gaze and smiled. "Positivity is overrated. I'll give you another R: Reality."

She stuck her tongue out at me. "I'll see your R and raise you another A: Accomplishment. Whatever letters you choose, you did something here today. You faced yourself and you came out the other side."

I laughed. "Did you think I might not?"

She shook her head. "Never doubted you for a moment."

I shook a finger at her. "You're only saying that because no one's ever been swallowed up whole by this twisty dirt path."

Cassie tilted her head to one side and tapped her lips with an index finger. "Hmmm. Now that you mention it, the pattern does remind me a little of intestines."

"Ugh, thanks for the image. Thanks more for not mentioning it before I got 'digested'."

Cassie put her mouth on her arm and blew to make a rather realistic, if crude, sound effect.

I rolled my eyes. "Raven was my age. You're her *big* sister? How old are you, anyway?"

She held up three fingers for me to see. "Tree. I'm tree years old!"

We made faces at each other, and she burst out in a giggle fit. It was contagious, so I giggled along with her. We laughed a lot harder than anyone watching would have understood, but I think we both needed it.

Cyndi Lauper sang from Cassie's purse. Cassie dug around and pulled out her phone, and she waited just long enough for Cyndi to complete the title of "Girls Just Wanna Have Fun" before she answered. "Hey Phil! I'm putting you on speaker."

Phil's words tumbled out of the phone at a breathless pace. *"We're on our way in the L.T.'s truck!"*

"What's going on? You don't even know where we are!"

Cassie shook her head. "Yes, he does. While you walked the labyrinth, I let them know our location, just in case something bad happened and I needed backup."

"No time for that. We've got to come get Skye, now!"

I squeezed my eyes shut and spoke slowly. "Now what, Phil?"

"You'd almost have to see it to believe it. It's like night just fell at your place. It's like that Hitchcock movie. Aaaaa! Crap that was close!"

The L.T. yelled at the birds describing something anatomically impossible.

Cassie and I looked at each other, eyes wide. I said, "Yeah, just get over here, Cassie can hold them off."

Cassie bit her lip, then said. "I don't know. For a little while, like last time, but Mother Wren may have other tricks."

A terrible screech, like fingernails on a chalkboard, came from the phone. *"Get it off, get it off! I don't know, use the windshield wipers, or something!"*

I breathed some impolite words, then said aloud, "Phil? Are you okay?"

"Those little monsters, what'd you call them, puknoogies? They're all over the truck!"

"Pukwudgies," I said, "So it's *that* dark, huh?"

Phil yelled something unintelligible.

I yelled into Cassie's phone. "Go into the light!"

"What? We're not dead yet!"

"No! Light, they hate light! The brighter the better!"

Cassie's phone showed that the call had been lost.

Chapter Nineteen

I scanned the skies for birds. I found them. "Damn! Look at that."

A dark cloud, much like the one I'd just faced in my mind, grew like an oncoming storm from the way we'd come.

"Get in the car, Skye," said Cassie.

"No way. I'm not leaving you to--"

"The car's made of steel, mostly. Get in. I'll do what I can until they get here, then I'll join you."

"But--"

"Please? I don't want to worry about you while I concentrate."

She turned away from me and began muttering to herself and stretched her arms up in the air, fingers splayed.

I didn't like it, but I did as she asked and sat inside the elderly beetle. I watched out the window as the cloud of birds loomed and rolled down Michigan Road toward us. I couldn't see the L.T.'s truck. I reached over and flipped on the car's lights. I almost honked the horn to help guide the guys to me but didn't want to interrupt Cassie's spellweaving.

The living mass of darkness turned the corner and flooded the parking lot. I cursed myself for being helpless as the storm front of flapping birds rushed straight for us.

Cassie stood her ground, her curly brown hair flying like a pennant in the sudden wind. Sparks crackled at her fingertips, and her voice rose over even the roar of the thousands of flapping wings.

"By the name of Artemis, I banish you!"

The wave of birds broke ahead of her, like a tidal wave split by a hillside. Two points of light emerged, and the tires of the L.T.'s truck screamed as he slammed on the brakes. The truck skewed sideways and shook as it came to a halt just a few feet in front of Cassie. Shadowy lumps that swarmed all over the outside dropped off and formed a line, eyes glowing even in the avian twilight. There had to be at least eight of them.

I leaped out of the beetle and ran up to Cassie. "Can I do anything?"

She shook her head. "I don't know! This is hard, Skye. I can't hold the birds off long, it's more than last time. A lot more."

My eyes wanted to slide off of the shadowy, indistinct pukas, but I forced my attention to stay on them. The eyes surrounded us now.

"Stay back!" I yelled at them, fumbling in my jacket pocket for my flashlight.

The doors of the truck flew open and The L.T. and Phil leaped out, wielding shovels. They swung at the pukwudgies, but missed, and missed again. *They can't see them well, maybe not even as well as I do.*

I found my million-candle flashlight and the night under the dome of birds turned to daylight. I swung the powerful beam in a semicircle, and the pukas screamed and fell to all fours and scraped their claws on the pavement as they scrambled to get away.

"We need more of those," said Phil.

"Got one somewhere in back," said the L.T. "Okay, Skye, what's the plan?"

I glanced at Cassie for ideas, but her face was scrunched up in concentration, her eyes somewhere else. Sweat shone on her forehead, even in the cold November air.

My thoughts whirled like the birds overhead. *If only if I could banish this darkness the way I had the dark in my daydream.*

Then it came to me. I shouted up at the birds, "Is this how you fight, Mother Wren? Sort of like flipping the chess board when you don't get your way, isn't it?"

I thought the birds thinned a bit, but then saw that they clustered in a dense knot to one side. A human-shaped knot that stepped into the circle, robes fluttering like great wings. "The Knight has become a Queen, against all convention, and she dares question the fairness of play?"

"I do! I question the whole game, Mother Wren."

Mother Wren's slack face stretched sideways, and I wondered whether she meant to open her mouth like the Kelpie to swallow one of us whole. A screeching, gargling, choking sound emanated from that stretched mouth, and it came to me that Mother Wren was laughing. "The game is ever in play, though pieces may fall, and even players come and go. The new Queen may not understand its rules, but that is not Mother Wren's problem. The Bird Queen was once so much more, before the desolation of mankind blanketed her realm. Was that fair? Was that right? It matters not, the game goes on."

My voice softened and I took a step toward the fairy Queen. "There doesn't have to be a game, Mother Wren. I want to stop it."

For the first time, Mother Wren's eyes locked onto mine. With no irises, her pupils narrowed, and white showed all around. "Queen or Knight, the new player has no power to stop the game. The game may not be played without pieces being lost by all."

"Skye!" called Cassie. "Hurry up!"

Eyes reappeared all around us.

Mother Wren smiled. "The Queen is in check, her bishop and pawns at risk. She must make a move."

No peaceful solution presented itself, so I yelled out, "Get her!"

The L.T. lunged, swung his iron-bladed shovel, and connected with Mother Wren's head.

Crows, ravens, and even pigeons burst from where she'd stood, all screeching.

The dome above us appeared to fall, and the four of us fell to the ground. I covered my head with my leather coat and covered my ears against the screeching of hundreds of birds. Small bodies bounced off my coat, and the scratching sound of their talons made me thankful for the thickness of the coat.

Phil's hoarse cry came from nearby, and the L.T. roared and cussed in defiance.

I dared peek, and flickering sunlight dazzled my eyes. There was no sign of the pukwudgies or Mother Wren, and the cloud of birds thinned even as I watched.

The L.T. stood, swatting at the remaining few birds with his shovel. Phil sat on the pavement, blotting at a wound on his shoulder blade with a knit hat, his shirt red and torn.

A shadow passed over me. I squinted into the sun to see an enormous bird whose wings spanned at least fifty feet, swooped down and picked Cassie up in its talons. Cassie shrieked and struggled, but the monster-sized bird screamed victory and pushed hard with its wings and rose up above the lot.

I knew who it was, so I did the only thing I could. I called him out. "Earl Winter, shame on you! That is my friend, and if you hurt her, I swear by my name, I will remove your head or run you over with a bus, no matter how long it takes me to do it."

In that moment, everything changed. The sound of birds muffled. The sky showed stars, though the sun shone dim and red without a cloud to obscure it. The crescent moon shone with a dazzling silver light, as though it were midnight.

To my left, the lines of the labyrinth glowed with a cold blue light. To my right, the steel body of the beetle practically hummed. Phil's coppery aura flickered and flared bright where he'd been wounded, and the L.T. shone with an angry red glow.

Up in the air, the beak of the giant bird of prey overlapped the visage of Earl Winter, scowling down at me. His aura shone like dirty pearls, shifting and iridescent.

Meanwhile, Cassie burned with a cobalt blue fire that outshined both the sun and the moon together.

"To the Queen!" shouted a gravelly voice, and it was joined by the roar of many others. My trolls had arrived, and they rushed out of the tree line, hurling rocks at Earl Winter. One struck a wing, and he faltered in the air. Another missed his head by a feather.

I wanted to kiss their rocky faces, but I yelled, "Stop! You'll hit Cassie, or he'll drop her!"

The trolls held their fire, but stood in Olympic shot-put poses, ready to throw at my command.

The Winter Earl let out a cry and faltered, spilling air through his feathers. He and Cassie dipped down toward the pavement, and the L.T. rushed forward, brandishing his shovel.

Then, Cassie's aura dimmed to half and then flared still brighter than before. She held something in her hand, and she thrust it against Earl's leg.

Where she struck, pearlescent light poured forth like a fountain of energy. Cassie fell, released by the talons, and landed on the L.T. His shovel clattered to the ground and the two of them lay in a heap.

Earl screamed and an icy wind full of sleet stung my face and made me turn away.

I didn't think about it, I just yelled, "Fire!"

A volley of six or so cannonball-sized stones arced into the sudden sleet storm where the giant bird had been.

And as soon as it had all started, the parking lot fell silent, the sky clear of birds or fairy Lords and Ladies.

It also reverted to the color of my dress and the sun beat warm and yellow against my face. All my friends' auras faded out, and the labyrinth was back to just dirt paths in the grass.

The trolls remained trolls to my eyes, however. Hematite stalked over to me. "Yer awright, majesty?"

I nodded and thanked her and the other trolls, then rushed over to where Cassie and the L.T. struggled to their feet.

"Are you two okay?" I looked them up and down for signs of damage.

"I'm fine," said the L.T., brushing dirt from his coat and pants.

Cassie's voice shook. "I thought I was dead there for a minute. Good thing I brought this," she said, holding out a dull black dagger.

I knew better than to touch it. "Iron. Guess you stung him pretty bad."

She nodded and glanced up at the sky. "So that was the Winter Earl?"

"Yeah. I'm not sure what his deal is, but it looks like he's working with Wren. And the pukas."

"Yes, it was kinda smart to use the birds for darkness so the pukas could come after us." Cassie glanced around the parking lot. "And those guys are trolls?"

"Yeah, I didn't even know I had bodyguards shadowing me."

Hematite's voice boomed from ten feet away. "Yah, gotta keep yer safe, Queen Skye."

"That's more than a little creepy, you know?" No expression crossed Hematite's shiny face. "How'd you guys even get here?"

"Hur. There're more tunnels under the city than you'd fink."

I shook my head. "I've got a lot to learn from you."

Hematite saluted. The others followed suit.

I looked around me. "Phil? Phil!"

The L.T. pointed at his truck. "I told him to get under cover after getting hurt."

I left the others and tapped on the window of the truck. Phil's face popped up, pale and moonlike, in the back seat. The window rolled down and he said, "Really, that was your plan? 'Get her!'?"

"I'm sorry, Phil, it was the only thing I could think of."

He smiled. "It' okay. I'm all right, Skye."

"Are you kidding? I saw that cut you got."

Phil gave me a weak smile. "Tis only a flesh wound."

"Really? Monty Python at a time like this?"

"T'is always time for Monty Python!"

"Shut up. Look, we should get you to a hospital or urgent care or something."

He frowned. "No. I think I just need some first aid. Besides, aren't you under a deadline? Sunset in a few hours, then the pukas roam free."

I turned so I could talk to the others. "Okay, here's what we'll do. Cassie, can you drop Phil off at my place? We've got first aid supplies at home. Is Frannie still there?"

Cassie and the L.T. answered "yes" together, to my separate questions.

I smiled. "Okay. So, my place isn't safe after dark. Get ahold of Larry. We'll invade his hotel room tonight."

Cassie's mouth quirked and she shifted from foot to foot.

"What is it, Cassie?"

She glanced at me and then away. "I can help Phil out, or maybe Frannie can, but I'm supposed to go to my parents' still for Thanksgiving."

"Okay, yeah, I forgot. Are you out for today, then?"

She shrugged. "Probably."

"How about tomorrow? The war's supposed to be tomorrow sometime."

She grinned. "Not too early, I hope? I like to sleep in."

"I really have no idea, but my gut says that if trolls, goblins, and pukas are involved, it's got to be at night. So a little over a day from now."

The L.T. said, "You think your trolls are ready?"

I looked at him. "Hard to say. I told them only to fight in defense. I have the feeling we're defending my throne room from the other forces in play."

"Throne room?" said Phil.

"Yeah, the room where the Chained Lord used to be imprisoned has a big troll-- throne in it now. The Monument's the focus of a whole network of ley lines, sort of like magical power lines. Whoever holds the center pretty much owns paranormal Indianapolis."

"So what *is* the plan?" said the L.T.

I shook my head and held out my hands. "I'm still in reacting mode, getting mugged by the Lords and Ladies."

He nodded. "Think you can count on the Transit King? Maybe get that magic lightsaber of yours?"

I smiled and sighed. "I don't know. He's been funny since Big Con. For a while before, too. I want to go see him. Tomorrow. Tonight, you and I have a mission at Eagle Creek, before dark."

The L.T. saluted.

Hematite butted in. "I'll get a squad out there, but we're gonna be outnumbered."

I thought about this for a moment. "No. I think it's better that we go under a flag of peace."

"Carrying iron shovels?" asked Cassie.

I shrugged. "And a peace offering."

Hematite added, "Oh, an yer majesty? Yer fergot this at the party."

A squat troll, the cinder block one I'd seen before, approached and handed me my purse.

I squeaked and hugged the rocky little guy.

"Guess that means you got your phone back?" said the L.T.

I reached in and came out with the phone. Low battery, but it still functioned. "Yep! I could really have used this earlier. Oh well. L.T. do you have a charger in your truck?"

He grinned and nodded. "Ready to go?"

Chapter Twenty

The L.T. amazed me as he B.S.ed the guys at the gate to Eagle Creek Park. He didn't actually come out and *say* he was acting under official business, but he did show his Marine I.D. and tags to them and said he needed to investigate a reported disturbance from last night.

I hid in the back seat under a blanket. No sense letting them see me and putting two and two together.

Of course, if they searched the bed of the truck, we'd be dead. Sure, the pukwudgie's body was under a bunch of brush made to look like trash, but more than a glance would show the body-shaped trash bag bundle, along with the shovels.

The L.T. schmoozed with the guard. "Yeah, it sucks to have to be out on Thanksgiving, doesn't it? I'm just going to duck in and check some things and get out. I've got a brewski and the last half of the game waiting for me back home.

I groaned as they delved into sports talk for a few minutes. The blanket smelled of dog, and the longer we sat here, the closer sunset loomed. I worried about the long shadows cast by the trees all around us as we'd approached.

I came close to nudging the back of the L.T.'s seat to move things along, but then he and the guard burst out laughing and traded insults over their favorite teams, and the engine revved and we moved forward.

I sat up after a minute and peered at the L.T. in the rearview mirror. "So, the key to getting in the park is sportsball?"

He grinned. "Do I make fun of your nerdy vampire games?"

"At every opportunity, yeah."

His eyes held a twinkle as he met mine in the mirror for half a second. "You're all right, Skye. Where're we going?"

"Just follow the road and take all the rights, and I'll tell you when to stop."

"Yes, ma'am!"

We pulled into the shelter parking lot. To look at it, no one would know that a battle had taken place here last night.

Each of us checked our flashlights as we got out of the truck, but I told the L.T. to keep it in his pocket as I put mine away.

I had the worst feeling of being watched, but the orange light of the sun still lit the sky and ground up to the forest's edge.

The L.T. and I carried our grisly, smelly bundle from the bed of the truck to the edge of the shadows and unwrapped it from the trash bags, taking care not to let the sun's rays touch the body. I had to hold my breath, as the day-old body stank of death and filth.

We returned to the truck and took out the shovels, along with a wreath I'd woven from some pine branches.

The L.T. held the shovel pointed ahead of him as Larry had, like a bayonet. I asked him to stay a few paces back, and to hold my shovel for me.

He frowned and glanced at the reddening sky. "We gonna bury it?"

"Maybe. Not sure we have time. I have to say some words first."

"Really?" he raised an eyebrow and frowned.

"Yeah, really. I have to try this, or we may as well have left it to rot under the bridge."

He gave me a shrug and a mock salute.

I ignored his sarcastic body language and turned and stepped up to the body, which now lay in the lengthening shadow of the trees. Yellow stars winked on in pairs in the deeper darkness in the forest, just twenty feet or so from where I stood.

I lay the wreath upon the body and said, "I don't know if we even speak the same language, but I want to say I never wanted a fight with the pukwudgies. I didn't know anything about you. I still don't want a war with you all. This is one of your warriors. He tried to kill me, so I had to kill him first. He was brave and terrifying, but I still feel bad for it. I've battled and won against the Queen of the Hunt, and I tricked the Lord of Trolls to his death. But this was a stupid death, an unnecessary death. I can't bring him back from the dead, but I give you his body back to honor in whatever way you wish."

The setting sun stretched the line of forest shadow past my feet, and halfway up my legs.

The yellow lights blinked, and several grew closer.

Blink. Closer still.

I backed up a couple of steps, and bumped into the L.T., who had closed the distance to me.

"Skye, we better go. This stinks, and I'm not letting you get killed trying to make nice with the critters."

I shook my head and pressed the palm of my hand against his broad chest. "That's the thing, they're not critters, they're people. Just small, angry, nasty people we don't understand. Look, you said you'd follow my lead, and I need you to do exactly what I say now. You hear?"

He nodded. "Yes, ma'am."

"Even if it means leaving me behind."

He shook his head. "No. You're not--"

"Lieutenant MacPhearson?"

He pressed his lips into a tight line. "Yes, ma'am. As you say, ma'am. Permission to speak freely?"

"Denied. Not in front of potential hostiles. Understand?" I swung my chin less than an inch one way, then the other, holding his gaze with mine. Behind him, the trees' shadows stretched nearly to his truck.

He slipped his hand in his pocket, then saluted me. "Behind you, Skye."

I faced deeper darkness than I anticipated, but eyes glowed yellow only a few paces away, as close on the other side of the body as I was on mine.

"Get to the truck and start it up. Get the headlights ready on my signal, and we'll run like hell if we need to."

"Got it." The L.T.'s boots crunched on gravel as he quick-stepped away from me.

My heart beat faster as the darkness deepened all around me. The pukas chattered in their monosyllabic language, their voices hushed and low.

At least they're not chanting. I held my ground, shivering more from anticipation than the cold wind whistling and cutting through my thin goddess dress.

A high keening wail from one puka scared the daylights out of me, and I almost ran for the truck. But I whispered to myself, "Hold fast, Skye. Hold fast."

The wail was joined by another voice, and then ten. And then a hundred. And then multiplied throughout the woods.

I shook, and hoped none of the creatures could see it, but I held fast.

The wailing stopped all at once, as if on an unheard signal. It was replaced by a growling, snarling, animal sound.

Now the pukas did chant. "Po jo gar! Po jo gar!"

I was startled as the truck's engine turned over and purred behind me.

To my relief, the pukwudgies did not flinch at this. The chant spread through the fifteen or twenty pairs of eyes, it seemed, and I had the impression the snarling came from the vicinity of the body.

I dared a little light. I turned on my fading phone. The glow of its screen lit a grisly scene; one of the pukas gnawed at the neck of its fallen brother.

My stomach turned, and I froze, not sure what to do. *If they're cannibals, are they too alien to reason with? Are they really so nasty as to be purely evil?*

I took a step forward. The puka kept up its gnawing, and the growling mixed with the grinding of teeth. The few pukwudgies that clustered around advanced to get between me and the body and the one that chewed at it.

A horrible thought came to me. *What if these creatures are like ghouls, feeding on the dead?*

I dismissed the idea as contradictory, since ghouls involved the shadow world and its death energy, not the fairy world and its magic. In fact, I'd seen the two energies cancel out in a disastrous way before. Minnie had also said they couldn't co-exist.

So, if not a feasting ghoul, then what was I watching?

The chewing puka strained and pulled, its clawed hands around the dead throat, its teeth gleaming in the faint light of my phone, and with an abrupt *snap*, something tore loose.

I fully expected to see that it had decapitated the dead puka with its teeth. Instead, something flashed in the light, and the pukwudgie spat something at my feet.

Something that clinked on the pavement.

Their chanting stopped, and they watched me.

I crouched to see better; a small metal disk, like a coin, lay at my feet, attached by a ring to a severed leather collar, as for a dog.

I looked up at the yellow-eyed pukwudgies, and the one who'd chewed through the collar pointed and mimed picking something up and holding it to his eye.

Moving slow, so as not to startle anyone, I picked up the coin. The collar fell free, and the tarnished brass token sat in my hand.

"Oh no," I said aloud.

The L.T. called from the truck. "What's wrong, Skye?"

A sense of heavy dread poured through me, worse even than my fear of the gathering pukwudgies. Worse than I'd felt at the center of the labyrinth, facing the darkness within me.

More engines rumbled in the distance, just barely audible. Many engines. Powerful engines.

"L.T., don't turn on the lights, but take the truck out of the lot and further down the road, and kill the engine. Hide if you can. I'll find you in a few minutes."

"You're sure about this?"

"No time to argue, Lieutenant. Just go."

The truck backed up and then crawled out of the parking lot far too slow for my comfort.

I turned to the yellow eyes and said, "Thank you for explaining. I'll figure something out."

The eyes blinked out, and I turned and ran for the shelter house. I propped a picnic table up on one of the supports and climbed up to the roof, then I kicked the table over behind me. I flattened as best I could on the side facing the woods, uncomfortable on the gritty roofing. I struggled to get my breath under control, then dared to peer over the peak of the shelter's roof.

The first of the anticipated vehicles rolled in on enormous tires that ground gravel into pavement. Its driver guided the huge bus, the kind bands use for touring, in on running lights only.

Another bus followed close behind, and another several behind that.

Hunched figures disembarked from the enormous buses, each carrying a pole tipped with shiny metal that glinted in the yellow running lights.

I tensed and ducked my head down and thought flat thoughts. I still struggled with my breath, feeling stifled; I forced long, slow, deep breaths rather than panting and gasping as my body craved to do.

I watched from my perch as a couple dozen frogmen fanned out in the clearing at the edge of the woods.

The woods were alive with glowing yellow eyes, and the air filled with a chant I could not make out.

The frogman soldiers burped and croaked and thumped their spears on the ground.

And then, the craziest thing happened. The pukwudgies filed out of the woods. A trickle at first, heads bowed, the mean little creatures had a conquered look about them as they went where the frogmen directed. Then the trickle became a stream, joined by another stream. Dozens became hundreds, marching past like prisoners of war, marching in ragged lines from the dark toward the parking lot.

As they moved as a group past the shelter, not a one of them looked up to where I lay hiding. I peered over the ridge of the roof to see them board the buses one and two at a time, careful not to touch the edges of the doorway or the metal railing along the steps.

I couldn't estimate how many the buses held each, and I lost count of the legion of pukwudgies that the frogmen boarded on the huge vehicles, but I'd be safe calling it a small army.

And then, as quiet and efficient as they'd come, the buses closed their doors and slid out of the parking lot like rolling ocean liners.

When I knew I was alone, I took out the coin that had been chewed from around the dead puka's throat. I studied it. I knew its markings because I'd held one before. The Metro Interurban token from early in the previous century was the calling card of my mentor, the Transit King.

Chapter Twenty-One

"You're shitting me!" said the L.T. as I told him what I'd seen.

We raced down the road, away from Eagle Creek, hoping to catch up with the convoy of buses. We held out little hope, since they had a ten-minute lead, and we didn't know which direction they went after leaving the park.

"All I can say is, my old buddy Bask has some serious 'splaining to do."

The L.T. started to say something, then paused, then started again. "Y'know, Skye, maybe this is a good thing. I mean, those things tried to kill you and Larry, right?"

I let out a dramatic sigh in a gust of frustration. "Yes, but what if they were *made* to do it? Or what if they were mad about being brought to Indy. Larry said they're usually up in Mounds State Park, that they shouldn't even be in Eagle Creek."

"How's that your problem? Mean little monsters come after me, it's not my job to figure out what some other dude's rounding them up for."

"Really? I mean, can you be that cold?"

He shrugged. "How's it cold? It's war, Skye, you said so yourself. If I pause to think about the other guy's feelings, his past, his family, how am I going to pull the trigger?"

"Maybe pulling the trigger isn't always the right thing to do."

He snorted. "You hesitate to philosophize like that in battle, and the other guy gets to pull the trigger first. He's not gonna think about *your* story. He's just trying to follow orders and survive if he can."

"Damn it, L.T.!" I struggled for words, and he gave me the silence to compose them. "Okay, look. Bask's got a mighty bus convoy of pukwudgies. I mean, who else could have that many big buses at his disposal? Not to mention the frogmen from his castle, and the Interurban token. All signs point to Bask. Even if we're heartless and don't care what happens to them, he's got them following his orders somehow, and he's got them mobile. And there's a war on tomorrow sometime. How's this a good thing?"

The L.T. shrugged and stopped at a red light. "He's been a good guy before when you worked for him. You think he's switched sides?"

I slapped the dashboard and groaned. "You don't get the Lords and Ladies. No matter whether he's a friend of mine, the Transit King has only ever been in it for himself. He's doubled, tripled, or more in power since I met him, mostly because of things he's gotten me to do one way or another. Now he wants me out of the fight? And he just added the pukas to his arsenal? I don't see how this turns out well."

The light turned green, and I directed the L.T. to continue straight. I had a vague notion of seeing if the bus convoy was headed to Bask's castle at Holliday Park, but hadn't thought much beyond that.

"You're assuming too much, Skye! I still say there's a chance he's doing this to stop the others. You know, the goblins. The Kelpie. Mother Wren and the Winter Earl. Those guys. You were making a good case for them being in cahoots. And if you hadn't noticed, none of them are looking out for your well-being. Meanwhile, Mr. Bask saved you from the pukwudgies once."

I wrung my hands. "Yeah, yeah, that's the sticky part. But his solution was just to get me and Larry the hell out of his castle. He talked me out of claiming the MacLeod Fairy Hilt, which could have been a big help tomorrow. And he wouldn't tell me anything."

The L.T. pulled into a gas station. "I'm runnin' on empty, and so's the truck. We're too far behind, and I'm kinda worried about you runnin' in half-cocked and pissed off at this guy. The more you talk about him, the more he sounds like the baddest of the badasses in Indy. Is that about right?"

I nodded. "These days he really is. I don't know the full extent, but I doubt even the other three together could take him on."

"Or you," he said.

I stared the L.T. in the eyes for a long, angry moment, then sighed. "No. Not me, either. I never was a match for him."

"So, let's think about this. You want to run back to his fortified castle, which neither of us can actually see, and call him out? Best case, I'm right, and he's got a plan we'd approve of. Worst case? He's gone darkside or he's had you fooled for years, and he squashes us like bugs under his big magical fairy boot. Squish."

I bit my lip, but just stared at him, waiting.

He touched my shoulder with a calloused but gentle hand. "Skye, we need to know more. We need a plan. And we need bigger guns, maybe."

"Corn nuts," I said.

"Huh?"

"If you're going in, could you get me some corn nuts? And coffee. Cream and double sugar, please?"

The L.T. laughed and squeezed my shoulder. "Yeah, sure, Skye. Why not come in with me?"

I shook my head. "You're right. I'm rushing in hot, like Drunk Skye would. I need to cool off a bit and figure it out."

He grinned at me and let himself out of the truck. I heard him go about filling the gas tank. I rummaged through my purse and found my phone's charger cord and plugged it in and looked at my messages.

There was one from Phil, asking if he could crash Friendsgiving.

There were a few from Cassie, who'd been checking before coming over.

And there were a bunch from Larry.

Larry had holed up in his hotel at first, and then started sending scouting reports.

One mentioned a big flock of birds swarming around the Circle off and on.

Another reported Jimmy barking his head off at eyes peering up at him from a sewer grate.

Larry also reported a lot of activity around the Monument and the 50 or so lines of lights strung from the top to a circle around it that formed the World's Largest Christmas Tree.

He followed that up with intel I already knew; the Festival of Lights ran every year on the day after Thanksgiving, and that there'd be a hundred thousand souls packing the two block radius around the Monument all Friday evening.

Something bothered me about his wording, but I couldn't put my finger on it. It also reminded me of something. Something I'd forgotten. Something important.

And then I got a text from Frannie that made it all come together: "Strange things are afoot at the Circle, 'k? Those aren't just lights. Spectral force field kept me from getting past. Meet @ Larry's."

And right on the heels of that text came another: "And hurry. He still creeps me the hell out. Jimmy's sweet though."

I texted back to both her and Larry that the L.T. and I were on our way.

"Hope you like plain, 'cause that's all they had left," said the L.T. as he opened the truck door and tossed the bag of snacks into my lap. He put two covered styrofoam cups of coffee in the cupholders and slung his butt into the seat.

"We gotta roll," I said.

"Trouble?"

I nodded. "Nothing lethal at the moment, but my gut says Frannie might get violent with Larry."

The L.T. started the engine and we swung out onto the road. "I don't know Larry. Can't decide if he's as much a bastard as they say or not."

I frowned, watching the streetlights fly by. "He's like anyone, really. I used to hate him for what happened to me. I used to hate myself for what I did, but you know, it wasn't my fault. Sometimes you get forced into things, and you think you're doing the best thing."

"How's kidnapping the best thing?"

"Yeah, I don't know. Maybe the demon made him do it. Maybe he's just that greedy. Maybe he's changed for the better since then? Or maybe I'm just stupid to trust him at all. But he's saved my butt a couple of times now. Do two rights make up for a big wrong? Does anything?"

"You tell me. Seems like some never forgive, like your Transit King, hmm?"

I watched the L.T. drive for a long moment. His face passed into shadows between lights, mysterious and, I had to admit, a little sexy. In the light, his features showed stark, scarred, and stubbly--not pretty, but honest and real.

"The Transit King is a fairy creature, no matter what else he is. He can't help being bound by certain conventions. I broke a promise, so that forever taints me in his eyes."

He snorted. "He asked for the one thing you needed to fix what you'd screwed up, Skye. He had to know you couldn't keep that promise. It was a setup if you ask me."

I sipped my blistering hot coffee and swallowed with gratitude. "Why do you think he'd do that?"

He shrugged. "Maybe it was a test. Maybe it was a power grab. Maybe he couldn't help it, like you said, because of his nature. Freakin' little Rumplestiltskin contracts are his business, right? The Fairy Godfather with offers you can't refuse? If the fairies are so black and white, then which is Bask?"

I looked at the L.T. as he turned the wheel toward downtown. The lights on Meridian so close together that instead of dark and light, his face was bathed in bright and dim light. It was as though I saw him for the first time as a light went on in my head.

I drew a deep breath. "I think that's just it isn't it? He's not so black and white. He works within the rules to do what he can."

"Then why's he roundin' up mean little monsters?"

I shook my head. "I don't have all the answers yet, but some pieces are falling into place. So, back to your original question, Larry really is a bastard, but he's not black and white, and he's not bound by fairy laws. He's human, like you and me."

The L.T. thought about this a moment, then glanced at me with a grin. "Think you can use those laws against the Lords and Ladies? Seems like a weakness to me."

"I sure hope so, L.T."

We drove down Meridian in silence. The buildings of downtown rose above the road to beckon to us. My thoughts wound in circles, dwelling on the buses, the Kelpie and his-or-her goblin army, on skies dark with birds, on my tough but thick-witted trolls.

But my mind returned to the Circle itself, and that walk I had on the bricks around the Monument. I could remember the Circle of Lights, Stuart had insisted we go a couple of years back, when we'd moved to Indy. He said we needed to assimilate into the local culture. The festival had been full of elves and choirs and television personalities, street vendors selling hot chocolate and coffee. And so very many people. Even in Chicago, I'd never been in such a packed crowd. More people even than I'd seen at Big Con, all packed into a small space. Even Ernie's zombie army was just a fraction of that sea of humans. The people gathered around the middle of their city to see Santa and the Mayor flip a big fake switch to turn on the ginormous cone of light strands to announce the Christmas season in Indianapolis.

I'd watched the same thing on TV the next year, cuddled under a blanket and glad not to be out in the cold and crowds, but still happy to feel like a part of the ritual. A pang came to me, thinking of Stuart's sacrifice to save me and the other gamers, after I'd given up too easily on him, on us.

I'd missed the Festival last year, helping Rebecca, Blue, Chip, and Phil down in Bloomington. I'd made a try at not drinking that month too, but I'd missed my Minnie too much to stop completely.

Until Big Con. Until Raven got bitten in two as I watched.

As I stared out the windshield. Passing streetlight after streetlight, I saw the reflection of my face lit brighter and dimmer, back and forth, round and round. If I could forgive Larry, if I could believe the Transit King could have both good and bad motivations, then maybe I could forgive myself one day.

I leaned over to rest my head on the L.T.'s meaty shoulder and closed my eyes, the play of streetlights as they passed filtering through my eyelids.

And then it came to me. To forgive myself, I had to forgive others. I had to let go of my pride and fix things.

I sat up and turned on my phone and picked a number I'd sworn I wouldn't dial without being called first.

I got her voicemail.

"Hey, Rebecca? It's Skye. Yeah, I know, it's been awhile. I'm sorry. I just want to say thanks. You know, for sending Blue to check up on me, and for the advice. And to say, I get why you fired me. And to thank you for that. I'm doing better. I'm still clean, and I'm working on rebuilding bridges I burned."

I almost hung up then, not wanting the call to end this way, but I swallowed more pride and said, "I hate to bother you on Thanksgiving, but something big's going down, and I might need your help."

Chapter Twenty-Two

"Just keep away from me, you monster!"

"Monster? Who's mostly ghost, playin' her body like a meat puppet, callin' me a monster?"

The moment Phil let us in the hotel room, I pushed my way between Larry and Frannie, who stood glaring at each other from inches away.

Frannie reached past me to shove Larry's shoulder. "Says the guy who had me tied up with duct tape in a van!"

Larry's face reddened. "Says the room-temperature ghoul who stuffed her face with meat, grunting like a damned animal!"

"Says the assassin!"

"Aw, those were paintballs!"

Frannie's voice pitched higher than I'd ever heard her. "Filled with silver! Did you know what would happen to me? I think you had a pretty good idea!"

Larry shook his head. "You're standin' here yellin' at me, ain't ya?"

I filled my lungs to shout at them both, but instead, I kept it to a low growl. "If you two don't play nice, I'll do this without either of you."

They hurled protests at each other like insults, each claiming to be more necessary to the plan.

From the far side of the room, Jimmy whined and barked at Frannie.

The L.T. spoke up, his voice calm and quiet. "Skye, why don't we get our own room, and let these two have their privacy."

"No! Don't leave me alone with him!"

"I can't take any more of her bitching! I can only say I'm sorry so many ways!"

I collapsed on the bed next to Phil. He had on a new shirt, a blue flannel number that flattered him, though it didn't seem as though he could button it over the Fantasy Free Form t-shirt underneath.

He murmured to me, "Skye, is it time to fight pukwudgies yet? Anything's got to be better than this, they're making me crazy."

I tuned him out and did my best to shut out the bickering for a long minute.

Then, I sat up and looked from face to face. Larry scowled and shouted. Frannie's face bloomed red with fury, her brow furrowed as she glared up at Larry. The L.T. leaned against the wall near the door, arms folded, poker-faced. Phil stared at a blank TV, his eyes as flat and blank as the screen; his shoulders sagged, and I could almost see his grey aura of fatigue.

Okay Skye, you're a Queen, so start acting like one. The voice came to me and I wasn't sure if I'd thought it, or if Minnie'd whispered in my ear. I looked around for her, but my tiny otherworldly sister was nowhere to be seen.

I stood. "Okay, everyone hush. Here's how it's got to go. Frannie, you're with me, we're going on a scouting mission."

The L.T. reached for the doorknob, his intent clear on his face; he wanted in.

I shook my head. "Boys, get some sleep. Phil here looks half dead, and I'm going to need you all to take second watch when we get back."

I ignored the guys' protests. "Look, I need to do this without attracting attention, and I need Frannie's special perceptions. But most of all, I need you all rested and ready to go tomorrow."

Larry ran a hand over his face. "This Queen crapola has gone to your head, Skye."

I shrugged. "You can follow my lead or do your own thing, Larry. Your choice. But if you're not going to help us, get the hell out of my way, okay?"

He turned to Jimmy. "See? See what I get for giving a crap? For risking my neck for her?"

Jimmy barked once, then crossed over to stand next to me. He wagged his tail.

Larry took off his hat and threw it on the bed. "You too, boy? Well, whatever. I'll take a nap while you get that b--"

I pointed a finger at him. "Careful how you finish that sentence, Larry."

He held up his hands. "You heard what she called me!"

I laughed. "What is this, kindergarten?"

Larry sat on the bed. "Whatever. Just as long as she's out of my sight for a while."

Frannie raised her voice. "Hey, I didn't ask to stay here!"

I touched Frannie on the shoulder. "Shush. Come with me. It'll be okay."

She relaxed and sighed and turned away from Larry, the color fading from her cheeks. "Okay, Skye."

"I still think I should go with you two," said the L.T., straightening his shoulders as though standing at loose attention. "What if you get attacked?"

"Out on the Circle on Thanksgiving night? Thanks, L.T., but I promise you, this is troll country; I couldn't be safer anywhere in the city. There's gargoyles hanging from half the buildings, for starters."

His poker face held, but he looked away and didn't have anything more to say to me.

I turned to talk to Phil, but his eyes were closed, his mouth open as he leaned against the headboard, asleep already.

I muttered, "At least someone knows how to take orders around here. Come on, Frannie, get your coat."

She held up a circle of silver and smiled. "Your crown, your majesty?"

" Thanks for taking care of it," I said as I took the thing from her and stuck it in the big pocket of my coat. "Best not to be conspicuous but can't hurt to have it."

Outside, it was a cold couple of blocks' walk to the Circle. Jimmy trotted ahead of us, his breath visible in excited gusts of panting as he looked this way and that. I was glad for his company, but I began to regret bringing Frannie along.

"And do you know, that jerk had the *gall* to flirt with me? How does his brain work, anyway? Guy like that should be behind bars. But no, he got out on probation. Then he got away *again* just because he--"

"Frannie."

"What?"

"Hush. We're being inconspicuous, remember?"

"Ugh, yeah. But come on, I can't stand one more--"

I put fingers over her lips for a second and shook my head. "Shhh. Now show me what you saw."

She sighed with excess drama and stomped off, headed directly for the Monument, Jimmy trotting along at her side.

I looked back and forth around the Circle, but other than some couples taking selfies on the steps, it was a quiet night. I hurried after Frannie.

I caught up to her right at the edge of the ring of electrical cables. She swept a hand to indicate the curve of the anchors that held guy wires that stretched taught to the top of the Monument. "I can't go past this point. It's like the pretty lights have some spectral energy to stop me."

I waved a hand between two wires, braced for resistance, but all I felt was a thin wall of cobwebby static-cling. "Doesn't stop me. What's up with that? Is it shadow energy?"

She nodded. "Yeah. Something on my side of the paranormal fence."

Jimmy snuffled along an invisible line between two of the anchors and whined, giving me the doggy equivalent of a side-eye.

I scanned the bricks for any sign of tampering. "I don't see how it's being done."

Frannie shrugged. "I don't even see anything in ghost mode, other than a sort of purplish lightning going up and down these wires."

I put a fist on my hip. "Is that all? Anything else you didn't think worth mentioning?"

She smiled. "Sorry, I forget sometimes which things only I can see. But what I meant was, I don't know what the source is, or how it got there."

Jimmy sat, his nose bobbing back and forth between us like he was watching a tennis match. His mouth opened and his tongue hung out to one side. I'd swear he was smiling in amusement.

"Okay, I've got an idea. You stand here, I'm going to circle around a few times, but don't stop me, okay? I need to concentrate."

She nodded, then hugged herself against the cold and put a mitten over her nose.

I thought maybe Jimmy might follow me, but he stuck to Frannie's side as I began my walk.

I tried to bring my mind back to the previous night; my steps took me around the Circle the way I'd done with Brick and Limestone. As I paced the perimeter, I didn't think it was working at all. I did get a good up-close look at the fifty-something anchors from all sides, but nothing supernatural presented itself. Not so much as a spark or glimmer of aura.

Frannie rolled her eyes at me as I made my first circuit, but I ignored her and kept walking. I drew breath and let it out slow, picturing myself at the labyrinth, as though this were the major arc around the outside where it had started to kick in.

And then, in my mind, the image of concentric circles formed. Not the twisty pattern of the labyrinth, which only seemed like circles at first glance, but an actual set of hoops that grew smaller and smaller into an infinite point. The hoops glowed a neon blue, and then instead of going around them, I seemed to fly *through* them. The smallest hoops grew as the largest ones passed out of my field of vision, making a sort of tunnel.

And then it all clicked for me. The walk on the Circle with Brick and Limestone was like my walk along the labyrinth, which was just like my walk around the fairy ring in Holliday Park. They were all the same. *Circles and circles and circles.*

I came back to myself, most of the way around my second circuit, and I spotted Frannie talking to a guy in a yellow hard hat and a fluorescent yellow vest with reflective stripes. They seemed to be in an argument, but I couldn't hear what was said over the roaring that had begun in my ears.

At their feet, Jimmy stood with his teeth bared and hackles up; on his back, Minnie cupped her hands as if shouting at me, but nothing reached my ears.

I walked as though in a groove, unable to divert my path toward them.

My feet seemed to scuff up neon blue sparks, and then I waded in a small ticklish shower of them. My fingers became blue sparklers, and the world changed, lit by a fierce crescent moon and a million brilliant stars.

Frannie looked right through me as I passed, but the electrical worker stopped and turned to watch me, its goggle eyes narrowed, its crocodile mouth snapping open and shut.

A crowd of elves, or children, surrounded me, pouring out of what had seemed to be a closed storefront. They menaced me with root-like claws and gnashed gravelly teeth.

I was forced to stop, and the claws became grasping fingers, the goblin faces became faces wrapped in scarves. Hands pulled at my clothing; panic rose inside me and I had the urge to shove them all away from me.

A flash, like an enormous static electric shock, burst from me and blew outward like an explosion.

The goblins, glamoured to look like children, flew back from me and landed on the pavement in a ring around me, five feet away in all directions. Narrowed eyes peered up at me from the brick street.

I needed an escape route. I made like Iron Man and held my hands out palms forward and *pushed* like I had in that moment of panic.

Nothing happened.

The small figures rose to their feet and began to close on me. I searched my pockets and came up with Larry's high beam flashlight and my crown. *Why the hell did I think it was a good idea to go out scouting unarmed?*

Chapter Twenty-Three

What could I do? I imagined plowing through the "children" to get to Frannie and Jimmy. Maybe the flashlight would blind the Kelpie and cause confusion enough for us to escape.

I had the flashlight out of my pocket and looked around for a weak point in the line. The illusionary faces of the glamoured goblins studied me with a mix of emotions. What stood out to me? Fear. These little jerks feared me.

And you know, it might have been a rush to Drunk Skye to have monsters worried like this. Drunk Skye would have taken advantage of that and used it against them.

No. I can't do that. That's not what I'm doing here.

I put away the flashlight and pulled out my crown and jammed it on my head. I held out my hands to either side like a crossing guard. "Wait. Stop. I don't want war with the goblins."

A voice from the back ranks spoke up. "Yer see? Dis is what I said she says. Di'n't believe me?"

I scanned the dirty little faces, and thought I caught glimpses of their lumpy true forms for just a second or two. "Who said that?"

"M'name's Ferd, mum." A goblin broke through to the front. I let him take a step or two toward me before I stopped him with a look.

Other goblins around him hooted and laughed. "Hur hur, looks like Ferd's got 'im a tall girlie!"

Jimmy burst into a fit of barking, and I glanced toward the Circle to see the Kelpie striding toward me. Jimmy leaped and capered ten feet away, but I didn't see Frannie.

The goblins gabbled and murmured among themselves, and they parted ranks to make way for their sewer Queen.

For some reason, I had no trouble seeing past the electrical worker disguise now, and the reptilian eyes of the

Kelpie bore into me. "Don't listen to this Oathbreaker! She lies, like any trawl!"

This roused the goblins to cheer, gnash their teeth and roll their eyes. I crossed my arms and waited for them to settle down.

I forced a smile, and I took my eyes from the Kelpie to talk to Ferd. "Why do you suppose I'm not dead where I stand? How come your Queen hasn't ripped my throat out with those teeth? Think she's afraid of my dog, Ferd?"

This brought a raucous wave of hur-hurs from the goblins. A hiss from the Kelpie silenced them all at once.

Ferd's gaze bounced from me to the Kelpie and back. "No, mum. S'cause yer the Trawl Queen."

The Kelpie took a step toward me. "Ah hah, ah hah, Trawl Queen's in check, know what I'm sayin'?"

More chess terms? I shot a look at the Kelpie. "How many pawns do you feel like sacrificing, Lady Kelpie?"

Before she could reply, I glanced at Ferd and laughed. "'Cause that's how war works. Some of you'll die. And for what?"

Ferd backed up, knocking down one of the other goblins behind him. He shook his head and the whites of his eyes showed all around. "Don't kill me, Trawl Queen!"

I touched the crown on my head in a little salute. "Not if I can help it. Told you, I don't want war."

The Kelpie took another step toward me. "Don't know 'bout all that. Uh uh, nope. Trawls, they crush goblins. Trawls rip goblins in two. What do they call yer, Ferd?"

Ferd's eyes narrowed, his expression hardened. "Gobbos, they says. Jest dirty little gobbos."

Think, Skye, think! "Doesn't matter what they call you now. They made me their Queen, and if I say they don't go to war with goblins, they don't."

"Says the Oathbreaker!" hissed the Kelpie.

The word, "Oathbreaker," echoed through the circle of goblins. Round and round. Ferd crossed his arms and stared at the ground. "Oathbreaker trawl," he muttered.

May as well own it. "It's true. I had an artifact in my hands, one that grabs your mind and pushes you around, and makes you crave whatever it wants. Makes you want power. More and more power. Too much isn't ever enough. Maybe I should have done as the Transit King said? Kept my oath? Maybe he'd be King of the Trolls now. Or maybe he'd have been gobbled up, and the Chained Lord would have snacked on a dozen goblins a day, every day, since then. Think the Kelpie could stop either of them?"

Several goblins shivered visibly, and all eyes shifted to the Kelpie, who growled at me and snapped long rows of teeth at me. "Hur. Yer playin' what-ifs, trawl pretender. Fact is, yer said no to him when yer had a deal. Even me, I wouldn't do that. Know why? I got honor. You got nuffin'."

Somewhere around the curve of the circle where I couldn't see, a dog barked, and metal grated on stone.

I pulled myself up straight, pleased to be able to glare down at the Kelpie. "You're wrong. I kept that cursed artifact out of honor. I might have promised Bask, but I had a debt of honor for having freed the Chained Lord. It was *my* screw-up to fix. It was *my* fight to fight. My battle. If I gave it to him, I might have kept a promise, but I would've lost all respect for myself. Call me Oathbreaker if you want, but I know I did the right thing."

The Kelpie took another step, within striking distance now. "Then yer dyin' with that smug pride and a dirty name."

I shook my head and grinned. "I'm not dying now."

The Kelpie snapped at me, and its sewer breath nearly made me choke. "An' why not?"

"'Cause I know something you don't."

"An' what's that, fairykin?" The Kelpie's eyes glowed, even in the streetlights of the Circle.

I refused to let my grin slip. "I know that you have a platoon of big, rocky trolls behind you, ready to smash you to pulp at my command."

The Kelpie darted, like a snake, and sharp claws dug into my leather coat from behind me faster than I would have thought possible. Inhuman strength of the fairy noble's grasp pinned my arms to my sides. As it murmured in my ears, only the reek coming off the creature was stronger. "Then I'd better rip yer throat 'fore you can say the word!"

My breath came in ragged gasps, my chest compressed by the Kelpie's embrace, its foul scent thick in the air I did choke down. I could only whisper, "Check."

"Eh? What's this?" hissed the Kelpie.

"You're... in... check... too. Watch... your... stinky... ass."

Yeah, okay, it was a reach, but since everyone else kept using chess lingo, I thought maybe it'd have some power with this thing.

Not like I had many other options left. *Hold fast, Skye!*

The Kelpie's grip loosened, just a fraction, but its breath was no less fetid. "Then we are at a stalemate, fairykin. I let you go, your trawls attack. I kill you, your trawls attack. Better to remove you from the board."

I took a deeper breath, then coughed. "But that's it, this board has more than two players. There's you and your goblins. There's Mother Wren and her birds, along with the Winter Earl. Maybe you're all in cahoots? But there's also the Transit King, his froggies, and the pukwudgies."

"Pukwudgies!" hissed the Kelpie. "Sssso, you admit you ally with those..." it paused and spat, "creatures? They're worse than you! Oathbreakers one and all!"

I shook my head. "You have it wrong. I'm not allied with anyone, and neither are my trolls. T.K. warned me to stay out, and so has every other player. And you know what? I never *wanted* to be in this game! But at every turn, I'm being forced to react to one or the other of you, and so, I'm here. Take me out, and my trolls will take out your army and probably you, too, before the endgame. Maybe they'll throw in with the Transit King, who knows? But without me, you're nowhere. Like I said, 'check'. Your move."

The Kelpie turned me around so we faced each other. "Call off your trawls."

Maybe it was an adrenaline high that made me channel Drunk Skye, but so help me, I said, "Why should I trust you?"

I thought the Kelpie couldn't get any worse, but then it *smiled*. The smile crawled across its face like a disease, baring sharp teeth as its predator eyes narrowed to slits. "Because *I'm* not an Oathbreaker. Call them off, Trawl Queen."

It had me there.

"Fine," I said, drawing myself up taller. At the top of my voice, I said, "Fall back, trolls!"

"But yer majesty—" Hematite's voice came from somewhere behind the Kelpie; I don't think I'd ever heard a troll whine before.

"That's an order!" I snapped.

The crunching of stone on brick told me that they obeyed.

The Kelpie's horrible smile broke out into an even uglier grin. "Didn't your preciousss Transit King ever tell you that promises made to an Oathbreaker aren't binding?"

It raised an arm and cuffed me with the back of its grimy hand, knocking me backward, on top of a few goblins. They cried out and scattered, depositing me without any care on the freezing cold bricks.

I scrabbled backward, crabwise.

A shot rang out. Then another.

The Kelpie's head burst into a splash of dark blood, and its body crumpled to the ground.

A sudden silence spread across the Circle.

Soft hands, small but human, grabbed my arm. Teeth bit into my sleeve on the other side. Frannie and Jimmy dragged me backwards through a crowd of stunned goblins.

I probably said something then or made some sort of noises. I couldn't tell you.

I must have asked Larry a question, because his face broke into a cat that ate the canary grin. He answered, "Iron bullets. And you're welcome. Hope we're square now."

"Huh?"

For some reason, he took off his hat and placed it on my head. "Take good care of Jimmy, would ya, Skye?"

And then, Larry turned his back on me; the goblins roared as one and rushed towards us like a gathering wave of flesh, claws, and blood-red eyes.

Chapter Twenty-Four

I never really managed to come to my own feet before I was scooped up by large stony hands and carried off, slung up onto a troll's back. I shouted in Brick's ear, "Save my friends!"

Brick's gritty chuckle came with a shrug, which made me cling on to his neck to keep from being knocked off. "Awready ahead of yer, mum. We've been gettin' ready since yer said not to smoosh gobbos, waitin' for a chance to grab yer all up an' run."

I peered back over my own shoulder and saw Frannie on Limestone's back, with Jimmy slung under one of the troll's arms, writhing and howling.

"Where's Larry? Who's getting Larry?" It took everything in me not to let my voice go shrill.

"Har," came Brick's unenthusiastic laugh. "Yer can go back and scrape what's left of him up with a rake tomorrow. Gobbos shredded him for killin' their Kelpie. Nuffin' we coulda done, it happened too fast, and we needed ta save yer, mum."

My skin crawled with chills that had nothing to do with the cold night air. My eyes stung. "Are... are you sure?"

"Oy! There's no comin' back from that, mum."

I swore a streak that would make Gonzo proud, though I felt nothing like that as Larry's demise sunk in. I wanted to look at Jimmy but couldn't face him.

I need a drink.

Larry's hat made me feel top-heavy. I took the hat off and hugged it to my chest with one arm.

Something cold and hard pressed against me from inside the hat. I peered inside and swore again. Held inside the hat by a special elastic band, Larry's hip flask mocked me.

Drunk Skye would have downed the whole thing at this point.

With images of Bask, Rebecca Burton, and my Annabelle whirling in my head, I did what I had to do.

I drank the contents of the damned flask. It burned all the way down and sat like molten lead in my stomach. I stuffed the flask back into the hat and jammed the hat onto my head. I felt every inch the Oathbreaker I was.

"Thanks, Larry," I whispered, not even loud enough for Brick to hear.

And then I wept.

I don't know how long Brick carried me that way, but it couldn't have been long before we passed under an arch made of his namesake and into a dim, wide, torch-lit hall, and down a broad set of stairs into deeper darkness. Except, I could see; lines of blue foxfire outlined everything. *No doubt, it's the booze taking hold.*

Trolls bellowed at one another, rushing the other way, falling in to block the way behind us, wielding axes and clubs and curved swords.

I caught my breath and wiped my eyes, still shaking.

Minnie turned out to be clinging to my sleeve. I couldn't meet her eyes. "Oh, Skye," she said, her voice soft and pitying.

I ignored her. More tears built up behind my eyes.

Between clenched teeth, I hissed, "Brick. Stop. Now. Put me down. Put everyone down."

Brick and Limestone both halted, exchanged a glance and a shrug, then placed me on the floor of the passage next to Frannie. Jimmy the dog bolted away from the trolls and growled. At least, I hoped his growl was for the trolls, and not for my miserable self.

Frannie called out, "Skye, are you all right?"

I snapped. "Does it *look* like I'm all right? Larry's *dead*, he got ripped to pieces saving me! I'm covered in Kelpie brains! I had a *drink* and broke my promise to Annabelle. And Raven! And the Transit King. And Rebecca. And worst of all, *myself*! I let everybody down, Frannie! I'm just freaking *peachy*, okay?"

Frannie blinked as though I'd slapped her hard across the face. She took a breath, and then said, "Skye, listen to me. It's bad. It's really bad. I know. But you aren't letting everybody down. Larry did what he did on his own, against your instructions. He was supposed to be in the hotel room. We still *need* you, Skye. There's a war coming, and without you, there's going to be a lot of innocent bystanders killed tomorrow, if not sooner."

I sagged and sobbed. "Why me, Frannie? I'm no leader. I get people killed. I didn't even want to be a part of this war. I didn't ask to be the Troll Queen. Everyone wants me out of the fight."

"Ever think there's a reason for that?" she asked, watching me.

For no reason I could think of, I felt like I could *see* Frannie's ghost floating just outside her body, just for an instant, like a halo of mist. Then, as though blown by a breeze I couldn't feel, the misty apparition melted away.

The gears of my tipsy mind turned, and I bit back the sarcastic reply I had been about to spit at Frannie. "What?"

A tiny smile touched Frannie's lips as she said, "You said it yourself, you've been warned off by every party in this little war. What if there's a reason? Maybe the Transit King is just looking out for your safety, but Mother Wren, Earl Winter, and the late Kelpie all told you to butt out. You're an important piece in this game, and they all want you off the board."

Before I knew what I was doing, I laughed out loud. I laughed with tears streaming down my face. I couldn't draw breath, and yet I still laughed.

Frannie stared at me with wide eyes and open mouth.

I caught my breath after a long painful moment, and said, "That's it. They've all been using chess terms. That's the key to this whole thing. I know why they want me out of the 'game' now."

Frannie blinked and said, "Do you? Tell me."

I felt the grin creep across my face like a death mask. "They're fairy lords and ladies. They have rules, just like chess pieces, that they *must* follow. The game has only so many moves, and they've all got their pawns and knights lined up for battle."

Frannie nodded.

I drew a deep breath and raised my voice so that it echoed up and down the hall. "Except I'm a dirty Oathbreaker! I don't *have* to follow their rules! I can move however I please, Frannie!"

Brick and Limestone took a step back from me and exchanged another look between them.

Frannie's Mona Lisa smile returned. "And?"

I finally dared look at Minnie, who smiled despite the tracks of tears on her tiny face.

"And that scares them," I said.

Chapter Twenty-Five

I touched Frannie's arm and led her down the hall. Minnie hopped off my shoulder onto Jimmy, who trotted along at my side. "Trolls, can we hold off the Goblins?"

"Fink so," said Brick.

Limestone added, "Har, we're watchin' for 'em now, mum."

I decided it best not to remind them about the coronation attack just then, but I kept eyes locked with Limestone for a longer moment. *Maybe he'll get the hint.*

Limestone nodded, then headed back the way we'd come.

I patted Brick on his bicep, to get his attention. "Can you get us back to the hotel on the sly?"

The big red troll grinned, baring teeth like a row of jagged rose quartz. "What hotel do yer mean, mum?"

I swatted him. "Don't play dumb with me, you big oaf. I know you too well for that. Any time I've gotten in trouble, trolls have appeared out of nowhere. You *know* where I'm talking about."

"Har. I'm just a big, fick, troll, mum. But yeh, we kin get yer there, wifout Wren, Winter, or His Majesty knowin'. Brick clapped his huge stony hands, making my ears ring. What seemed to be my tabletop court of mini-trolls scurried out of the masonry. They clustered around, and Brick muttered to them in some trollish tongue. The toy sized trolls clambered over each other and scattered, vanishing into the walls again.

Frannie peered up at Brick. "What was that about?"

Brick shrugged. "Need to clear the way for yeh."

I nodded at him. "Can we use those guys as runners to communicate later?"

Jagged teeth glittered in the corridor's torchlight. "We got better ways, but yeh, they'll do."

Minnie said, "What are you thinking, Skye?"

I shrugged. "Not sure yet. I don't think planning is the best, er, plan right now. I need to be unpredictable. But I need everyone to be ready tomorrow night. That's when things are going down, and we've got to be ready to mess up the works. Or help it along. I don't know. I need more information, I don't know what this war's going to be about, but it involves the Monument, and the hundred thousand people who'll be huddled around it."

Frannie shook her head. "I don't think it can be anything good, given the spectral energies I saw crawling up and down those cables. It could be really bad, Skye. If it were just us at stake, I'd say we need to take a trip out of downtown. Maybe out of the city entirely."

I stared at her; her eyes held a fear I hadn't seen in her before. "I have a bad feeling about it, too. What I don't get is what game the Transit King is playing. Can he really be so mad with power that he'd risk harm to that many people?"

"You fink he sees 'em all as people?" said Brick. "Har. He's a fairy lord, a King. Yer don't get to be King wifout steppin' on heads."

I cleared my throat.

Brick fell behind a step and his grin disappeared. "No disrespect, mum, but yer *did* kill the Chained Lord. An' cut off Howl's head. An'..."

"Fair point," I said, more to cut him off than to concede. "But Bask has always been fair, even if not always gentle. And his business is trading favors. Seems like he's going to lose a lot of business if he gets a reputation as a mass murderer."

"Yer never know, mum. Mebbe he's done tradin' favors because he's about ta get everything he wants without callin' in any more."

A cold lump formed in my stomach. I thought of Bask in his dead wife's castle, looking down on me from up on his high throne. Hardly the creepy-but-genial homeless gnome I'd met only last year. Was he capable of that much deception? Was I *that* gullible?

Frannie's voice sounded rough as she said, "What do you think he's going to get?"

Brick shook his head. "I told yer, I don't know nuffin'. But that fing out there, it's bad news, even a fick troll like me can see that. An' if he's lettin' this fing exist, an' he's plannin' ta fight over it, there's a prize involved, mark my words, mum. An' mebbe it's so big, no one cares what happens to bystanders."

"*I* care," I said.

Frannie touched my shoulder. "Might be that's another reason they want you out of this. You're not willing to let harm come to the bystanders."

I had no answer to that, so we walked without speaking for a long time.

The passage forked many times, and narrowed a little each time it did, until Brick was stooped over nearly double, and I had to take care not to knock my head on some archways we passed under.

And then, the passage ended in an elevator.

I gave Brick the side-eye. "Really?"

He blinked at me owlishly. "What?"

"You guys have elevators?"

"Har. No. We don't, but the Hilton does, and it's connected underground ta a buildin' that connects to your hotel."

I thought nothing could surprise me more, until the elevator door opened.

Inside, stood a red headed woman in a fedora and a heavy trenchcoat. I could feel the intensity of her gaze, even though her eyes were hidden behind dark sunglasses.

I couldn't help it, I laughed. "Rebecca? What--"

"There's no time, Skye," said my former employer. "Come with me, we need to talk."

Brick, Frannie, Minnie, and even Jimmy all looked from Rebecca to me.

"And how do you do, Agent Burton?" I said, crossing my arms in front of me.

"This is no time for games," she said, her tone icy.

"No games, babe. Honest. I hate to remind you, but I don't work for you. You fired me, remember?"

She sighed. "Look. I need to talk to you. You can ignore my warnings again, but there's a lot more going on than you realize."

"I mean," I went on, as though she hadn't spoken. "How did you even find me here? Even I had no idea I'd be here, that this elevator even *existed* until about thirty seconds ago."

A crease formed between her eyes. "You'll regret it the rest of your life if you ignore me, Skye."

"You want me ta take care of dis lady?" said Brick, cracking his stony knuckles.

I shook my head. "No, but I think I'm done being told what to do. Let me guess, you're going to give me dire warnings to stay out of tomorrow's festivities, am I right?"

The elevator began to close, but Rebecca took a step forward onto the threshold and the doors rebounded. "Quite the contrary. If you'd just *listen*..."

I made a snap decision and pushed past her into the elevator. "Fine! Let's go."

Jimmy slipped past, a sour-faced Minnie riding on his back. Frannie and Brick moved to follow.

Rebecca Burton held up an elegantly gloved hand, palm out. She shook her head. "No, we need to talk alone."

The others stopped short but looked at me for direction.

I snorted. "Look, I know you're used to being in charge, but while clearly you can't trust an Oathbreaker like me, and after the termination of our professional relationship, maybe I can't trust you, either. I am not going alone."

"Trust has to start somewhere, Skye." She removed her sunglasses and those green eyes pierced me.

She reached out a hand to touch my arm, but I shied away. Rebecca's touch had changed minds, and more, before.

"No. That's not how trust works. Trust starts with respect, and if you're going to use mojo on me, you don't have that for me."

Rebecca pulled her hand back from me as though I had burned her. "I promise you, no tricks. But it needs to be private. Please, Skye? I would consider it a personal favor."

"You know you're talking to the Queen of the Trolls, a fairykin, right? Personal favors mean quite a lot to my people," I said, trying my best not to giggle. Even as I said the words, however, I felt a sort of electricity in the air, like a static buildup. *Is this a hint of what T.K. feels when he makes a deal?*

She nodded. "I know what I'm saying, and what promises mean."

"Even to an Oathbreaker?"

"Even so," she said. She drew a breath, and I thought she was going to add something, but she let it out and waited for my reply.

The elevator tried to close on Rebecca again, and its buzzer rasped, echoing down the tunnel and back.

"I've got to get to my friends soon, and plan a battle," I said, "But I can spare a few minutes for a friend. Are we friends, Rebecca?"

I couldn't tell if the twitch of her lips was a smile or not, but it looked prettier than the expression she'd worn before. "I'd like to think so."

I met her stare for a long moment, then touched the brim of the hat Larry'd put on my head. "Okay, but this dog just lost his best friend, he comes with me." *And Minniekins too.* If she had ways to detect my little friend, she could call me out on it. And I'd point out that Minnie is a part of me.

Rebecca frowned at Jimmy, then shrugged. "Very well."

"I'll meet you all at the room," I said, looking at Frannie. "If I'm not there in a half hour, gather the trolls."

Frannie's eyes grew wide. "Really?"

I nodded. "Get the L.T.'s help to organize them."

Brick rubbed his hands together. Red sand fell to the floor.

Rebecca sighed and said, "Always so dramatic, MacLeod. Let's just go. It won't take that long." With that, she stepped back into the elevator, and I watched Frannie's worried face as the doors closed.

Neither of us spoke as the elevator rose. I stared at the floor indicator, rather than meet her eyes again. The numbers counted up, and we didn't stop on any floors, and after the top floor went by, we kept going.

With a ding, the elevator opened to a mechanical room, full of large motors, a transformer, and things I couldn't identify.

Rebecca led the way out, not watching to see if I followed. She crossed the room and opened a door to a rooftop. A light flurry of snow blew past on chill winds. The icy crystals stung my cheeks. Larry's hat managed to fend off some of the chill, and I pulled on thin leather gloves that I found in my coat pockets.

I looked up and saw a few stars, despite wispy clouds lit orange by all the streetlights of Indianapolis. The moon was as slight as a nail clipping. Something passed between me and some of those lights, darker than the sky.

Jimmy growled low and stayed close to the door to the mechanical room. Minnie watched the sky as well. I decided to trust them to keep an eye out while I talked.

I spoke first. "I don't know if you know all that's going on, but I don't think this is a safe place."

"Mother Wren? I feel certain her attention is elsewhere at the moment. So long as we're quick, this will suffice."

I looked at her. "So, what's so important?"

"Blue encouraged me to speak with you, Skye. I have been watching something unfold in this city. Something with a frightening scope."

"You know what, Rebecca? You were right. I was reckless at Big Con. I let loose something that caused a lot of damage. There's at least one death on my hands. That was pretty big. But I already know something big is going on tomorrow. There's a war scheduled, and ground zero is where a hundred thousand people are going to be gathered. I don't want to be involved in this, but I think no one is going to watch out for those people if I don't."

She nodded. "Good. Go on."

I paused a long moment, then said, "I've been given this stupid crown, and I've been abducted, threatened, attacked, and Larry just sacrificed himself trying to save me. I know I have to be all in, or it's going to go so much worse."

She didn't even blink at any of that. "So, what are the stakes?"

I shrugged. "Beats me. It is big, though. Those hundred thousand souls fuel whatever is happening at the focus. All the bigwig fairy lords and ladies have a stake in it. I'm not even clear whether there are alliances or if they're all in it separately."

Rebecca leaned in close and said, "Skye, always consider what each side *wants* in a war. What's the Transit King want? What do the goblins want? Mother Wren? The pukwudgies?"

"But--"

Rebecca shook her head. "No, time's up. We both have to go. Just think about it."

I turned to go, but she stopped me with a word.

"Skye? I know you think I don't care, but I do. For a time, you were unreliable. Even dangerous. But I've been watching, and I've seen the change in you. If we make it through all this, I'd like to work with you again."

I smiled. "Thank you. I know it took a lot for you to say that. Yes, I'd like that. Just maybe more on even terms?"

She paused a long moment, then mirrored my smile. "Fair enough."

I grinned. "I appreciate that respect."

She touched her nose with a finger. "Exactly. Respect means more than promises, and certainly more than fear."

The sky above us dimmed, stars winking out in waves. I shivered.

Without another word, we dashed for the door.

Chapter Twenty-Six

I woke, tangled up in Annabelle. She and I clung to each other in an embrace that was both awkward and fierce. I had to pee, so I extricated myself carefully from her.

I passed through an intense sunbeam, my eyes dazzled, and almost tripped over Jimmy. He snored nearly as loudly as Cassie, who had crashed with Fran on the other bed in the hotel room.

I opened the bathroom door to find Fran sitting, clothed, on the toilet, in the dark. She stared straight ahead, past me, rather than at me.

"Fran? Are you okay?"

"Hmm, yes," she replied, in a dreamy voice. "I'm not all here."

"Your ghost is elsewhere?"

She nodded.

"Where?"

She shrugged. "Looking. Searching."

Nature called more insistently. "Fran, could I get in there?"

She shrugged, stood up, and we switched positions. After I finished my business, I opened the door to find Phil had joined Fran outside the door.

"Creepy much? Is the L.T. hogging your loo?"

Phil shook his head. "You just gotta look outside, Skye."

Sunlight was nearly too much for me, but I found myself hangover-free, deserved or not. "What am I looking for?"

"Look down. On the Circle."

"Holy crap," said Fran, who seemed to be much more herself now.

I peered out and down at a sea of humanity covering the concentric circles of sidewalk, brick roadway, and concrete, surrounding the Monument. Stages had been erected while I slept, and work crews still crawled all over their surfaces and gantries. Large figures towered over the crowd, spaced out every few yards on the inside of the Circle, just outside the base of the lights of the "World's Largest Christmas Tree".

I squinted my eyes and the figures resolved into trolls, casting watchful glares all around them, nodding to each other occasionally.

I echoed Fran's sentiment. "Holy crap!"

Phil leaned in to look with me. "I know, right?"

Annabelle squeezed in between us and let out a curse, then said, "I mean, this is how it's supposed to be, but not until night."

"Gonna start getting dark in about an hour, boss."

I turned to see the L.T. hulking in the room's doorway. I frowned, and said, "Huh? How long have we been asleep?"

He shrugged. "You got in pretty late. What was it, about...?"

"Around five," said Annabelle, slipping an arm around my waist. She blew a lock of her tousled bangs out of her eyes and added, "And *then* we started drinking."

I checked my memory and said, "I'm so sorry, love. I know I said..."

She shook her head and put a finger across my lips. "No. *We* were all drinking, it was an unfair temptation."

"That's no excuse, I promised..."

Her eyes narrowed. "Skye, you were safe here with us, not galloping around with fairy swords or raising hell with the trolls. You were the one who told *us* to go to bed."

Right. I *had* been the one to call it a night, after celebrating awhile. "But-"

Her eyes met mine and my heart froze at their hardness. She whispered, "It wasn't about the drinking, Skye. It was the irresponsibility."

This time, I didn't speak; I was afraid it'd come out whiny. Or as a sob. I just nodded.

She smiled, and it was like the sunbeam behind her dimmed by comparison. "Stop it. You've worked hard, boo, I've seen it. And you did it for me. For us. I'm proud of you."

Phil coughed. Frannie stared off into space. The L.T. looked outside like he had other places he'd rather be.

To hell with how I'll sound. I took a deep breath and sobbed, "Oh, Belle, I'm still kind of a screwup."

She shook her head. "No. You've been pulled into this. I was wrong to second guess you. I was being too controlling, Skye. You need to be you. If that means being a Knight errant, a paranormal secret agent, or even Queen of the Trolls, I need to back you."

I met the eyes of everyone else in the room in turn, and then returned to Annabelle. "No, love. I need you. To keep me grounded. I get swept up in things, and without someone to watch out for me, I do stupid stuff."

She nodded. "Maybe, but you held that promise, to yourself. Not to me. And you're an adult. If you want to have a couple of drinks in a safe haven with some people who love you on the night before a war, who's going to deny you? Not me."

"But *Belle*," I hated the whine in my voice. "I *broke a promise*!"

She smiled. "Sure, you're the Oathbreaker, hmm? But what's more important? Keeping a promise, or being true to yourself? Hmmm? You may be part fairy, but you're not one of them. You're not *bound* by those things. You're like the rest of us flawed mortals that way."

Over her shoulder, I saw the L.T. crack a grin. Phil had turned a couple of shades of red. Frannie stared at her shoes.

I buried my face in her shoulder and ugly cried for a long minute. I heard Phil cough again. The door creaked.

I stood up straight and pulled myself together. "I'll remember that," I whispered to Belle. To the rest of the room, I said aloud, "We'd better get moving."

The L.T. held up a box. "Not before breakfast. Bagels and coffee, then saving the city, okay boss lady?"

We descended on the L.T. like Mother Wren's cloud of crows. The big Marine backed away as we devoured his delicious gifts. I don't think I can remember ever loving coffee as much as I did just then. Its dark power flowed through my body and chased away wisps of cloudiness in my thoughts.

Phil saluted the L.T. "Truly, you are a warrior worthy of song, L.T., and today, many lives have surely been saved by your actions."

I laughed and flashed Phil a grin. "He's a lifesaver, for sure." I waved a hand at Brick, who loomed behind the guys. "Just think, I might have bit a troll's head off."

Brick stiffened his back and *whuffed*. "Like to see yeh try, Majesty."

For the first time in days, Frannie laughed out loud. Annabelle giggled, which made Frannie laugh even harder, and Annabelle couldn't help but join her.

Minnie leaped from a perch on Brick's shoulder, hopped to Phil's head to the L.T.'s shoulder. She stood her full three-apple height and glared at me, fists on her hips.

"Oh hey, Minniekins--" I began.

She cut me off. "Shut it, Skye," she said, with a bit of a rasp in her voice that reminded me of the Transit King. "We got problems. Clouds are rolling in."

I frowned. "So? We'll get wet while fighting a war. What else ya got?"

She shook her head. "No, you don't get it. That moves things up. That's not natural weather, those black clouds are going to bring darkness sooner. Which means..."

"Oh crap," I said.

Frannie's laugh drained away, and everyone's eyes were back on me again. "What, Skye?"

"Guys, we gotta get to the trolls, and fast. Minnie just told me the weather's about to get dark, and I'm thinking that means the pukwudgies are going to make their move before sunset."

A shadow passed over the window, darkening the room for a split second. I heard a bird's cry, and the massive form of a turkey buzzard did a slow circle around the Monument.

Chapter Twenty-Seven

I had to wonder what the people around us in the Circle saw as Brick carried me on his shoulders, wading through the crowd. Did the fairy glamor make me disappear, or did they see a football player carrying a girl around as though she were a child?

Behind me, I heard the L.T. doing crowd control, leading Frannie and Cassie in our wake.

Earlier, I wished Phil safe passage down in the tunnels, on his errand to summon the trolls for battle. Then, I had kissed Annabelle goodbye before she disappeared into the crowd. She hoped to warn the civil authorities that there was going to be trouble, to try to keep everyone as safe as possible, under the circumstances. I smiled and murmured, "my hero," after she left.

My faraway thoughts passed as Brick came to a stop. "Er, mum, I fink I'm seein' things."

When a troll thinks he's hallucinating, it's time to pay attention.

I peered at the sudden haze ahead of us. People seemed to recede like the tide going out. Except it was like, I don't know, like space stretched to make it happen, the people continued their shuffling, seeming unaware of the rift opening up between us and them.

The gulf widened to a full lane's width, and then a yellow checkered car pulled up in front of us. The taxi's back door opened wide, and the Transit King peeked out the window from the driver's seat.

Before I could say a word, he met my eyes and said, "Get in, lass."

I hesitated only for a breath or two, then hopped to the wavy pavement and did as he asked. Brick protested, but I waved him off. He tried to insist, but I pulled my crown out of my pocket to flash at him. Brick sagged and nodded.

The door to the cab shut behind me, and somehow the Transit King drove straight through the crowd as though they weren't there.

I couldn't think of anything bright to say, so I waited. When seconds became minutes, I gave up and spoke the line he expected from me. "You're late, we were supposed to talk yesterday. What do you want, T.K.?"

"An a happy 'Black Friday' ta ye as well, Queenie!"

I winced. "You know that's what I called your ex, don't you?"

He nodded, glancing at me in the rearview mirror. "Yeh. Sometimes I'm clever like tha'. I don't s'pose you'd listen to me any more than she did? Y'know, if I should tell ye ta quit now before I have ta kill ye?"

Ice shot through my spine. "Bask, you don't mean that. We're friends, right? You coulda killed me a few times over, in the last few days alone, I'm sure!"

He let out a chuckle, though he still didn't smile. "Exactly, love. It's 'cause we're friends that I'm warnin' ye. It's because of that bond 'tween us I'm askin' if ye'll listen to me."

I knew I should be scared. I sat in the back of a car driven by the most powerful being within a hundred miles, one who'd just threatened my life. I didn't feel fear. Instead, a hot, slow anger began to simmer deep in my guts. "Why should I start minding you now?"

The Transit King hit the brakes and swung around to face me. "*Exactly*! Ye remember that, when it comes down ta it, right? Tell me ye will, please lass? Ye may be Oathbreaker, but consider it one last favor ta an old friend?"

The lines on Bask's face lacked the mirthful cast I was used to, nor the hateful mask of someone who wanted me dead. No, Bask's face held only raw, pants-soiling fear.

Thinking of just what could frighten a being as badass as my old mentor put a chill in my feet that crept upward with each second that he and I locked gazes.

"You... want me to... T.K., what is all this, can't you be straightforward for one minute? Lives are at stake," I gestured to take in the hundred thousand souls of the Circle.

He snapped a curt nod at me and pursed his lips. Carefully, one word at a time, he said, "That is *jest* why I cannae be straight wit' ye, girl. Ye keep on nae listenin' ta the crazy ol' Transit King."

Something inside me snapped. I fished out the token I'd gotten from the pukwudgies and held it up for him to see. "Sure, I won't listen to you. I'm not sure I'd believe what you say, anyway. Like if you were to explain the meaning of this trinket I found."

The little old king's eyes narrowed. "Yer right, lass. All th' more reason not ta listen ta me. All the more reason ta know I'm not yer friend this time around, Skye."

"But *why*, Bask?"

The Transit King slammed a fist on the steering wheel, making the horn bleat in protest. "I cannae tell ye that, lass! I cannae help it any more than I can help the wind, the weather, or yer damned meddlin' in me business!"

"But--"

The door to the cab flew open. The Transit King's face twisted into a sudden mask of rage, and he roared, "Now get out of me cab! An' when next we meet, it's as enemies, Skye. Don't make me kill ye."

Hair stood up on every inch of my body, and as sure as if lightning had struck, my body obeyed his command and scrambled to get away from him.

As the door slammed behind me, so did the rift in space, and I found myself down on all fours on the bricks, hemmed in on all sides by humanity.

I wanted to hug every single one of them.

Chapter Twenty-Eight

When I stood up, I found myself in front of a stage full of dancing children, all dressed as Santa's Elves. A local meteorologist with a hundred-watt smile clapped to the time of the Christmas song, her hair dusted with snow.

For a moment, I forgot where I was and all the worries piled up on my shoulders and just watched the show, let myself just be one of the thousands crowded around me in the audience. The scent of hot cocoa wafted by, and I let some of the tension drain out of me, there in the center of the Circle of Lights Festival.

My respite shattered as a commotion arose behind me. Brick plowed his way through the crowd, Frannie following along in his wake. A man yelled at Brick; his cocoa had spilled as the troll pushed him aside. Brick ignored him, only stopping when he and Frannie reached the front of the crowd where I stood.

Brick scowled down at me. "That were kinda stupid, yer Majesty."

Frannie pushed ahead of him, and for a long moment, I thought she might slap me. Her eyes flared with anger, but she drew a deep breath and shouted, "What the actual hell, Skye?"

I held up my hands in protest. "Look, it may not seem like it, but sometimes I do know what I'm doing."

"Like getting in the cab of the King of the Pukwudgies?" she spat back at me.

I shook my head. "I'm not sure it's like that."

Frannie held her head in her hands. "The token, Skye? The *buses*?"

I sighed. "Okay, fine, yes, something bad is going on. T.K. as much admitted it in the cab. But he didn't harm me. He only warned me. He says we're enemies from here on tonight. Trust me, if he wanted me dead before I got into the cab, I'd already be dead."

"That's so reassuring, Skye."

I needed to get back on plan. "So, something is going down in the middle of the Circle, something involving all these nice people around us. Something that Bask himself is caught up in. What else do we know?" I looked around "And what happened to Cassie and the L.T.?"

Pinching the bridge of her nose, Frannie sighed and said, "Cassie and the hunk went looking for you on the other side of the Circle. Jimmy, and I think Minnie, went with them. Cassie said something about trying to do something about the powerful Shadow magic on those cables, but she didn't sound too sure. If they can find us in this mess, maybe we can get word to the rest of the trolls when we know more."

Brick spoke up. "Yer girlfrien' and the nerd gotta be under the Monument by now."

A roar went up among the crowd. I turned to see the children jumping up and down on the stage as Santa's sleigh, pulled by animatronic reindeer, had arrived. There was something familiar about the jolly old elf who climbed out to greet them.

"Oh, shit!" I said. "That's Earl Winter."

Frannie snorted. "What, Santa's an evil fairy lord?"

"Yeah! What's he up to?"

Frannie put a hand on my arm. "Skye, he's got to be part of whatever this is. Maybe he's behind it all, and he's in there to set it off, whatever it is."

I stared at her. "Well, you know Santa's job at the Circle of Lights, don't you?"

She shrugged. "Being jolly?"

I pointed at the comically large lightswitch on stage. "He flips on the lights on the World's Largest Christmas Tree. Or rather, he picks a person who does that for him. If anything is the trigger for whatever's going to happen, it's got to be that. It's the moment everyone waits for. All eyes will be on him when it happens!"

People around me shushed me as Peggy Roberts, the TV meteorologist, walked toward Santa with a large glittery wrapped box.

Frannie's eyes widened as she watched the proceedings with new horror. "I think you must be right, Skye. We have to stop him!"

"I wish my Minnie were here to give the word to the trolls to make their move now!"

"Right here, Gigantor!" came a squeaky voice from the neighborhood of my knees.

I looked down to see Minnie astride an excited-looking Jimmy the dog.

"Minnie, go to Annabelle and the L.T.! Tell them to stop Santa if they can!"

My tiny soul sister saluted me. "You got it!"

Jimmy bounded off toward the circle of cables and disappeared.

"Frannie," I said to my friend, "can you ghost out and get up on stage to interfere? Or get us some intel?"

She shrugged. "I'll try."

Her body slumped, eyes losing focus and clarity, as most of her soul departed. I put an arm around her shoulder to steady and comfort the dull husk that remained.

With nothing else useful to do, I returned my gaze to the stage, where Santa was opening the gift box. His head snapped to one side and his eyes seemed to focus right on me. His bushy eyebrows knit together, and he swatted at the air with his raised hand.

Frannie's body crumpled into a heap on the bricks beside me.

I let out a cry and fell to my knees to tend to Frannie. The people around me ignored this, their attention still only on Santa.

I sighed relief when I felt Frannie's breath on my face. Still, her face seemed even paler than usual, and her skin shone with a sheen of cold sweat. "Frannie," I said, "girl, are you in there?"

Frannie's eyes fluttered, but then shut again. She made no other reply to me, so I looked up at Brick. "Can you take her to safety?"

Brick shook his head. "Nuffin' doin', Majesty. I'm ter guard your royal self."

"I'm your Queen, you will do as I say!" I snapped.

Brick stood at attention. "Yeh, 'cept when yer in danger, Majesty. Fing is, that's part of my oath."

"Oath? But I'm an Oathbreaker! How can you be bound to me?"

Brick shrugged like a pile of gravel settling. "Har. Oath's not to you, person'ly. It's to the crown. To yer job, so ter speak."

"You're all so frustrating!" I fumed.

Brick grinned, broken-toothed. "Ya fink?"

Before I could reply, a commotion erupted somewhere inside the thick strands of lights that circled the Monument. As I turned to look, trolls appeared at the base of the cables, stalking in an ever widening, and thinning, curved line. I didn't see my Belle or Phil anywhere.

Over the PA, the newswoman cheered, "Ladies and Gentlemen, your Indianapolis Colts!"

Nice. The trolls' glamour is working for us!

"*There* you are!" the L.T.'s voice boomed over even the roar of the crowd. He led a flustered Cassie by the hand to where I crouched over Frannie's inert form. His voice softened, and he said, "Is she, I mean…"

I stood up. "She's alive, but she's unconscious. I think something happened to her ghost self. I hope it's just temporary. Brick won't follow my orders, could you get Frannie out of this crowd, somewhere safe?"

The L.T. gave me a salute that felt genuine. "I can try, but the exits are closed off. Those big tour buses have the streets blocked."

I frowned. "Oh. And with the storm clouds rolling in?"

He gave me a strained grin. "Pukwudgies can come out to play any time now."

Chapter Twenty-Nine

Santa held up an envelope, even as the trolls advanced outward. He handed it to the TV newswoman, who opened it and read off a name. "Skye MacLeod! She's twenty-four years old, a bit older than our usual kids, but she's our very special guest tonight, let's welcome Skye to the stage! Come on up and help Santa turn on the Circle of Lights!"

Everything stopped. My heartbeat thudded in my ears. How could this be?

Santa and the newswoman beckoned me to join them next to the giant glittery lightswitch. Hands all around me pushed me toward the stage.

I mean, I could say no. I could duck into the crowd and disappear. But at the same time, I wanted to get up there to stop this from happening, didn't I? Now I had an invitation, no army or fighting required.

The L.T. put a hand on my arm. "It's a trap, Skye."

I nodded. "Of *course* it is. But if I can get up there, maybe I can do something, and then no one has to die today."

He frowned but let me go. "Be careful," he said, pressing something into my hand. I could tell by the shape that it was one of Larry's million candle flashlights. I gave him a smile and began to walk toward the stage.

I paused, and said to Cassie, "Be careful, okay? I lose too many friends this way, and I don't want to lose you before I get to know you. Like... like I lost your..."

She shushed me. "I know. But I know this is big, bigger than me, or you, or any of us. We have to stop it, whether we make it out alive or not."

I wanted to tell her to shut up and leave right now, but I knew that, like Brick, she wouldn't follow that order. So, I made my way up to the stage.

Feeling kind of stupid under the spotlights next to the fake Santa, the newswoman, and a light switch the size of my front door, I pasted a smile on my face and got between Earl Winter and the switch.

The woman shoved a microphone into my face. "How does it feel to be moments away from being the one to make the magic happen, Skye?"

"What if the magic didn't happen, Peggy? What if I told you that flipping that switch would kill everyone here?"

Peggy Roberts stared at me for a long moment. "Is that any way to talk in front of Santa? You don't want him to leave you any coal, do you? Boys and girls, do you want coal in your stockings?"

As one, the kids in the audience booed me.

The Winter Earl growled, making me look at him. And once I did, I couldn't tear my gaze from his eyes. One word at a time, he said, "Flip. The. Switch. Girl."

In that moment, I wanted to. I really, really did. Everything seemed to slow down. My arm began to move on its own, reaching for the silly prop light switch, inch by inch. The crowd cheered me on.

Behind the fake Santa, I saw a small figure climb on stage, dragging what seemed like a giant snake. She wore a firefighter's raincoat and helmet. She had the face of an angel.

My Annabelle aimed a firehose at the Winter Earl, who began to turn, ever so slowly, to see what I stared at behind him.

I could have warned her off. I could have shaken my head no. I could have tackled the Winter Earl. Instead, I just stood there and watched the hose lift her off her feet as the water blast hit Santa in the middle of his chest. The powerful stream flung him off the stage, screaming.

Earl's voice boomed from off stage; a bolt of lightning struck Annabelle down. My beautiful angel of mercy fell to the pavement and let go of the now flailing hose. I heard Phil cry out somewhere behind the stage, and the water shut off.

I screamed and ran toward my girlfriend, feeling as though my legs had suddenly turned to rubber. I fell to her side, ignoring the stink of singed flesh and burning hair. Her breaths came in ragged hiccups, her eyes wild and unfocused, didn't seem to see me.

"Oh no, Belle, oh not my Belle! Please, please, please," was all I could stammer out as I took her in my arms and looked down at her face.

"S-skye?" She said, staring right past me.

"Yes, it's me, Belle!"

"I love you, Skye. Take care… take care of yourself."

"No, no, no! You can't. I need you! I love you!"

Her eyes focused on me and she raised her little, soft hand to touch my face. "It's my job. Even… even better that I got to save you doing it."

And then she was gone, limp in my arms, breath escaping her in one last sigh.

I did what little I knew of CPR. I tried to breathe life back into her lungs. I did chest compressions. I slapped her face and yelled at her to come back.

A heavy hand rested upon my shoulder. I glanced up into Phil's concerned face.

And then, I sobbed over Annabelle's body, lost in my misery and grief. The world could save its own damned self for all I cared, now that I'd lost her.

I don't know how long I stayed there, but a sudden bright light sprang up all around me. I snapped my head up to see through my tears that the cables all lit with bright, colorful lights.

Peggy Roberts stood at the switch, pretending like it'd all been part of the show. She must have flipped it on to keep things rolling for their major sponsor, the electric company.

Black light electric arcs played between the cables, and a darkness flowed outward from the ring at their base. My army of trolls littered the ground between there and where I stood.

All except for one cable, one strand of lights. Cassie stood at its base and beckoned to me. "Skye, run! I can't hold this long!"

I didn't want to leave Annabelle's body. I didn't want to do anything at all, ever again. But there was no way I could let anything happen to Cassie. Not like Raven, Stuart, Larry, and now my Belle.

No more.

I sprang to my feet and sprinted to where she stood. A large bolt held the end of the braided steel cable, and the electrical cable ran off toward another. I noticed the electrical cable had been severed, and a troll's axe lay on the ground nearby.

A sunny aura glowed around Cassie as she clutched the steel cable with one hand and drew patterns in the air with the other. "Quick, climb up! It'll save you from the darkness!"

"What about you?" I said, putting Larry's hat on top of her head. It'd only blow off on my way up anyway.

She shook her head. "I'll be okay, I'm warded. But you said it yourself, the magic is going to be like a solar collector, and the focus has to be at the top of the Monument! You're the only one who can do anything about it, Skye!"

"How do you know that?" I asked as I began to shimmy up the cable. I was happy that I'd changed into jeans for the day and had my gloves on.

"I just do. Trust me, Skye?"

"Okay. Don't die, Cassie."

"I'll do my best!" she said with a crooked grin.

Chapter Thirty

"What. A. Stupid. Idea," I gasped out as I climbed the cable. I thanked myself with every hand over hand that I'd had suede gloves in my coat pocket, or my hands would be bloody, frozen, or both by now. I don't know how many glass bulbs I'd broken on my way up, but I remained thankful that Cassie had cut the power to the lights before my climb. Both for the relative cover it gave me, and for not worrying about electricity. Well, and the lack of Shadow energies that flowed up and down the other strands around the middle of Monument Circle.

A factoid kept haunting me. Two hundred and eighty-four feet, that's what Peggy Roberts had said earlier about the height of the Monument. I had to climb two hundred and eighty-four feet up to the top. Stupid Peggy Roberts. More worried about ratings than anyone's lives. Not that she likely understood what would happen when she flipped the switch, but she'd doomed a hundred thousand people.

Unless I could stop it.

I risked a glance down now and again. A fall from here, already a couple of stories up, would likely kill me.

Further away, the tide of inky darkness flowed out among the crowd, so that they seemed to wade knee-deep in sooty smoke. Everyone in the crowd stood and stared inward, their gazes now raised to the pinnacle of the "World's Largest Christmas Tree", the very top of the Monument.

Out at the edges, past the street, I couldn't tell what was happening, other than some sort of fighting. Remembering what the L.T. had said, it seemed to me that the pukwudgies were on the loose, wreaking havoc.

Night birds, great swarms of them, filled the air above the crowds. I froze anytime one flew near me, but so far, none had attacked me directly. This seemed wildly improbable, but I decided it must be more of Cassie's magical influence sheltering me.

I tried not to think of Annabelle, that memory was too red hot and recent, if I let my mind wander in that direction, I might just let go of the cable and end it all.

But no. I had to go on, to make sure her death wasn't for nothing.

I worried about Frannie and the L.T., somewhere in that inky mass of stupefied people. I hoped that the L.T. had found a way out, but it didn't seem too likely at the moment.

I had more hope for Jimmy and Minnie, who might still be inside the cone of light cables, or better yet, inside the trolls' underground domain.

I hoped the trolls who'd been knocked down in the path of the Shadow magic had some way to resist. Instead of attacking, maybe they should have brought axes and cut all the power like Cassie had. I had no way to know if that would have been enough. Or what state the inert trolls might be in.

I didn't worry all that much about my old mentor, the Transit King. I knew where I'd find Bask. I had no idea what I'd do when I met up with him, but he'd been right; we'd meet again as enemies. More than he knew when he said it.

I pushed away thoughts of lightning and last words for now, though. I just climbed, hand over hand, legs wrapped around the cable, shimmying my way all the way up. I wouldn't have thought myself capable of a climb like this even an hour ago, but at the moment, I had nothing left to lose except my burning desire to carry on saving people. Making her final act count. Living up to her belief in my ability to save all these people.

I began to notice what I thought might be fireflies winking on all around the Circle. Pairs of them. Like stars scattered in the inky darkness below. Unlike actual fireflies, these never blinked off, they just stayed lit.

And then, it made sense. The eyes of the staring people lit from within, by some magic or other energy.

The image from my dream came to me then, of the suns laid out all around the Circle, and the analogy of the solar collector. My mind made a little play on words right then:

"It's a Soul Collector!" the sound of my own voice startled me as I hadn't meant to say it out loud. But now I knew that was the intent. The soul energy of a hundred thousand people was about to be focused on Lady Liberty's torch at the top of the monument.

The pairs of stars below me brightened into binary suns bit by bit. While I wasn't in the direct focus of that energy, I got enough of it to feel buoyed up, stronger, like I was a part of something much larger than myself.

I peered up above me; Lady Liberty shone with an incandescent brilliance that dazzled my eyes. A widening bubble of energy eclipsed her form. The circle's edges hardened, and something dark and squiggly moved within its confines. Just then, Blue's words from yesterday came to me, "don't look when everyone else is looking" and I averted my eyes from whatever formed inside the bubble of soul energy. After-images swam all around my vision as I redoubled my climbing efforts. My spirits lifted a bit. I was going to make it!

I saw stars of a different sort when I banged my head on the stone ledge at the top of the Monument. I'd made it! I clambered around to get a grip on the edge of the observation level. With Super Soul Skye strength, I hoisted myself up and threw myself through the open window.

As I picked myself up off the floor in the close quarters of the observation deck, I felt his presence before I saw or heard him.

"I warned ye, Skye. There be no turnin' back now, lass." The Transit King's voice held more sadness than menace. He held a sword that looked too big for him, but he handled it like he knew how to use it.

I dusted myself off and met his icy gaze. "Call it off, Bask. This isn't you. You're a Lord, a King, this isn't your style."

He favored me with a thin smile. "Thank ye, that's the kindest thing ye could say ta me right now. And no, tis not me doin'. Tis Mother Wren's game, not mine."

"Then stand down. Let's stop this Soul Collector before all those people lose their lives."

Outside, weird shadows wiggled in the light of the souls. A shrill wind shrieked somewhere just above; dust and debris whipped past the windows.

He shook his head. "Ye know I wish it were otherwise, Skye. But I cannae. I gave me word ta her. Long ago, before this city had a name. I needed a favor, and she gave what I needed at the price I always ask; anythin' she asked o' me the future. Anythin' at all."

"So, your pride's worth that many lives?" I took a step towards him.

He raised the point of the sword to aim at my heart. "Nae, and neither's the power. I'd give it all away to stop this. Ye have no idea the stakes. It's more'n these souls, much more."

"Then why not stop? Break your word. We could be Oathbreakers together. It'll be fun."

Something boom-boomed like monstrous kettle drums amid the whistling winds. Pulsating waves of light and dark spread outward. The light in the observation deck strobed; light, dark, light, dark, over and over again.

He sighed. "I cannae break my word. You may do so, because yer mostly human. I cannae. I'm compelled, lass. Even against my best interest, even if it means my life. And it surely does, as well as yours; when tha' portal above us opens, *things* will spill forth that ha'ent been seen on this world. Things that eat such as me fer breakfast with a side of beans on toast."

I put a fist on my hip. "So, you're saying the souls are being used to let friggin' Cthulhu or something come through to Indy?"

A bass growl, like a dozen angry diesel semi-truck engines revving, shook the tower and cracked a few panes of glass around us.

Bask's face held no mirth as he nodded. His face gray and lined, he said, "Aye. Ye ha' no idea how close yer joke is ta th' truth, my friend. They'll walk this little world and pound humanity into the dust. Gone and forgotten, ye'll all be, and it makes me sad."

Anger welled up in me. I balled my fists at my sides and almost threw myself at the little gnome. "Sad? Do you want to know sad? This fiasco has already k-killed Annabelle. You bastard! What will you do if I just kick that sword from your hand and use it to cut off your head?"

Bask smiled. "I think ye'll find that a wee bit trickier than ye may think. It'd be a better end than what waits for us. But nae, ye cannae stop me with force, no matter how terrible yer grief may be. I'm sorry about yer sweetheart, Skye, I truly am. She were brave an' beautiful, an' the light in the world's dimmer for her loss."

I made an anatomical suggestion that's rather difficult to take back right about then, but he took it with grace.

After I wiped some tears from my face, I said, "Why aren't you killing me right now? You've got the sword."

Bask shrugged. "Mebbe I jes want company in my last few minutes?"

"Suppose I had the Hilt with me, and I cut you in two like I did Queen Howl. Would that stop this…" I waved at the dimming and brightening light outside the windows.

Something sinuous wormed around in silhouette in one of the windows, but it was gone after the next dark-light cycle. The stones that formed the Monument groaned and trembled, as if now supporting an enormous additional weight.

He nodded. "Tha' it would, if ye had it and got to me very soon."

"Then give it to me," I said. "You gave your word."

He smiled and shook his head. "I don't ha' it with me, lass. An' yer an Oathbreaker, I'm not bound by promises ta ye anymore."

I took a deep breath and said, "No, you don't owe me. But you owe the MacLeods, my family. Your kin, too. You made a promise to my family that we'd always have the Fairy Hilt when we need it. It's like the troll said, not to me personally, but to the job."

The Transit King's face went blank for a moment, then his eyes widened, and his mouth formed an "O" of surprise. "Lass… you cannae…"

"I can, and I will. Bring me the Fairy Hilt, Bask. Fulfill your promise to my family. Do it *now*."

He stood there, staring at me with that dumb expression on his face for a long moment, then he burst out laughing. "Aye, Lady Skye MacLeod, I shall do as ye ask. Tha' promise is much older than th' one I made to Mother Wren. So as much as it hurts me to break my oath to her..."

I felt some pity for the fairy lord as I said, "Someone wise once told me, 'to get better, sometimes it's got to hurt', hmm?"

Bask nodded and dropped the sword.

The soul-light from all directions winked out all at once. For a long moment, I couldn't see due to dazzled eyes. The stones of the Monument's structure sighed relief, and the winds calmed and died. Something large, wet and slithery fell past the window, producing a revolting splatter upon impact far below.

When my vision cleared, I found myself alone in the room.

I'd won. The portal wouldn't open now. No one else had to die, not even Bask. Not even me.

Before I could even breathe a sigh of relief, a black bird flew in through the open window. It was followed by five more black birds. Then eight more. A cawing stream of black birds poured in after, and I knew I wasn't alone after all.

Chapter Thirty-One

As the birds formed into a familiar shape, I backed away from the open window. I nearly tripped over the sword the Transit King had dropped when he left to get me the Fairy Hilt. I picked it up and found it to be much lighter than it looked, as though it were made of aluminum. Something told me it was made of something more exotic than that. Some sort of curvy runes covered the mirror-smooth flats of the sword. The runes glowed a sick greenish yellow in my peripheral vision, but not when I looked right at them.

I held the sword out in front of me, aiming the point at the middle of the mass of birds.

"Awwwwwwwkkkk!" cried the birds in some kind of unholy unison. All the plate glass windows of the observation deck shattered; their glass blew outward into the darkness surrounding us. I hoped flying glass shards nicked some of the other evil birds circling out there.

"Right back at ya," I said, faking bravado as best I could.

My vision blurred as the birds merged together, and Mother Wren stood across the small observation deck from me. She cried, "Foul, foul! The game was mine, false Queen! Mother Wren had you in checkmate, and you cheated!"

I shook my head. "I won, within the rules. I just removed a key piece from the board and made up my own moves. And why the hell am I talking in chess metaphors? That's your thing, not mine. I stopped you. I stopped your eldritch horror portal from opening. You ancient cryptic bitch!"

Mother Wren's eyes glowed a deep, dangerous red. "Cheating fairykin! Vile Oathbreaker, unworthy of your family's name! Crooked victories win you only malice. So now, Mother Wren will devour you whole!"

The fairy hag advanced on me, growing larger and more terrifying with each step. Her hands grew into stiletto-tipped claws, her mouth enlarged into a jagged-toothed maw, and her eyes smoldered with a red-hot hatred. Her wiry hair trailed along the ceiling of the small space we shared. I backed up step by step, menacing her with Bask's spooky sword, but if it intimidated her at all, she showed no sign.

Glass shards crunched under my feet; I knew I'd backed up to one of the open windows and could go no further.

This is it, Skye, your last stand. Hold fast!

Instead of fear, or anger, I felt a calm descend upon me. "Annabelle died because of you. You took away the best thing that ever happened to me. But you know what? Even if you do eat me all up, it's worth it. If I die finishing Annabelle's heroics for her, that's a good death for a MacLeod. I might not be a match for you one-on-one, Mother Wren, but forever more in your pathetic immortal life, you'll have to live with the fact that *we beat you.* A firefighter, her fairykin girlfriend, and their nerdy friends. I hope it gives you indigestion every time you think of it."

Mother Wren let out an incoherent screech and lunged at me with her claws. I ducked and swept at her legs with the sword, but her lower half burst into birds and reformed within seconds.

Her talons closed on my shoulder, icy agony spreading from where the points touched me. Nearly blind with pain, the sword fell from my hand with a clang. She kicked it away from me.

She used her talons to force me to the ground, back against the low wall below a window. She brought her terrifying parody of a face inches from my own and hissed at me, her breath fetid and rotten. "It doesn't matter. You're beaten, girl. Queen takes Knight after all!"

I was pinned like a bug on a collector's board. I'd run out of smartass things to say. She had me, and no amount of snark could save me this time.

She savored the moment, and an awful, wicked smile crept across that nightmarish face. She could have done me in, but I knew she wanted to draw it out and prolong my fear. It worked; I desperately wanted the pain and despair to end.

"I have a special delivery fer a 'Skye MacLeod'!" Bask's voice came from behind Mother Wren. "Think fast, lassie!"

A bejeweled silver cylinder skittered between the fairy hag's feet, toward me. I scooped up the Fairy Hilt, and its magical bright blue blade sprang out. I didn't waste any more time on banter. With my left hand, I swung the weightless blade through the body of Mother Wren over and over.

She didn't just burst into birds this time, she *exploded* into feathers and smoke.

Everything went dark. And silent.

For half a moment, I thought I must be dead.

Slowly, my vision began to clear. The smoke poured out of all the open windows, blowing upward and outward, the echo of Mother Wren's final screech echoing off the buildings surrounding Monument Circle.

And then I was alone with the Transit King.

"Took you long enough," I said to the gnome-like little king.

Bask laughed. "Tis a wee bit harder ta get from here ta there an' back again with most o' me power stripped from me. Breakin' her oath took it all out o' me, lass. I had ta run up sev'ral flights o' stairs at the end. Seems it were just in time, eh?"

I studied my old mentor. He seemed smaller, more shrunken and shriveled. Older, so much older. I asked, "Are you dying?"

He shook his head. "Nae, nae. Such as me may ne'er die, Skye. Nor Mother Wren, nor even Queen Howl. They'll be back one day, though I scarce believe ye'll be around ta see it. Jes' gone fer a long, long time, an' when they come back, they'll have ta start over. Like yer ol' Transit King."

"Only you're not dead," I said, still holding the Fairy Sword out before me. "Yet."

Bask's eyes bulged in his head and he threw his hands up before him. "Skye! Ye would nae kill yer own kin, would ye?"

I took a step toward him, sword point still aimed at his heart. "Tell me why I shouldn't? You threatened to kill me. You used me, Bask. From the very beginning. You took advantage of me when I'd hit bottom, offered me a way out that made me do your bidding. With everything I did for you, your power grew until you became the scariest thing in Indianapolis. And when you got played like you play everyone else, it became my problem to stop you. And you planned that one, too. Leading me here with pukwudgies and their token. What did they owe you for, anyway?"

"Lass, I…"

"I'm tired, T.K. Just answer the question."

He swallowed a couple of times, then nodded. "The wee monsters needed a way out of Mounds Park. Their home was bein' crowded out o' existence. They're terrors, but they're still people, o' a kind. They live on the edge of the magical realm, with one foot in this world, too. Like you, Skye."

I ignored the plea in his voice. "Go on."

He wrung his hands and continued. "So, I bussed the lot o' 'em to Eagle Creek, on th' promise they'd fight fer me when the time came. I didnae know you'd run afoul o' the buggers."

"So, why did they fight the froggies at your castle?"

He let out a nervous chuckle. "Th' hell o' it is, they didnae know it were *my* castle. I had ta get rid o' ye so I could end that fight by makin' an appearance. If I'd done it while ye and Larry were there, ye'd know somethin' was up."

"I knew it by the way you acted anyway. For what it's worth, Larry's dead, so you can't collect on that debt."

He waved a hand. "Does nae matter now, and I'm glad the pup's doin' so well. He makes a fine friend fer yer Minnie, hey?"

I stared at him, with his watery smile and bedraggled clothes and humbled, frightened eyes. I lowered the sword, and the blade disappeared back into the Hilt. "Look, there's been enough death and destruction already. But I want you to know why you're still alive. Do you know?"

He shook his head and said nothing.

I held his eyes with mine as I spoke. "It's because respect is more important to me than oaths. I may have broken my word, but it was for the right reasons. And I accepted the consequences of my actions. I get that you're physically incapable of breaking your word, I do. But there had to be a better way to get me to help you than to trick me into it, Bask."

"But lass, ye see, the bargain I made so long ago with her, I had ta do what she said, in good faith, without tellin' anyone it was her bidding. It had ta seem like my own free will."

I let out an exasperated sigh in a gusty breath. "I am so *sick* of fairy rules, fairy promises, fairy favors, fairy business! You're all so caught up in your webs of who promised what to whom, and what you owe each other, I don't think you *have* all that much free will."

He smiled then. "Now yer gettin' it, lass. It's why my kind and yers, well, we'll always be alien ta each other."

"Bask. Listen to me. We were friends. I cared about you. I thought you cared about me—"

"But lass, I did, I do!"

"I wasn't finished," I said through clenched teeth.

He made as though to lock his mouth with an invisible key.

"And it's that friendship, that respect, that's why I won't just kill you, even if it'd be temporary for an immortal such as yourself. Maybe we'll be friends again someday, I don't know right now. My heart hurts too much from losing—" I held back a sob. "—you know what I've lost, and why. For now, I can't stand to look at you while I feel this way."

"Skye—"

"Shut it! King Bask of the straight tracks, I hereby banish you from Indianapolis until I specifically invite you back. Do you understand me?"

He opened his mouth, then shut it again. He nodded. "Aye, lass. I do."

I wiped at the dampness on my face with the back of my hand. "I don't want to end it like this, but please, just go. Now."

He held up a finger, then pointed it at the sword. "Lass, before I go, I ha' one last gift for ye. The portal's closed, but this is a place of Shadow fer the next few minutes, y'see. When I'm gone, swing that runesword around thrice widdershins an' ye'll have more goodbyes ta say."

I stared at the sword, and I almost spoke to ask him to elaborate, but I didn't dare say anything more to him, or I might change my mind. And I didn't want to change my mind. Not yet. So, I just nodded to him.

He waited a few heartbeats, then returned my nod. "I'll be on me way, then. Fare well. An' Skye?"

I let it hang in the air.

He removed the battered crown from his head and held it before him. The corners of his eyes crinkled as he saluted me. "Fer wha' it's worth, I thought we made a damn fine team."

Then Bask turned and descended the stairs.

Chapter Thirty-Two

I'd never admit it to him, but after Bask left, I wept. As I stood there, crying in the dark, I listened to the sounds outside. Sirens blaring. People crying out in pain, loss, or confusion. I wondered how my friends fared down there. I knew I'd have to go face the chaos and aftermath soon enough, but I needed a moment just to myself.

The sirens were the worst. I'd never hear one again without thinking of her.

I felt sorry for myself awhile longer, pacing around the observation deck, glass crunching under my boots. I almost tripped on the runesword again, so I picked it up. The runes had lost most of their glow, retaining only a sickly foxfire light. Whatever this was, it'd been part of the ritual Bask had used to open the portal for Mother Wren. I'd be foolish to do as he'd said. It could finish the ritual and open a portal. It could summon a demon. Only Drunk Skye would do something that stupid, right?

But I held it point out and swung it around me anyway. Three times, counter-clockwise. Why? I don't know. I think it was the little guy's charm. Or my continued misplaced trust in him. Or because respect is more important than oaths.

On the third time around, a greenish line trailed the point of the sword, describing a circle around me. The circle, once complete, widened and descended to the floor, and everything outside of it blurred and fogged, seeming much further away.

And I wasn't alone.

Three figures stood within the circle with me.

Larry, Raven, and Stuart.

They looked real enough to touch, but I froze and dropped the sword with a muffled clang. I didn't dare speak. I just looked at them, one after another, in disbelief. My face felt wet, and my heart thudded in my chest.

Larry met my eyes and touched the tip of his spectral cowboy hat. He favored me with a crooked grin and a nod.

Raven pumped her fist and bared her teeth, eyes smiling.

Stuart—I'd be lying if I told you my heart didn't skip a beat seeing his pudgy form—made a V with his fingers and winked at me.

But where was Annabelle? Was it too soon for her to be a ghost? Had she moved on?

I burst into tears. "I'm so sorry! I didn't want any of you to die. I'm so, so sorry. I don't know what to—"

In the blur of my tears, I only caught motion from all around me, and then I found myself held in Stuart's strong arms. They held me silently as I sobbed on them. My nose filled with the musky-sour scent of my lost love. He whispered things like, "It's okay," and "It's not your fault," but the icy ball of guilt in my gut told a different story.

At the same time, I never wanted that moment to end. Sometimes when I can't handle being trapped in my head with my own thoughts, I try to go back to that moment again.

The moment did end, though, and he stepped back. "We don't have much time," said Stuart.

I barely dared speak my question aloud. "S-stuart, where is she?"

"I dunno. She *was* here, but then she was gone."

"Do you think she... that is, maybe she..."

Stuart stroked my hair. "I don't know. Maybe she moved on to the next place already. Maybe because you finished her final act for her?"

"B-but I wanted more. More time with Belle," I blubbered. As I watched, he seemed less solid by the second. I could see through him, making out the outline of one of the windows behind him.

His smile was sad. He nodded. "Believe me, I know the feeling. For what it's worth, I haven't minded sharing you with the living."

I couldn't help myself, I laughed. "Great. Only I could get caught up in a ghostly polycule."

Stuart laughed along with me, but his laughter faded, seeming farther and farther away as all of the ghosts became more and more transparent.

"Wait, don't go!" I cried.

The mist that filled the room cleared, and the greenish circle faded.

From somewhere far away, Larry's voice called, "You take care of Jimmy, y'hear? So help me, I will haunt your ass so bad..."

Before I could break down crying, a painfully bright spotlight filled the room and I had to shade my eyes with a hand. The chopping sound of a helicopter rotor accompanied winds whipping debris and dust in the room around me.

"Care for a ride?" Rebecca Burton's commanding voice blared over a megaphone. Without waiting for an answer, the helicopter raised up, plunging me into darkness once again. A rope ladder fell in front of the open window, within arm's reach.

Well, why not?

I used the leather belt of my duster to tie the sword to my waist, then reached out and took the rungs in my hands and swung my legs out after. For a terrifying moment, my feet failed to find the lower rungs, and I flailed crazily almost three hundred feet in the air. Once I did get my feet in place, the helicopter moved outward and down.

Below me, the Circle had cleared out for the most part, and I caught no sign of pukwudgies, trolls, or even night birds. In fact, I worried I might have slipped back into the mundane world so much that I couldn't see anything but our own world anymore; just when I thought I'd gotten the hang of my Second Sight when sober, too.

But then, as I approached ground-level, I spotted a golden retriever dashing along below me, chasing me. The dog had a tiny figure riding upon his back.

"Minnie! Jimmy!" I cried into the wind.

Jimmy barked. Minnie waved her arms with abandon.

I cried, happy tears this time.

The helicopter carried me toward the understated sign for Heath's Brewpub. I expected to see a lot more damage out on the edge of the Circle, but other than debris you might expect from a gathering of a hundred thousand people, there wasn't any noticeable wreckage. People on the street looked up to watch my progress. Some of them cheered and waved to me, some just looked stunned.

As my feet touched the ground and I let go of the ladder, I caught sight of red hair and a fedora peeking out of the Lifeline helicopter that had fetched me from the top of the Monument. I gave my former, and possibly future, employer a salute as the helicopter flew up and out of the Circle.

The L.T.'s voice boomed from behind me. "Someone sure knows how to make an entrance!"

I turned and let him sweep me into a bearhug that literally took my breath away. I squeaked.

Before I could catch my breath, Phil squished me in a somewhat less aggressive hug. In my ear, he said in a quivering voice, "We kinda thought you were dead, Skye. Glad to see we were wrong!"

I stage whispered to him, "Me too!"

Minnie rode up on an excited Jimmy, who barked at me twice and presented his head for petting. He accepted the affection with dignity, then let his tongue flop out in a doggie smile. Minnie leaped from his back to climb my arm and perch on my shoulder. We wrinkled our noses and grinned at each other. Few words are necessary between sisters like us.

I looked around and asked the L.T. "What happened to Frannie? Is she...?"

He jutted his chin to an outdoor table, where Frannie slumped in a chair. "She's still out to lunch, if you know what I mean."

We exchanged concerned looks, but I nodded at him. "Thanks for getting her body to safety, but that blast of Shadow magic couldn't have been fun to ride out as a ghost. I hope she'll be okay."

I thought of the assembly of spirits in the runesword circle. Frannie hadn't been among them. I held onto that little bit of hope. *I can't lose another friend today.*

Which reminded me. I whirled and looked around the Circle with sudden alarm. "Cassie! Has anyone seen her?"

Minnie tugged on my hair and spoke in my ear. "I forgot to tell you, Cassie—"

"Here I am!" Cassie's chipper voice was the best sound in the whole world right then. As she appeared, approaching from behind the L.T., I rushed up and tackle hugged her.

"Skye! You're alive!" she laughed as she said it, but her body trembled as I held her out in front of me.

"So are you! I didn't know if you'd make it, but you saved the day by holding back Mother Wren's spell so I could climb—"

"What-ever! You're the daring hero who climbed—how many stories—and kicked butt! When I saw that portal opening at the top of the Monument—"

"You saw it start to open? What did it look like?"

She shook her head and closed her eyes. "I can't think about it. It was horrifying. Like a hole in the sky, but somehow... darker than black. It hurt to look at, Skye. It was awful."

The others murmured agreement.

I let her go and my attention returned to the inert form of Frannie.

"What's wrong with her?" asked Cassie.

"Her 'ghost', most of her soul, wasn't in her body when the Shadow wave hit," I said. "She could be lost, or even destroyed. Her body lives on with a sliver of her soul, but there's not really much of her in there. I wish I could think of something to do."

"If only you had a witch who knew something about Shadow magic," said Cassie.

I stared at her. "You can do Shadow magic?"

She smiled and nodded. "Some."

I frowned. "If that's so, why did you need Frannie to talk to your sister?"

Her smile faded and her gaze dropped to her shoes. "Well, for one, I wasn't sure I wanted to open that can of worms. For another, I'm not very precise with it, and I didn't care to let anything bad through while I dabbled. But I could send up some kind of Shadow signal flare. If Frannie's anywhere in the area, she should be able to follow it. I just need some kind of focus. Something silver, maybe?"

I pulled the sword from my belt and showed it to her. "It's not silver, but it's definitely been used for heavy duty Shadow magic."

Cassie's eyes were huge as she took the hilt of the sword. "Holy crap, Skye. I asked for a match and you just handed me a blowtorch!"

"Will it do?"

She giggled. "Will it do? Oh my, yes. Stand back."

I did as she asked. My new friend closed her eyes and said some words I didn't catch, and she and the sword faded from view, like the sun going behind a cloud.

I traded nervous glances with Phil and the L.T.

Cassie gasped and snapped back into solidity and full color once more. "That had better do it! This thing is scary as hell, Skye, I think you shouldn't use it unless it's a dire emergency."

I frowned. "Is it evil?"

She shrugged. "Is a gun evil? Is any sword? It could be used for great evil, but it really depends on who's wielding it, and why. I wouldn't give it to Mother Wren, for example."

"I don't think that'll be a problem," I said.

Frannie groaned.

We all turned to look. She straightened up in her chair. Her eyes fluttered open. She swept her red bangs out of her eyes and turned to stare at us. "What are you all looking at?"

Frannie isn't much of a hugger, but I pounced on her anyway and kissed her cheek. "Frannie! We thought you might be—"

She shook her head. "Lost, maybe. Scrambled, definitely. Thanks for the Shadow beacon to lead me back, it sure helped me get my bearings."

"I'm so glad you're back!" I said, as Cassie handed the eldritch sword back to me.

Frannie eyed the sword. "Jeez, Skye, that thing is on fire in the Shadow world. Bright enough to wake the dead."

Her words knocked the wind out of me. "Did you say—"

Frannie nodded. "I saw her. She's not all dead, Skye. Just *mostly* dead. Not much time."

I grabbed Cassie's hand and took off at a run, dragging her along. "This is a dire emergency, come on!"

We arrived at the foot of the cable, and Annabelle lay just as I had left her, guarded by Phil.

My heart ached, but I had to try anyway. "Cassie, if this thing has incredible Shadow power, do you think it has power over life and death?"

She scrunched her nose and held her hands out, palms up. "I mean, maybe, but—"

I waved off her "maybe" and said, "Take the sword and swing it around three times counter-clockwise, okay? And keep Annabelle in mind as you do?"

Cassie bit her lip, looking from me to Annabelle's body and back. She took the sword and nodded. "But Skye, if this doesn't work—"

"I know. I won't blame you. Just do what you can, okay?"

She smiled at me. "Okay, sweetie."

I sat on the ground next to my fallen angel and pulled her head into my lap. I called her name over and over as Cassie swung the sword as I'd asked.

One time around, nothing seemed to happen, and my heart caught in my throat.

Twice, and a hush fell upon us, sirens muffled and distant now.

Thrice, and the world outside the circle receded and became indistinct.

My Annabelle stood between Cassie and me, looking down at her own body. Then she met my eyes with hers. "I knew you'd come for me."

Tears welled up in my eyes, and for a long moment, I couldn't speak. An icy fear shot through me, thinking of how the other ghosts had faded after such a short time. I had no idea what to do, and very little time to do it in.

"Oh, my Belle! I thought you were gone—"

"I was. But I don't want to go. And I figure, if anyone can cheat death for me, it's you, Skye. So, I came back here, to wait for you."

My breaths came short in my lungs. "Belle, I don't know how to bring you back, what do we do?"

She reached out a hand to touch my shoulder, to comfort me, but her touch was feather-light, as though she were just a soap bubble that might pop right before my eyes at any moment.

She shook her head and said, "You're the magic one. Cassie, too. I'm just a firefighter. Maybe I can't be brought back. Maybe this is just one last goodbye, Skye."

I wiped at my tears with the back of my hand so I could see Annabelle clearly. "No! It can't be, I won't let it end that way. This is my story, and I... you... *we* deserve a happy ending, Belle!"

She just smiled that sad little smile at me. "Yeah. I guess we do."

"As you wish," said Cassie. I thought I could see her outline through Annabelle now, and my breath caught in my throat.

"What?" said Annabelle.

"All this fairy business. It's a fairy tale, right? How would you save the dying princess in a fairy tale to have that happy ending?"

Annabelle crouched on the bricks across from me, more transparent than just moments ago. Her eyes fixed on mine, she said, "Kiss me, Skye. Like in a fairy tale. It's all we've got."

I set her body down and knelt next to it. Annabelle laid down *inside* her body, and I could only tell she was in there by a slight shimmer as the body and spirit were still separate.

I took a deep breath, leaned in close to her face, and pressed my lips to hers. They were still warm; she tasted of soot.

And after a long moment, Annabelle pulled away from the kiss and drew in a breath with a gasp and coughed. Her eyes fluttered open.

Sparks filled the air around us, and the sword clattered to the bricks and shattered into shards. My ears rang from the sound.

Along with that, the sounds and colors and commotion of the world around us rushed back all at once.

"Oh, my goddess, did it really work?" shouted Cassie. "I held onto the sword as long as I could, but it—"

"Call 9-1-1, Cassie. Right now."

She pulled out her phone to dial.

"But I'm already here," croaked Annabelle, smiling.

"Hush. You were hit by lightning. You *died*."

"But I'm back," she protested.

"You still need an ambulance." I kissed her forehead, my heart pounding with joy inside my chest.

"Actually," said Cassie, "Here come some EMTs already! Along with that red-haired lady in the hat."

How did Rebecca know where and when to bring them?

Annabelle still protested. "Can't you just get the Transit King to heal me? I figure he owes you something or another."

"He won't be by. I sent him packing."

Annabelle stared at me. "You *what*?"

I shrugged. "He was forced into making this whole mess happen. But then, I was duped into helping him rise to power or he wouldn't have had the juice to do it. Bunch of Fairy nonsense, really."

She blinked at me. "So, without T.K. around, who's going to keep the fair—the lords and ladies in check?"

I reached into my coat and pulled out the circlet and placed it upon my head at an angle. "Guess there's a new sheriff in town, even if she doesn't really want the job."

She groaned, with a smile on her lips. "I was afraid you'd say something like that."

As the EMTs put my love on a gurney, she called out to me, "Babe, I'm buyin' you a beer when they release me, you hear? You earned it for sure!"

I shook my head. "You know what? Heath's got this amazing ginger soda. I think I'd rather have that."

About the Author

E. Chris Garrison writes fantasy and science fiction novels and short stories.

Her urban fantasies feature ghosts, demonic possession, and sinister fairy folk delivered with a "lightly dark" side of humor.

Her latest series is Trans-Continental, a steampunk adventure with a transgender woman protagonist. The series is set in one of the worlds in Chris's dimension-hopping science fiction adventure, Reality Check, also published by Silly Hat Books. Reality Check reached #1 in Science Fiction on Amazon.com in 2013. Silly Hat Books released Alien Beer and Other Stories, a collection of her short stories, in 2017.

Chrissy lives in Indianapolis, Indiana, with her wife, step-daughter and many cats. She also enjoys gaming, home brewing beer, and finding innovative uses for duct tape. Keep up on the latest news and releases from Chris at https://sillyhatbooks.com/

Photo Credit: (c) Ellie Sophia Photography
www.elliesophia.com

This book is part of an author-cooperative urban fantasy universe. Characters created by E. Chris Garrison (including Skye MacLeod and the Transit King) and R.J. Sullivan (including "Blue" Shaefer and Rebecca Burton) interact in a shared world. For example, Chris's Transit King appears in R.J.'s Haunting Obsession, while R.J.'s Rebecca Burton lends a hand in Chris's Mean Spirit. So if you love what you just read and want the entire story, here's a handy guide and timeline to:

The Skye-Blue-niverse

Haunting Blue by R.J. Sullivan *
Four 'Til Late by E. Chris Garrison**
Haunting Obsession by R.J. Sullivan
Sinking Down by E. Chris Garrison**
Blue Spirit by E. Chris Garrison
Me and the Devil by E. Chris Garrison**
Virtual Blue by R.J. Sullivan*
Restless Spirit by E. Chris Garrison
Mean Spirit by E. Chris Garrison

*Also part of The Collected Adventures of Blue Shaefer by R.J. Sullivan
**Part of the Road Ghosts Omnibus by E. Chris Garrison

Enter the Skye-Blue-niverse at:

**https://sillyhatbooks.com/
and
https://rjsullivanfiction.com/**